THAT TINY LIFE

ERIN FRANCES FISHER

Published in Canada in 2018 by House of Anansi Press Inc.
www.houseofanansi.com

22 21 20 19 18   1 2 3 4 5

Library and Archives Canada Cataloguing in Publication

Fisher, Erin Frances
[Short stories. Selections]
That tiny life / Erin Frances Fisher.

Short stories.
Issued in print and electronic formats.
ISBN 978-1-4870-0366-1 (softcover). — ISBN 978-1-4870-0367-8
(EPUB). — ISBN 978-1-4870-0368-5 (Kindle)

I. Title.

PS8611.I837A6 2018   C813'.6   C2017-904733-7
                          C2017-904734-5

Cover design and typsetting: Alysia Shewchuk

*We acknowledge for their financial support of our publishing program
the Canada Council for the Arts, the Ontario Arts Council, and the Government of
Canada through the Canada Book Fund.*

Printed and bound in Canada

CONTENTS

We are survivors of immeasurable events,
Flung upon some reach of land,
Small, wet miracles without instructions,
Only the imperative of change.

Rebecca Elson, "Evolution"

VALLEY FLOOR

THE SAWBONES SQUATS, his satchel by his knees, his back to the cart and the mules and their feedbags. He runs his forefinger along the tourniquet above Roy's knee, rubs the pus between his fingertips and thumb, sniffs the lot, and says he's taking Roy's leg.

"Like shit you are," I say. "What's he left with it gone?"

The sawbones pushes his specs up his disjointed nose and says that if he leaves the leg attached, Roy'll be gone. Roy's girl, just three, explores her mouth with her fingers. Her eyes big and gold as coins. She squats in the dirt in front of some thorny shrubs, a whelp in piss-stained trousers, the night growing fathomless above the hills behind her.

Girl's new with us. I guess it was three years ago Roy and I passed through the settlement her mother lived at with Roy on the lookout for comfort. I hope he found it, 'cause now we're hampered with the product of said comfort—Roy fetched the girl from the mother less than a week back. Don't know why he accepted the child, since, one, he knew the child's age from the letter, and two, he already had that crushed toe sending stripes up his foot.

The sawbones' specs shine flat-lensed in the light from the firepit. I suspect they don't so much alter his vision as give him a look. He bends over Roy, who's laid flaccid under the cactus. Roy's hair and skin and clothes are tacky with basin dust. The firelight blinks over his silhouette, pretties his discoloured leg and cracked lips. His cocky flip of curls thrown back from his ridged nose and cheeks and spread over the dirt. His eyes closed. Been passed out a while. I grab his good foot and jostle and release.

"Might go anyway," I say.

The sawbones rocks on his haunches, eyeing the mule I promised him for the trip. One of a pair. Sorrel, sturdy—three hands short of draft—and recently acquired, though Roy and I have been hauling supplies through Arizona and the Southern Californian deserts good on seven years. That's seven years of spiny fruit and sunburn while carting basics to men batshit enough to have settled this particular desolation. Brutes searching a vein of gold-quartz, coal, oil midst the saltbush and boulders. The work gives Roy and me a nice, healthful pay, but only because not many want the job. Heat's hard on the mules and water takes up half the wagon.

The girl pulls her fingers from her mouth and wipes them across her shirt. Sawbones removes his specs, holds the lenses to the light, then plucks his hanky from his coat and polishes. His kerchief's done up old-style — stitched around the trim with cream dashes — same era as the jacket, which has buttons top to bottom, but hangs wide open. Plush fabric, carpet-like, worn thin down the back. Like he's spent his life sitting. He settles his specs back on that crooked nose and loops the wires around his ears.

Roy, flat-out, chest hardly lifting each breath. I put a hand on my lips and jaw. All the grit there, in the lines and loose skin — the valley sucks away fat. Roy and I, we seem to have aged twenty years though it's only been those seven, and we were both young men when we acquired the route. He and I been partners too long now to know who owes who — though I suspect at this moment it's him who owes me. We have a friendship. Which is why I said nothing when Roy kept the girl.

I recline against the wagon and set a knuckle to the forehead of the nearest mule, and the mule leans into it. Soft-nosed beast. "Take the leg then," I say.

Sawbones opens his satchel and reaches out a pan, a leather roll, and a hard-cased cautery set. Kicks the logs and exposes the coals and balances the pan. Unsnaps the cautery case and sets the long-handled irons into the fire.

"Water," he says.

I uncap a jug and fill the pan. The sawbones fiddles with the knot and unrolls the leather wrap. Tools inside flash blade to spine: tongs, scissors, various knives. He thumbs the clasp on a worn medical bag. Vials strapped to the underside of the lid. The interior's full of glass flasks and spools of silk and gauze. He tips a vial of iodine into the pan, then opens a jar of alcohol. Wipes down each blade with a soaked bit of cotton and sets the equipment ready on top the leather sheath.

Sawbones removes and folds his coat and lays it on the bow of the wagon. He steps to Roy's side and snips the torn pant leg. Twice the normal size below the knee, and two of the black toes sport open sores.

"Lift." Sawbones waves at the foot. I lift. "Higher." I lift the whole leg off the ground. He slides a sheet of oilskin under the thigh. "Down." He and I loop rope around Roy's wrists and good ankle, then tie the rope onto stakes and pound the stakes into the dirt. Sawbones pulls a big wad of cotton from the bag and wipes Roy's thigh a good half-foot above the tourniquet.

"That high," I say. "Christ almighty."

"Sit on him." Sawbones tests the tourniquet already in place. I take my spot kneeling on Roy's shoulders, and the girl comes up beside me. Kid's already kicked off and lost her shoes and stands barefoot in the cooling sand.

"Turn round," I say, and when she won't, I grab her. Press her face into my chest.

Thing is, Roy thought he'd be fetching a son. The mother played on that, had the kid's hair cropped. Boy's trousers and shirt. Course he didn't see it. So little difference between sexes at the child's age — the ability to piss off the back of a cart is about it. Which was how we discovered it was a girl — she wet herself. Roy should have left her when he realized. Tiny tot, good for nothing but cuteness, and what use is that? Wouldn't even grow into use.

A half-week out of town with the child, Roy's foot could no longer abide the wagon ride. We camped. He panted in the dirt and I helped him unwind his bandage. Hot red streaks up his calf. I tied the tourniquet.

Evening arrived. Roy went feverish, mumbling, tossing under the cactus. The girl, at least a quiet child, stared into the coral stain of clouds as the sun struck off. And then she stared at nothing. No, not nothing. I followed her look up the dust and barbs of the cactus trunk to thick white flowers, petals the size of fingers.

Morning, the flowers were gone, and the red poison ran as high as Roy's knee. I saddled a mule and rode to the nearest settlement. Left the girl with water for Roy.

By the time I returned to the wagon with the sawbones, Roy's leg was pusing and hot to the touch from something internal. Pit ash blew over him and clung. The girl sat with her face against her knees in the twilight. The water looked untapped.

"Roy and I are partners," I tell the sawbones. Why, I don't know. I suppose I mean to remind myself. The sawbones straddles Roy so his back is to where I'm kneeling on Roy's shoulders, the girl still in my chest. Her breath against the thread of my shirt.

"Fellows," I say, although Roy hadn't shown a degree of consideration after he received that letter and demanded we go out of our way and fetch the kid. The child would only slow us, but he was so fixated on it that when I objected, he jumped from the cart to walk off his anger and let the wheel lurch over his foot. Time we reached the mother, we knew the damage was bad. After we'd already taken the kid and discovered it was a girl, he said, "I owe you. I owe you, but if you leave me then you'll owe me too, and you take her. You repay me by taking her."

He made me look to his face and give my word. He'd an inward stare that said pain, and the whites of his eyes gone yellow. A child—and a girl at that. That's what he broke himself going back for, what he refused to leave behind. That girl might be, I figure, the very first thing he doesn't want to leave behind.

Roy's head lolls between my legs, his wiry chin unclenched. Stubborn a-hole. The sawbones' blades are dented, scrolled and likely inherited, but do look, at least, maintained. So there's that for comfort. Roy — goddamn. That it took this. What was he thinking? Should have given in days ago.

I keep the girl's face to my chest with one hand and clap my belt in Roy's teeth with the other. The girl's hair tufts between my fingers in a way that suggests if it grows, it might have his curl. The sawbones bends, and over his sloped shoulder is a pristine view of Roy's leg.

Sawbones cuts a flap of skin with his straight knife and peels it from the flesh. Blade slices through the brackish muscle, and dark clotty blood seeps over the oilskin and sand. I lift my head and listen to the ripped croak of toads that resounds off the corroded hills and over the basin, over those berserk, captive men who search the dust for what the dead streams brought down. Sawbones sets the knife aside and reaches for his final blade. I adjust my grip under Roy's chin. He's been unconscious for the best part of two days, but you never know.

Sure enough the blade's bite brings him around and I'm forced to use both hands on his jaw so he can't spit out the belt. The girl's head sneaks out of the crook of my body.

"Be calm, Roy," I say. "Be calm."

Roy's eyes roll every which way, including backwards where they stop. His sight has met mine, I assume, then I realize he's looking lower, into his girl's gold gaze. There's the wet rasp of sawed bone. Christ, I think, but don't say. Why? For what? Then it doesn't matter—his pupils flit further back and it's only his eerie whites showing.

Sawbones takes a cautery from the fire and sizzles the cut. "Christ," I say, aloud this time. "A bitta warning would have been nice." I let go of Roy and his jaw goes slack. A chunk of belt falls from his teeth.

Sawbones returns the poker to the fire. He tongs a flask of iodine water from the steaming pan, lets it cool, and pours it over Roy's stump. Washes yellow foam and bits of burnt skin. I stand and slap life back into my legs. Roy—I can't decide whether or not it feels a relief to him. Sawbones trims the loose flesh, folds the flap of skin over the wound, and stitches. Packs the wound with cotton and wraps it with bleached silk. I pull the stakes from the dirt, untie Roy's hands and ankle, and rub the rope burn at his wrists. Toss the pant leg over the dead limb. Roy's chest moves shallow but steady.

Sawbones cleans his tools. "Want me to take the girl?" He towels his hands.

The night is, for an instant, uniformly silent. Then it fills again with the stuttered flit of bats and scuttle of billy owls.

"No," I tell him. He packs his gear and loads a mule, and then crosses himself and presses two fingers to Roy's brow. This action — this and the yellow seepage out the severed limb — well, it's obvious the infection's throughout. The girl's returned her fingers to her mouth. Sawbones saddles the big bay mule and mounts. Straps his satchel over his shoulder with a sling and I see it's the case that wore his coat thin. He takes the trail. The mule's steps echo down from the hills long after I lose sight of him. Fainter, farther away, and then too far off to recall.

An hour passes, and Roy's bandage is soaked reddish black. His breath — uneven. I'm wishing I'd done what the sawbones suggested and let him take the girl.

I dig a hole while we're waiting for Roy to go. Not a wide one, but deep. Big enough for the leg now, and the rest of Roy when that's needed. The soil is loose and sandy. Easy work. I drag the leg over. It already smells green — only thing in the valley that does. Although Sawbones didn't say it, I know we won't have to wait long. The girl helps me toss dirt back in. I use the shovel, she uses her hands.

The fire turns low, smoky. Streams into the blank beyond.

"Leaving us behind," I say. And there is confounding vertigo in watching the soot trail into the cold black whorl.

The embers slip between red and white and crumble apart with heat.

Predawn or dawn, Roy passes. All his efforts go with him. I bury his body. Harness the mule, yoke it to the wagon, and hoist myself up front with the whip. Girl climbs into the bow beside me, piss-stained and pointless, and yet, even in her exhaustion, her features display Roy's self-righteous hurt: Why had I fought him, he asks me. Why even the discussion?

Colour breaks into the sky above the cliffs. Roy's left. I don't owe him nothing. I owe him squat.

I lift the girl down. "Get." She doesn't get, but stands on the wagon tracks and watches when I flick the mule and quit the place.

Takes me half the day arguing with myself to lose my anger at Roy. Another chunk of time to face the fact the girl won't last on her own. I pull the reins and halt the mule.

I turn back hoping, but the heat already wavers off the valley and I haven't seen as much as a wasp in the desert scrub. Rocks strewn across the basin clamp unyielding on their own shadows. The solitary mule shudders from pulling the cart by itself in the sun, but my thoughts are of Roy's girl and I hurry it with the whip.

When I get back to the camp, the sky's such a torturous blue the beast kneels. I pour water over my handkerchief and wipe back the sweat on my forehead. Something's been scratching at Roy's grave, which isn't a surprise in this land of scavengers. Whatever it was didn't get deep. From the marks I can't be sure it wasn't the girl herself, or a bobcat or coyote—an animal that might be the reason I can't locate her. The girl's nowhere. Cactus, charred wood of the camp-fire. Beyond that, timeworn dirt carried down from the mountains on the backs of long-gone sheets of ice. Boulders pock-full of spineless crabs that came and went with nothing to show for it. I'm shaken by the brevity of it all.

"Girl," I call. "Girl," until I wonder why I'm here.

I pour the mule a bucket and let him dip his nose to it, and then I loop my finger in the handle of the water jug, thinking to set it at the base of the cactus in case she returns. I don't. No point. I damp my kerchief and wipe my neck. What I left is gone, as I had known it would be when I vacated. Why? I ask myself, and know I'll keep asking. What was the sentiment? More relevant, what was the hesitation that I had—for him, or her, or any of it, in the first place?

WINTER ROAD

I'D BARELY CLOCKED out of my shift bolting roof screens at Diavik Mine when Trista rang.

"Dad highsided the Husqvarna at the ice races and his back is messed," she said. "Couple of pins and fused vertebrae. He's okay, but he's in a wheelchair for now and can't manage himself. And Jack," she raised her voice when I tried to interject, "you're not going to believe this — Mom has dementia. Early-onset. Dad's been hiding it."

"Why would he do that?" I sat on my dorm bunk with the phone.

"Why does he do anything?" she said.

I couldn't get my head around it. Fourteen hours of hydraulics and circulated air in the mine shaft — I wanted sleep. "Didn't the neighbours notice?"

"Notice? Probably. But most of them have left. Lots of houses boarded up. And Dad was there to care for her. He hides shit from us, not them." She sounded tired, and I wondered how long she'd been at the parents' place. "You know Dad," she went on. "He gets his first pension cheque last month and still thinks he can tear around like a teenager. Says he lost traction on the rear wheel over-steering into a turn, then the studs caught the ice and the torque flipped him head-first over the handlebars. Bike came after him, ripped right through his parka. Good thing he held his hands up or he'd have stitches down his face not his forearms. Plus the damage to his back."

I unlaced my boots and stretched my legs and waited for her to continue. She sounded like she was waiting, too. I didn't know what to say. I had a hard time picturing Dad in such bad shape—and Mom? My mind started to wander, to lope inward to its own hinterlands. The parents still lived where I grew up, a tiny cluster of trailers at the edge of the Beaufort Sea. No roads in or out except in winter, when you drove the frozen Mackenzie River. I remember Mom's twelve husky-cross runners tugging the titanium sled over the packed snow at the dog races, or to the traplines. Dad revving his Ski-doo or motocross down the Run-What-You-Have ice track the town plowed on the frozen ocean. Dump fires in summer and the watery croak of the ravens.

"I can't do this alone." Trista broke the silence. "I can't deal with the two of them and the dogs by myself."

"How about the neighbours? They'll take the dogs at least."

"Didn't you hear me? It's not the same. Everyone's moved south. You haven't seen how bad she is and how sick the dogs look. No one's been running them — I honestly don't think anyone's fed them."

"All right," I said, although it wasn't possible everyone had gone. And I'd seen the community come together over drilling and poverty and childcare, hell, even to organize the tea-boiling race for jamboree. If there wasn't family, there was always some gossip or do-good to enlist. Of course Trista could still *feel* no one was helping, and that people were shirking responsibilities — by people she'd mean me. "Fine. I'm coming."

I hung up. The snow patted the window in gusts. I wished I'd missed the call, or was asshole enough not to go. It had been years, a real chunk of time, since I'd been to the parents' place. Parents, neighbours — I didn't want to deal. I suppose the land, too: the planned retirement of the ice road, and the migration south coupled with the melt and refurbishment of that part of the world — I was sad.

I pushed myself to think about next morning's shift — the blast of the heated air in the mineshafts and the chug of the water-pumps. But I was only trying to think about work, and memories cracked open like the ice late spring—one frozen sheet then boom, fragments on open water.

TRISTA AND I were kids when the local government started its push against rabies. Pamphlets tacked to the hunting board at the Trader's Co showed sketches of bats, wolves, and skunks in various stages of disease: drooped head, sagging jaw, stiff gait. The presentation slides were graphic, intended to scare, so after the first image of a sick hound—arced body, scummy muzzle—the adults cut us loose. Trista and I and a couple neighbour kids, we bought chips and Coke at the Trader's Co (the only store in town) and headed to the ocean.

Tides had piled ice along the shoreline of the Beaufort. Long spears of it, both clear and flecked with bubbles, jutted into the air and the sunlight. Beyond that, the sea in early freeze: deep navy, filled coast-to-horizon with small plates of white pancake ice. We walked the beach. Trista pushed her hood back and tugged her braid from her parka. I turned up the shore and opened the ice hut—a small wooden structure, similar to a fishing shelter, built on top of communal storage that had been tunnelled into the permafrost way back in the sixties.

Inside the hut, a trapdoor filled most of the floor space and the bottom, when we lifted it, was crusted over. A ladder sank into the permafrost like a lure. Of course we went down, all of us. The wooden rungs were slippery, and the walls of the tunnels coated with rime. In the hut people had stored caribou, whale blubber, a frozen seal, tubs of ice cream, fish for sled dogs. One of us lifted the lid of a cardboard box and found the heads of four decapitated dogs. The heads were to be sent south for rabies testing, something that happened regularly, but the stiff fur and the bullet hole between the tan dog's ears startled us.

The first kids back up the ladder stood on the trapdoor and kept the rest of us in until they got bored. (We had the worst games. It would have been dangerous if we'd locked someone in and forgotten, but we never did.) Later I snuck back to look at the heads. Why not? It was as good a place to hide and smoke as any, and cold even in summer. When the heat had Mom's sled dogs panting in the shade of their houses, when Dad gave up on his dismantled motorbike because of the clouds of mosquitoes, in the ice hut nothing changed.

Only now, I guessed it had. I went through my drawers and packed a couple shirts and a pair of jeans, and then realized I should probably book a ticket before hitching to Yellowknife from the mine.

AT THE DIAVIK human resources desk, I told the girl I needed time off.

"Gotta plug some pups," I joked. I mean, I was serious, the dogs might have to be shot, but I wanted to keep the conversation light and away from the parents. Not a chance.

She knew all about my family issues, she told me. My sister had called her, and had no doubt gone on and on in detail about the accident.

"So I can have the time?" I said.

"You can have the time."

I asked the girl to give me the number of the airport.

"No worries," she said. "We've got you on a company plane. Yellowknife to Inuvik, and there's a supply rig leaving the mine in fifteen if you're ready now."

I thanked her, trying at the same time to think if I knew the girl. It seemed out of character that Trista had spilled personal details to a stranger, but she was overwhelmed, so, maybe. The girl and I continued our back-and-forth with her talking like she knew me — knew my family — and me scrutinizing her but unable to place her. Was she from the hometown? There were a lot of people at the mine from the Territories. But she looked city-based: her fluffy bleached hair and sharp nose, the pierced eyebrow she was going to regret if she ever went outside in the cold, and the edge of a blue tattoo — a vine or maybe a snake or the arm of an octopus—creeping around her neck from under her collared shirt.

No, I couldn't place her, and I had to give up. Which made me wonder if she had me right, or if there had maybe been another accident with another family, and I ended up thanking her again for arranging the plane instead of asking her if we did, in fact, know each other.

The doubt hung around, bothering me while I packed my bag, and I was distracted throughout the drive to Yellowknife with the supply rig. Had I known her, the girl? I held my hands to the heater in the cab of the semi. The driver blasted country music and I relaxed a little. I had to force myself not to chuckle. So I couldn't remember a face. What must it be like for Mom?

MY PARENTS CAME to the north from the south, which was almost unheard of. Dad was RCMP, and Mom lived for the dogsled races. Which could explain why they led the roundup—town safety, and threat of disease circulating into the sled dogs. Each summer they'd gather a crew, catch and load any unchained dog into a pickup, and then drive the pack to the landfill to be shot. I hated it, although I ended up helping swing the dogs into the pit when I was older and working for Search and Rescue.

But Trista and I, we didn't think of dogs the way our parents did—as dangerous. Even now my memory of the roundup strays is their scrawny, joyful rutting in the box of the truck on the way to the dump. We didn't see the land as violent either. Trista and I'd harness a bear dog if Mom had her sled dogs out. We'd borrow the lightest-weight sled we could, and run the fast edge of the floe—where the frozen ocean held the shore. If we couldn't find a sled, we'd repurpose plastic siding, half an aluminum culvert, or anything else that let us run the mirrored sheen of puddled ice late spring, stupidly happy over fathoms of black ocean.

On the ice, water splashed and pooled teal, like the colour of the Diavik office girl's tattoo—that tentacle that snuck up her neck from under her white-collared shirt and made me wonder what it was attached to, and how far down it went.

THE DRIVE OVER the company ice road from Lac de Gras to Yellowknife was a routine whiteout of snow and cloud for 373 kilometres. I didn't know the rig driver, and after we lost the radio we filled time with small talk that made me wish Dad had nearly killed himself in summer instead of winter.

When the road from the mine is thawed, which is most of the year, the company flies its crew between

Yellowknife and the Diavik excavation site over the tundra. The view from the single otter — green in spring; red, pink, and purple near the end of summer; a real fiery autumn. Big stretch of crowberry and bearberry heath, moss, and lichen, splashed with lakes that throw the sky back at you. Blue creeks and waterways run everywhere, since there's nothing to stop them in that flat, treeless place. And then Diavik itself: that open-pit mine — an outlandish, chalky hole corkscrewed in the centre of Lac de Gras. That first time I saw it, it blew my mind — that the water doesn't fill the pit is a feat of engineering. Astonishing.

The driver dropped me in Yellowknife. I had time before I had to be at the airport, and I needed a drink. The bar was crowded with one of the young mining crews — I guess it was payday.

"Next round is on me," I said. Why not. The kids were fresh from their first three weeks and, following their solo shifts, stank with the relief of company. In that crowd I felt I owned the city — the dirty snow, the gravelled strip, the saloon, the stuffed muskox that eyed us from the loft above the bar. I carried a couple pitchers to the table.

"How'd you end up at the mine?" someone asked.

"Before this I was Search and Rescue," I said.

"How long at Diavik?" They topped my pint.

"What, maybe fifteen years?"

There was a pause, and then a kid asked, "How old are you anyway, man?"

A few years into my forties. That's nothing—barely started. I paid for the pitchers and tried not to take it personal. So they couldn't understand why I didn't want to leave the north. Hell, *I* barely understood, and I definitely couldn't explain it. Fuck them.

"Like," I said. "What about the time I decided to snowshoe the lake? The air was cold and blue around the horizon, pink-and-orange twilight overhead. So pretty I didn't watch where I was going. It was forty below and remote as shit. What was there to run into?"

The kids were onto pint three or five. They leaned toward each other and yelled above the music and noise of the bar. I rambled on and pretended I didn't notice no one was listening.

"I ran into a caribou, what was left of it, caught by the legs in the ice. Wolves'd stripped the flesh from its back and rump. I had a view of the spine and ribcage, since, by some miracle of balance, the animal had frozen standing."

"You want another?" The waitress cleared the empty pitchers and gauged the mood of the mine crew around the table.

"Keep it coming," I said. That caribou on the lake, it carried a huge rack on top of its gnawed face. If you haven't seen them, caribou antlers spread at the tips like they've been pressed with a spoon—big scoops of bone flatten into a palm, edged with any number of points, and this pair held palms at the top, mid, and brow. A spectacular set, each splayed palm twice the size of my hand. The breadth of the rack gave me a headache, how an animal could walk around with a pair like that.

I raised my voice. "In case anyone thinks Diavik is the ass-end of civilization, it isn't."

"Keep it together, dude," someone said.

But isn't the ass-end. Same way the parents' place isn't the ass-end of nowhere. Not quite. Wintertime, Diavik's ice road extends beyond the mine. Keep trucking north from the hole in Lac de Gras and in thirty-eight kilometres you'll hit Misery. I'm serious, Misery Lake. Misery Camp—a satellite of Ekati Diamond Mine. Check the maps. And 220 kilometres further, yet another mine spirals into Jericho Lake clawing even more diamonds from kimberlite. Beyond that there's the islands, and a few kids who've never seen trees.

Outrageous, sure. Maybe even fable-esque, but not shit. Not ass-end.

YOU WANT FABLE-ESQUE, let me go back even earlier than the dog heads and the rabies scare to when I was four or five, and my parents told us about where they were from. Most people in our town grew up there, were born at home or in Inuvik or Whitehorse hospital. Dad, his family sprouted so far south I couldn't picture it: Edmonton.

"What's it like there?" Trista asked. We were raking hay in the summer dog yard. The dogs draped themselves behind their houses, dug under the frames, and collapsed anywhere there was shade — it was mid-July and the sun had been up nine weeks straight.

"For starters," Dad said. He had his motocross pulled apart in the open shed. "The sun sets each night, even in summer. Rises year round."

"No way," I said. "There's *no way.*"

We had no doubt he was pulling our leg, and couldn't understand why he insisted.

"I know," he said, "the sun doesn't always do that here. But trust me, they wouldn't believe this place exists either."

I CAUGHT A TAXI from the bar to the airport, slightly drunk and disgruntled by the attitude of the younger crowd. To top that off, my flight was delayed and I had nothing to do. I scrolled through the contacts on my phone and decided to call an ex-common law, but hung up when I heard her voice. My ex, Rachel, she'd had a kid when I moved in with her, and he used to come in the bathroom and pee while I was showering. No big deal, I'm no prude, but it was all stops and starts with the kid's urine stream. I asked him what was up and the kid showed me. He'd pinch his foreskin closed and pee into it until it ballooned, and then let the piss splash into the toilet bowl.

My ex called back thirty seconds after I pocketed my phone and said, like old times, "What the fuck gives you the right to hang up on me, fucker?"

"Rachel, you sure you got the right guy?" I asked.

"Call display, Jack," she said. "What do you want?"

"I wasn't thinking straight," I said. I told her Mom had Alzheimer's and I wanted to reminisce. She didn't say no, so I went on. "That pee trick. Where'd Joey learn that?" It hadn't come from me — I'm circumcised.

"How the hell should I know? Kids pick things up."

"I guess that's why the bathroom stank."

Why'd I say any of that? Maybe the same reason that, after we found the box of decapitated dog heads as kids, I kept sneaking back to the ice hut and staying as long as I could. Which was a long time in the winter, when I could layer myself in a parka and snow gear, and a very short time in the summer. It was so weird I wanted to make sure I remembered it right. That it'd been real.

Rachel hung up on me this time, and I'd barely set down the phone when it rang again. It was my parents' number. I didn't pick up. It would be Trista wanting to know why I wasn't in the air yet.

OUTSIDE THE AIRPORT windows mechanics rose in bucket trucks and sprayed pink, foamy liquid over the wings of the plane. The flight wasn't anywhere near ready. I wanted a smoke, but I'd quit years ago. That's something that follows you — old habits. I could chart my life into smoking, quitting, craving. Shake up the order and the list would still be accurate.

I first smoked when I visited the dog heads as a kid — and thinking about that made me a little excited to see Trista. To rehash all the shit we pulled, everything we thought we got away with, who'd ratted on who. The time Trista and I had the guns taken away for popping ptarmigans — one shell from a 12-gauge and the fat birds exploded in gratifying puffs of white. I almost hit callback on my cell to chat with her, but I didn't want her to tell me how far gone Mom was. Not yet.

Maybe, I told myself, maybe she remembers the old stuff. Like, finding me when I was eight in the ice hut next to the box of heads. After she shouted me from the hut she lifted the twelve-dog sled (lightweight, aluminum) from its hooks and had me hop the lead dogs (Hill-Billy and Cash) to the front lines, harness them, and drive into the night with her.

When it grew dark she had headlamps and then when the dogs grew tired she footed the brake. Secured all twelve husky-cross runners on a long chain pegged into the ice and fed them caribou joints and fish. She lit a fire, spread hay for the dogs, and stepped each into a sleep-sac. They curled into balls. When I woke, a light skiff of snow covered them, and she sat by the fire boiling a massive pan of kibble. I'm not sure what she wanted to teach me, but the labour of basic movement under all that winter clothing—I was exhausted before we'd left the yard.

AFTER I BOARDED the flight I realized I had nothing to read but the safety guide—orange and grey cartoons of women and men inflating lifejackets on a flaming plane, expressions absurdly tranquil. Before Diavik I'd worked Search and Rescue out of the military base near the hometown, and there was nothing calm about it.

Mostly I'd duct-taped my seatbelt together in a helicopter and leaned from the craft, on the lookout for a missing hunter's orange safety vest, a stream of smoke that rose in the distance, or the upturned hull of a trawler or skiff on the choppy ocean. Sometimes young idiots jumped ice floes with their Ski-doos. I'd done it when I was a teen—worked up enough speed for a leap and revved over open water, hydroplaning to the next bit of ice. If the Ski-doo didn't reach the floe, we were on recovery.

The plane hit turbulence and the nervous flyer beside me, a huge man who must have been way too hot in his parka, jerked his hand from the armrest and gripped my fingers. He kept his eyes screwed shut and didn't acknowledge the action, so I sat there and let him squeeze, and tried to think of anything besides the way my stomach lurched with each jolt of the plane.

Some of Search and Rescue had been good: I'd worked with Cindy. Five feet tall, pointed chin, black hair she wound in two buns above her ears that gave her face a kittenish shape. She'd volunteered at a fire department way south — Watson Lake, practically British Columbia — at the squat end of the Yukon. That led her to High Arctic Rescue Training at the military base outside my hometown, which led her to me. The first summer, when we were both in Basic Firearms, the deerflies slashed and sucked blood like a bitch. She was worried about tularemia, anthrax, eye worm, et cetera, and it was hot — the sun wobbled around the horizon like a helium balloon low on spunk. I suggested the ice hut.

Some thoughtless hunter had plucked geese in the corridor. Feathers and bits of blood were frozen into the gravel and on the walls. My family's locker was okay, sparkly ice crystals coated the roof, but it was more like

being in a deep-freeze than it was romantic, and when
Cindy opened a cardboard box, she found — I shit you
not — the same dog heads I'd obsessed over as a kid.
One grey, two black, one tan.

She didn't say anything, so I lit a smoke. Then
remembered she wanted me to quit (lung cancer — she
knew about the asbestos workers from Cassiar and said
it was unholy hell) and I put the cigarette out in the
tan dog's eye.

When she calmed down enough to listen, I explained
about the routine dog culls, that the town couldn't let
strays pack up. I said strays, but I meant sled or bear
dogs that had slipped the chain and soured. Wild, feral
animals plagued with mange and starvation — nothing
friendly or rehabilitatable about them.

And once I started talking about the culls, I remembered those particular dogs. How had I forgotten? The
first dog had turned up quietly — stretched in a green
patch of dwarf birch by the Trader's Co late August, its
matted coat thick with flies. Town shot the nose off the
second on the gravel strip outside the food bank. Third
I couldn't recall. But the fourth was a frothy-mouthed
bitch the town ran down on Ski-doos and blew to pieces.
There were kids to think of. I guess no one sent them
south for testing. No one got around to it.

Cindy must have forgiven me, because later on we
pushed a canoe into the Beaufort and dropped a fishing

line. She twisted around to look at me in the canoe, her shiny black buns a little lopsided, the long-sleeve shirt she wore to fight bugs and sunburn one of those old-fashioned ones. You know the type, the colourful plaid cotton that was so popular in the mid-eighties. "Why are they still there?" she asked.

"The heads?" I let the fishing line spin out. Who knew? The town must have forgotten about them. I forgot. I wouldn't have brought her down there if I'd remembered.

Baby-blue sky and clear ocean, the yellow canoe, the speckled red lure, Cindy's shiny twists of hair. My eyes followed the weight and jigging spoon down, way down—I could see depth that hadn't been there a moment ago—and then the glint of red fell too far into the black.

MY FLIGHT LANDED in Inuvik in the early morning, and the aircraft marshals waved us off the tarmac with their orange beacons. I hustled to the bathroom. My hand-holding neighbour from the plane pushed past me and locked himself in a stall. I spit in the sink and washed my face, but the sounds and smell from the cubicle didn't encourage relaxation.

"You all right?" I asked. No response. I went to the desk and put in a request for a rental, one with chains that could travel the winter road north to the hometown.

"Are you okay?" the boy at the desk asked.

"I'm fine," I said. "Turbulence." But I wasn't sure that was why I felt like shit, why my face was grey and had greenish bags under the eyes, the eyes a bit red and more yellowed than I was comfortable with. There was more to it than the flight; it was a mind trip heading home. I knew what would happen when I arrived.

I'd bang on the door, wait for Trista to open it, and haul my backpack into the living room. Some of the furniture would be different — probably a satellite dish, a flatscreen — but the house would still have the same dusty, burnt smell of newsprint and kindling, and like whoever vacuumed used too intense a setting on the shag carpet. Dad in a wheelchair in his housecoat, both his legs propped on an ottoman, greenish-yellow bruises over his shins and knees. He'd have lost weight in the hospital and his skin would hang off him. He'd take my hand and then, seeing me note the stitches down his forearms, he'd lift his arms to shield his face.

"Studded tires coming right at me," he'd say. "Ripped straight through the parka."

"Don't brag," I'd respond, and he'd excuse himself: "They got me on opiates."

I wouldn't be able to bring myself to ask about Mom.

All that thinking about what waited, when I could do nothing to fix it.

"Here's the keys." The boy at the rental counter handed me a fob. "You'll find the truck in the lot. Chains are in the box if they aren't on the tires already. There's a key for the storage on the ring."

MID-WINTER THE MACKENZIE was three feet thick and black and the only vehicles I passed were plows or water trucks sealing faults. Not much snow, but what powder there was had been scraped clear of the ice and piled along the sides of the frozen river. The pickup's headlights lit the fog, and then the sky caught a lick of sun and glowed rosy to the south. Ravens perched on fishing boats dry-docked along the banks. A couple of foxes scoured for hares and roadkill with the lanky, airy gait I remembered alongside the dogsled trails. The radio played eighties classics, interspersing the songs with chatter about an NHL charity game in Whitehorse, and then an update on the berm construction Tuk to Inuvik—an all-season highway over the permafrost. I'd seen it leaving Inuvik: stockpiled geotextile rolls and silvery culverts.

Of all the modern marvels.

The all-season road had been talked about for decades, opposed by the south because of the price, and in the north we had mixed feelings. Win some, lose some—the new road would be a bit of both.

Back when I was in the hometown, and right into my Search and Rescue years, you flew in or waited for the freeze. Water one day, ice the next, and vice versa. You had to watch yourself. Like when that overloaded rig cracked through the ice road—eighteen-wheeler bent at the coupling and hung on by the front axle and rear wheels long enough for the driver to pray his way out of the cab. The town patted the man's back, handed him a coffee as the tractor raised its nose and slipped backwards into the water. Nothing to do about it, and the rig vanished into the black without a burp, the whole picture eerily quiet.

It was a shock, but we went on. That same year: first haze of green in May, we harpooned a beluga. Cut and dried slabs of blubber and skin on the rock shore of the Beaufort. Cubed the fat into muktuk and stored it in the ice hut. Yellow warblers returned and perched in larch and white spruce that managed stunted growth in sheltered valley dips even this far beyond the tree line. Buds turned to meaty leaves. Hares and foxes shed their winter colour and the muskoxen gathered with undercoats hanging from their backs in mossy strips.

Summer. The last piles of snow collapsed and the entire town became a puddle. Water reflected the sky, heather bloomed and the horizon took on a yellow-white sheen. Fireweed, green-keeled cotton grass, Arctic huckleberry. The sun careened around the horizon. Mosquitoes and blackflies rose from the tundra in clouds.

Another roundup, we shot strays at the dump and swung them by the legs into the landfill. Anything that looked sick rather than starving got decapitated (carving knife between the vertebrae base of the neck) and tossed to a box. Once it was done, we'd empty a canister of mixed-gasoline on the pile and light it up.

Then fall, then winter. Then another spring. And again, the ice breakup—sudden, impressive, and loud. Groans for weeks, and then a boom that thundered over everything. The ice gave and flowed.

Rose-coloured shit, I told myself, navigating the pickup around the cracks in the frozen Mackenzie.

THE MACKENZIE ICE road hit the Beaufort and I drove the last leg of the winter road over the ocean. And then I was there. The hometown. The sign marking the weight capacity of the ice was pocked with bullet holes, and a couple mangy strays tugged at a muskrat hide. Dry-docked boats by the frozen shore. All the buildings on stilts above the permafrost, all the stilts buried in snow. Trailers coated in frost. Aluminum utilitdors, silver and pink in the twilight, snaked electric and plumbing and phone between houses. Insulated with foam and yellow fibreglass, those tubes are full of voles, and come summer the couple tattered cats that've survived the foxes will spend sunny days on top of the warm metal.

I parked outside the Trader's Co and threw my bag over my shoulder. I trudged through the snow over the Ski-doo trails up the hill, past too many boarded houses, to the parents' place, where I stopped. They must've tossed caribou antlers on the roof every single year they lived there, and the trailer looked fortified for the apocalypse. Dad's busted motocross sat in the shed beside the Ski-doo. A satellite dish (I was right, they'd installed one) pointed due south. And in the yard, Mom's dogs. Fifteen to twenty husky-cross chained to square-frame doghouses. Tan and black, pale-eyed, most curled and asleep on straw and snow. A torn ear, a raised head. Walking closer I saw most had yellow crust in the eyes. Shit stains down the legs.

I stood for a while. If I had Cindy's number I'd have called her. She'd probably hang up on me like my ex had, but I only wanted to make sure they remembered everything we'd been through. The embarrassing fuck-ups I used to wish I could forget. I mean, if we can laugh over it, we should be okay, right?

I watched the dogs squint through pus and chew their sores.

Until then—until I saw the condition of the dogs—I'd kept telling myself the situation wasn't as bad as Trista claimed. Same as Dad had done with Mom's illness, probably. Probably what kept him from calling for help—he couldn't get past the sadness.

I can forgive him that.

From the look of the animals, I guessed I would suffer a bit of heartbreak inside the house.

I CLIMBED UP the frozen stairs and banged on the parents' door. Trista opened it and we hugged. I handed her a bottle of Malbec I'd snagged in Inuvik.

"Wait here." She set the bottle aside, zipped into a parka and joined me on the steps. "I got to fill you in on the damage before you see them."

"That bad?" I said.

I didn't want to interrupt her, but I couldn't bring myself to listen either. In the yard, Mom's skinny dogs gnawed frozen char. Trista must have fed them. And watching the dogs eat I suddenly remembered when the other stray from the ice hut had turned up: a grey bitch, milky at the teats, wandering slowly from the eastern lake area. The dog's stiff gait, her relentless stumble along the rocky shore. The ice hut, I wanted to ask Trista. When you got the fish did you see the box with the dogs' heads?

"Okay," Trista squeezed my arm.

I grabbed the doorknob.

It's been thirty years since Trista and I were kids, but I remember this one winter when the snow came late. Dad and I ski-dooed the trapline with two neighbour boys, baiting foot traps with stink salmon. I scratched together the scattered, powdery cover—more frost than snow—at the river's outlet to hide the traps. We'd thumped a couple snared foxes earlier that morning and had a rogue, cherry-coated male and one white vixen lashed to the Ski-doo trailer. The light bounced a warm orange over the ice—the sun scraped around the south horizon and set fire to colour, every red enriched and backed by blue shadow. We lowered our hoods, the neighbour boys' toques bold yellow against the wolverine trim on their parkas. Dad and I planted marker logs near the traps and loaded the bucket of stink salmon on the trailer. Below—honest to god, I remember this as clear as the ice under us—we realized we could see the silty rocks of the riverbed and good-sized sheefish swimming in the brackish water. Course we broke out the auger and then took maybe thirteen fish total. Each time we dropped the lure we hooked and pulled a flopping, tinny fish onto the ice.

Mom was a long shadow on the horizon, running her titanium sled, six dogs off the gangline. Trista followed on the four-dog behind—there's no sound when you run, nothing but the breath of the dogs and the hiss of the sled over the snow. They caught us unawares, and helped haul the catch home.

Later we barbecued and ate. The white, flaky meat sweeter than halibut. While Dad cooked, I hung the two foxes from the shed by their rear legs and wrapped their noses in paper towel and duct tape. Cut a slit around each ankle and peeled the skins from the carcasses like a sock.

Standing with Trista, opening that door—

No, the fish is what I want to leave you with. Never saw anything like it again. We kept reeling one after another, saying, as their tails flashed in the sun and pounded the ice, "Would you look at that."

DA CAPO AL FINE

CÉCILE, I hope you'll hear what I'm saying—

September 1783, Taskin and I carried a fortepiano through the gold gates of the Palace of Versailles. On the patterned black and white slabs of the marble court—Louis XVI, not yet thirty, in a wide, ostrich-feathered tricorn, cream culottes, and jacket. Marie in pale blue. Courtiers flanked the royals at a distance, in their finest stockings and wigs, ribbons and lace. Taskin and I set our instrument to the cobbles near the gates and waited.

Buoyed by hot air and tethered under grey clouds: an immense balloon of sky-coloured taffeta. Roped to the base of the cloth, a basket held a sheep called Montauciel, a duck, and a common red-and-green rooster. The Montgolfier brothers, who had built the aerostat, conferred at the balloon's anchor. A sign from the monarch and the anchor released—the basket raised the animals. You, Cécile, soprano in the Opéra Royal, paused at the edge of the courtyard mid-fitting— everyone had stopped what they were doing and come from the palace to watch. Court astronomers and artisans clenched their hands, the Enfants de France kept still in the grip of their new governess, and the King and Queen—all faces lifted.

Cécile—or should I use your full name? Anne-Antoinette-Cécile Clavel, known as the soprano and diva Madame Saint-Huberty—you wore canary and amber stripes, and in memory, at least, outshone the Queen. Though no one looked at either of you—the Montgolfier aerostat strained under the clouds. The rooster crowed. The tailor, kneeling at your hem, let the pins fall from his mouth, and the young dauphin of France retrieved them.

After the balloon flew and sheep, duck, and cock became the first living beasts carried into the air (they were the first to crash as well, after the rope broke and the brothers chased the aerostat's flight over the palace) Taskin and I picked up our fortepiano and followed you from the courtyard to the Opéra Royal. The largest theatre in Europe—another marvel of engineering and decorative refinement—it could seat an audience of over a thousand in its stacked galleries. The seats were empty when we arrived, with only set workers and a few members of the pit orchestra rehearsing. Above us, mirrors created an illusion of depth and reflected the warm light of the chandeliers. Woodwork, embellished with gilded fleurs-de-lys and wreaths of leaves, ornamented every surface. On the ceiling, Apollo prepared crowns in a pale sky, and a winged horse reared behind him.

Taskin and I set the fortepiano on stage; I raised the instrument's lid. Your tailor, Cécile, went for the hem of your gown with his pins, and you ran your fingers over the ivory and ebony keys, brushed the Val di Fiemme spruce that composed the soundboard.

"*Gravicembalo col piano e forte,*" Taskin said. "A fortepiano, not a harpsichord. A new design. String sets replace plucked quill—hammers instead of plectra—and, as you can see, we coated the exterior with gold. Moulding, stand, corner rails, and box. A perfectly leafed and brushed rosette." He pointed to the carved lattice that shielded the sound hole under the wire strings. "Burnished flutes on the legs and at the base of each foot add elegance."

You played a chord. "Tobias," you said to me. "You've gilded a lily. I adore it. It may stay."

A lily—

Did I read too much into your praise, Cécile? Neither of us was that young—and you, already twenty-seven with one annulled marriage, supported yourself as courtesan. I loved you, you must have known that. Taskin and I both loved you. I suppose all your patrons loved you.

The tailor manoeuvered you to a mirror and bowed. "Voilà."

You turned sideways, looking at yourself, and tugged at the breast of the gown. "Taskin, Tobias — you know this opera?" you asked. "*Iphigénie en Aulide*? Do you think the ancient Greeks wore panniers and corsets?" You waved aside an exasperated look from the tailor, the set builders, and said, "A redesign. A change in costume. Something plainer. Let that shock them."

HAVE I TOLD YOU, Cécile, how Taskin and I became friends? Instrument making via a heritage of cabinetry — my father, an *ébéniste* from the Low Country along the Rhine, sold oak tables, jewellery caskets veneered with tortoiseshell, gilt copper, and pewter. On the death of François-Étienne Blanchet II, my father had me decorate and gift an armoire to the family. Seeing the quality of our marquetry, Taskin — the new master of Blanchet Harpsichords — took me on as craftsman.

The Blanchets were instrument makers to the King, and with Taskin I was honoured to detail the soundboards and cases of clavichords and harpsichords (and later fortepianos) for the French court and the Institut National de Musique. Printed paper overlay, ebony naturals, Chinoiserie, silver gilt rails and moulding, elaborate painted landscapes — on such instruments Claude Balbastre and Armand-Louis Couperin, grandson of Couperin le Grand, composed their works.

You remember Paris. Mid-century, during the rush of sciences, arts, and industry, it was the innovative that rose. A new steam pump drew drinkable water from the Seine, street lamps lit the larger roads, Cassini de Thury mapped the topography of Paris, and the Observatoire de Paris mapped the distant planets. In music, the Viennese fortepiano was our turning point. We gutted and converted harpsichords from quill and plectra to soft leather hammers, heads that struck the string with varied force and allowed for change in volume. With Taskin, I built the best.

Although, these days — you would have to hurry if you wanted to view the instruments now, as in this new era France raises an Emperor and it's rumoured the Conservatoire de Musique burns their keyboards for heat.

We might have continued to build the best —

What is progress, anyway? Why the human need to cleave a path into the future?

Almost ten years after the Montgolfier brothers flew their first aerostat, after Taskin and I presented you with our best work, we three — Taskin, you, myself — we were all in Paris. You had followed the royal opera, which had followed the royal family in fleeing Versailles — there had been a scarcity of bread, ransacking, violence, and the crowds had besieged the palace and pressed their demands upon the King —

CÉCILE, I find every draft of this letter riddled with excuses. I scrap the composition and rewrite. I start again. I keep getting it wrong. This time, let me just admit the friendship: Charles-Henri Sanson, headsman to the King, and later to the French Republic. Sanson and I met when Taskin, refusing to visit the headsman's house to repair a harpsichord, sent me.

Sanson — executioner of France, red tunic and hood, the blood on his hands, the blood in his heritage. Infamous for his lack of hesitation and his precision with the sword. The condemned could expect a solid death from Sanson, so solid a death it was rumoured he enjoyed the work. But Cécile, he also played music and studied medicine — he could take a cadaver and give you the history of the man's life through the injuries. His wife served pot pie and his sons had wit.

Sanson and I played music. I visited his home, and had him come to mine. How could I turn away his friendship? His requests? I was curious — as was Sanson;

he requested to see the latest instruments built by me and Taskin at the shop.

The Blanchet shop in Paris—a mess: sheets of cypress clamped into shape on moulds (the bent sides of harpsichord and fortepiano cases); workbenches full of rosettes and cornices; crates of pins and leather and kapsels (forked ribbons of brass that would hold hammer-shanks on newer models). Long-toothed keys waited—aligned, sanded, and numbered—to be painted and installed. Nests of wire—spools of flattened gold tape, buckets of bleached cattle bones, sliced sections of ivory, paint, and soundboards illuminated with flowers and inscriptions (the ever popular *dvm vixi tacvi mortva dulce cano*—*In Life I Was Silent, In Death I Sweetly Sing*). Sawdust, locks, and other hardware, custom conductor's batons, and, on that late evening, a fire in the woodstove, two glasses of wine, Sanson, and myself.

I opened the latest fortepiano: "The soundboard is composed of spruce flitches, glued and sanded. Each checked for knots or pitch pockets. See under the strings? Swiss pear hammer-heads and -shanks, escapements, damper jacks, and back checks—the fortepiano's action. All the anatomy between the key and the string."

I ran my hand over the walnut veneer.

Sanson sat and played the opening theme of an overture. The sound—Cécile, you remember the instrument we delivered?—a tone similar to the lute, but rounder, more resonant. Rather than the pluck of a finger, this was a cushioned blow of felts (we no longer used leather to pad hammers) that touched the strings for only an instant. Blanchet instruments demanded a patchwork of finesse, and I'd spent hours on that one: a metallic rattle silenced by a pinch to the kapsel arms; the replaced prell hinge eliminated a wooden thunk; constant ringing corrected by fluffing the chamois with a needle; adjustment to let-off prevented a hammer blockage—

I sat on a bench, then stood again at a sound from upstairs.

"Who's there?" Taskin held a candelabra in the stairway from his apartment above the workshop. It was late, and he was dressed to retire. I should have realized he'd stayed in town rather than at his estate (or with you in your Paris townhouse, Cécile. By then you'd long been mistress to him, to me, and I suppose to your Comte).

"Tobias, what—" He saw me first, and then crossed the room and held the candles to Sanson's face: ridged nose, flat cheekbones and chin, and a wide-spaced, almost bovine expanse between the eyes that gave him a calm but pensive expression.

Taskin, recognizing Sanson, stepped back. His eyes looked wet and prominent in the candlelight. "Get out."

"You'd criticize a civil servant for his career?" I said.

"You should know better — 'civil servant'?" Taskin swallowed whatever he would say next.

Sanson took his time, finished his wine, buttoned his jacket — rouge d'Andrinople, the jacket had belonged to his father and grandfather, and would be worn by Sanson's son when he inherited the post. (The great-grandfather had a black coat with puce sleeves and gallows embroidered in gold front and back, but Sanson's uncle burned that bit of history in a fit of disgust — or was it thankfulness? — after Paris's final quartering.) He straightened his wig and stowed his cello in its case. Taskin kept calm until I closed the door.

"I hired you for inlay," he said. "To apprentice, and then as journeyman — you were a child." He turned to the fortepiano and I thought that might be it, he might have finished the reprimand, but he went on. "You taint the name of Blanchet with that *bourreau*."

Light shone through Taskin's ratty nightshirt and showed his body — his potbelly, the shadow of his sagging chest, the hairs on his thighs. Cécile, I saw how his cheeks and neck drooped and had a soft, pocked texture. His hand on the brass candelabra column was lined with scars.

"Be serious." I topped my wine. "How would you explain my dismissal?"

"You'll see." Taskin embarrassed, in a rage. "Get out. Go on. Last time you, or any other Low Country shit, makes his mark on the King's harpsichords." He waved the flames near my face and I jerked back from the sputtering wax.

"But since the aerostat—" I started. I'm still not sure what I meant, other than we were sharing a mistress— you, Cécile—and not just a company; that I'd made a name with Blanchet's and that Taskin and I were (or I'd thought we were) friends. "Your finishing quality will go down."

"Tobias." He'd managed to calm down and added: "You know, I heard Madame Saint-Huberty displayed her breast on stage."

"Is this about Cécile?" I drained my wine and he said nothing. Though Cécile, I'd heard the gossip— the whole country knew of it. That opera, *Iphigénie en Aulide,* where you had designed the costumes yourself—

At first the audience had been charmed by the loose togas of the chorus—Thessalian guards, Greek soldiers, women from Aulis, slaves from Lesbos, and attendants on the princess sang and danced on stage. The singers were envied, even, as the chorus was certainly more comfortable in light clothing than the audience were in their layers and wigs, and seated at close quarters under the heat of the candles. It could have been a success, Cécile, until you, singing the titular role of Iphigénie, rode to centre stage half-naked on a chariot. Your waxed legs, your breast and small pink nipple welcomed the gaze of hundreds of opera patrons for three long Acts.

After the first performance, the King had forbidden the new costumes, and you were returned to the corset and panniers. Lewd sketches appeared in the streets (your likeness, though the size of your breasts and thighs were exaggerated) and the opera forced you into smaller roles. Your confidence fell. Your voice had difficulty with the higher register. You retired from the stage and accepted a different type of patronage — Cécile, we were both outcast.

I LEFT TASKIN to his rage and walked by your Paris townhouse, thinking I'd stay with you, since my home had been above the Blanchet workshop. Your townhouse was lit with chandeliers and music, and I let myself in. If you don't recall that masque, that's fine; it was one of many, with everyone in costume. The men wore crimson or black cloaks. Women pierced their wool-filled hair and wigs with jewelled scratching sticks. Everyone was covered in lace and brocade, and on their breasts, cut-glass gemstones caught the light and threw it laughingly back. The tables were covered in porcelain gambling chips, dancers took over the foyer, chamber players and music sounded at the top of the stairs, and drunken riddle games made little sense in the parlour. Your personal chambers were empty. In the garden, I saw only shadows that leaned toward each other behind bushes and the gazebo. At the pond, a fountain frothed into the pool and silver carps mouthed the surface.

Cécile, if I found leaving my father and brother and the Low Country difficult, expulsion from the Blanchets' instrument shop was devastating. Over the next week, under the guise of repairs and at the expense of restoring painted landscapes and Chinoiserie, Taskin scraped my signature from every Blanchet instrument in Paris. After hearing the news, I dragged myself to Sanson—his wife withdrew to the house, his son and apprentice Young Gabriel to the shed to clean the tools of the trade, and Sanson and I sipped water and played a game of backgammon in his garden.

"In the old days," he offered, "when a newsmonger caught my father with a bowl of broth in a bouillon, his presence bankrupted the restaurant. These days, if I go to a market and touch a melon, the fruit is tossed to the street. Not even the swine are allowed it. My wife has only her sister for friendship, and that in secret."

"Very nice," I said. "*Bienvenue*—welcome, fellow pariah!"

"Here's a distraction," he said, and presented a problem—Dr. Guillotin and the Assembly had determined

France needed a unified method of execution. "But can you see nobility at the gibbet? Or the reverse: an apple-vendor standing for the sword?"

"Easy." I sketched a simple combination of gallows and blade. *Le Mécanisme*. *La Monte-à-regret, le Moulin-à-Silence, le Rasoir National, la demi-lune, les Bois de Justice*—

The contract allowed me to rent furnished apartments and a workshop in the Cour du Commerce, rue Saint-André des Arts, Paris.

CÉCILE, here's another moment this letter varies—each new draft I say to myself, "What do I include?" Priests, forbidden to wear ecclesiastical costume outside of church. The moment Louis XVI bowed to the new constitution, or when we went to war (Austria and Prussia, Hungary and Bohemia)—it's not as if you didn't live it, Cécile. You know how France festered.

April 1792—Sanson and I built *le mécanisme* in the street in front of my new shop: the device that would behead both commoners and nobility with *Liberté, égalité, fraternité!*

We drew a crowd. An audience, rather, despite the weather. Rain drummed the roofs of the terraced apartments and the signs and heralds of businesses (clinic, dentist, printer); it flowed in rivulets down the sides of buildings to spit from the carved ram's head below each scrolled window ledge. Sanson piqued the voyeurs of Paris. His horses, harnessed to the family carriage and content with their bags of feed; the broken bell-crest that stated "headsman"; the bull-calf and the three meaty, mutton-bred, Bleu du Maine sheep Sanson had brought with him—all these promised a diversion, I suppose.

Typesetters leaned against the double-wide print shop door, their hands and aprons black with ink. Above them, servants peered at us from apartment windows, and down the street café patrons sipped coffee or spooned gelato at the indoor tables. Drink peddlers hawked wine to curious bystanders seated on crates under the eaves. Even some of the wealthy idled under wax-coated parasols.

By noon Sanson and I had the straight-edge blade screwed into the weight and yanked to the top of the bald uprights. Sanson, drenched, buttoned his tunic and straightened his cuffs. We would test the device on the livestock he had provided.

Have you ever sat a sheep, Cécile? I know your brother became a pork butcher, and your mother was a grocer's daughter, so although your father was *répétiteur* for the Elector Palatine, you might have gone to the fields with your cousins. If you haven't: sheep are surprisingly solid—heavy. Sanson grabbed the muzzle of the first and eased the wet animal onto its tail, where it remained in a daze, while the other two sheep — a lame wether and a botched castration with maggoty wool, both polled — looked on. Once the sheep was strapped to the bascule we slid the plank and animal under the blade and clamped the lunette on its neck.

The first drop cut cleanly. The second, the blade hooked into the wooden beam as it fell, and the lurch took down the speed. (With the heft of the thirty-pound weight the blade still managed to slice the wether's neck.) But by the time we had the calf cinched to the bascule the wood of the device had swollen with rain and blood, and friction slowed the fall. Sanson finished the calf with a knife, which brought taunts and an "Is that all, then?" from the crowd.

"Steel grooves," I said. "And the mechanism won't stick."

Sanson tucked his fingers into the nick the blade had gouged into the beam. He was pleased and gave *le méch-anisme* a name: "Louisette," he said. "After the King."

Indoors, I threw my wig onto a box of kapsels and wire and poured wine into pewter mugs. Violins, recently varnished — I took what work I could, as did you, Cécile — hung from the ceiling, and I'd purchased and repaired a spinet for practice in the new shop.

Sanson folded his jacket over a chair. He lifted his cello from its case and rested the butt of the instrument in the crook of his calves. We drank and played operas—mostly Gluck—until the oil burned down and the scores became illegible.

I lit a candle. Sanson rested his cello beside his chair and eyed the Louisette. The clock ticked and vied with the rhythm of rain in the gutters. We refilled our mugs and set the drinks on the wood stove to heat. I moved from the spinet to an armchair and stretched my legs.

"At eighteen," Sanson began.

"This again."

He pointed his bow at me and I raised my hand—all right, I'd listen. He went on: "We botched an execution, my uncle and I," he said. "We had the condemned strapped between horses, and the horses straining in four directions. The crowd in the auditorium reduced to silence and vomit—rare for them. Of course the man wasn't coming apart. I didn't know, neither I nor my uncle knew, to slice the ligaments first. How often did we draw and quarter? Never."

He ran his thumb over the hair of the bow and continued. "Sanson Père, my father, angry as fuck, and paralyzed down his left side, tried to correct us—the language he sprayed. I'm chuckling over it now, I know. What else is there to do? I was trying my best, barely eighteen. I cut the tendons, and the limbs finally ripped. We burned the torso at the stake." Sanson swirled his wine in its pewter cup. "Ah," he said. "Well. What comfort could I expect?"

I closed my eyes and listened to the wind, the dripping gutters. With wine and the smell of sawdust and varnish, I could have been back at the Blanchet workshop.

"But comfort came," I prodded.

"Comfort did follow," Sanson mused. "That was the final quartering." The diagram for the Louisette sat between us, tall pillars of wood, blade, a lunette to clamp around the neck of the condemned. The real device, dismantled and stored at the back of the room, had a faint smell—meat, and fresh-cut cedar.

He tapped the paper with his bow. "A simpler execution. Good will come of this, too."

IT WAS CLOSE to midnight when Sanson left my shop, and nearer to dawn when my city-wandering brought me to your house, Cécile. You weren't expecting me, and I caught you returning from some masque—you stood on the street near a lamppost, a carriage rattling away.

"Tobias." You pinched your cloak around your throat. "If you must. Follow me, then."

In your apartment I threw my coat on a striped sofa and scanned the curiosities and books in your library. Jewellery caskets decorated the side table. The smallest was two inches square, and on the lid, mother-of-pearl

Greek nudes. (Did you acquire the box before or after the explicit costumes, I wonder?) Delicate work, with well-cut miniature forms, but the box was empty. I set it down and opened the largest, ornamented with flowers — nothing of value inside. You were pawning your jewels, I realized. And I hadn't seen a servant, either. I closed the box. Standard marquetry material: bone and turtle-shell stems, thickly petalled peonies, and roses heavy with jasper and jade — veneers that carried with them all the weight of their composition.

I reached for your hand, but you were humourless and asked for money. I said I didn't have any. You told me you knew I had been given the contract.

"What do you mean?" I asked.

You unbuckled your shoes and pried them off your feet. "You would lie to me," you said, and set a paper from the print shop next to the jewellery caskets.

It read: "It's been asked by us, 'What manner of man is Sanson, with his steady hand at sword or gallows?' Now, though, we predict the crowds will cry out for a return of his 'dash, panache, and impeccable timing' (we quote ourselves) — and, indeed, are citizens not entitled to the spectacle of justice? The so-called Louisette is too quick to the cut."

"He'll hate it," I said.

"You demonstrated in front of your own shop, Tobias."

The brocade of your footwear and gown flickered lavender in the candlelight. Your face, pale with a coating of powder and paint, became suddenly tired. I caved and gave you money. Admitted the contract.

"Do you remember the aerostat?" I asked.

"I suppose so, Tobias." Cécile, you looked bored, and, at the same time, beautiful. Your violet skirts filled the chair and spilled over the arms and on the floor. The heel of one silk stocking had worn thin enough to see through, and you folded your fan and tossed it to the table.

"Everyone gathered on the marble courtyard — the King and Marie. How your tailor fussed." I reached down and picked your shoe off the floor. "Do you ever regret the costume innovations —" I started to ask. I often wondered, Cécile, if you would take back that costume change, the gasp your naked legs and breast caused the audience. If you regretted being shunned, performing less, and that you became known as erratic. Your forced retirement in Paris.

"Yes, yes. I remember the aerostat." You slid down the chair and rested your head on the crest. "I remember the rope broke and the Montgolfier brothers chased the balloon over the palace into the gardens, and when it landed the basket was green with duck shit."

"Are you still sleeping with Taskin?" I asked.

You took your shoe from me and set it with its pair.

"There's wine," you said, but didn't bring it, and you didn't let me touch you.

The walk back to my new workshop took me by the lumberyards and the swimming dock—still rowdy that late in the night. Some of the nudes called out, but I only thought about accepting their invitation.

THERE WAS MORE than one test to the Louisette, Cécile, but with the gossip and newsmongering on promenades in the parks, you would have known. The test took place at the Asylum de Bicêtre, a huge building with two pavilions, gardens, and several ornate wings that showed their age—new bricks were tightly packed between older, yellow slabs of stone. Superintendent Pussin greeted Sanson and me at the stairs, and had some of the able-bodied residents carry the Louisette down the halls of the seventh ward and assemble it in a small courtyard. The people in the Asylum—men who rambled when we passed their rooms, or sat absent and listless for purges and leeches; others with scrofula behind the ears: bluish-purple tumours, and open abscesses that overtook their face and neck. (Startling, thinking back, that within half a year the patients and prisoners would be dragged into the street and onto bayonets.)

An account of those present: Superintendent Pussin and his assistant Pinel; Antoine Louis—the developer of the angled blade we were about to test; Dr. Joseph-Ignace Guillotin, on whose recommendations the National Assembly brought in changes to execution; Sanson, Headsman; myself, harpsichord maker Tobias Schmidt of the Low Country *ébénistes*.

Guillotin had arranged for three cadavers and directed our attention toward a linen sheet under a row of chestnut trees. Sanson lifted the sheet and noted the bodies were as he had specified: strong, male, and victim of sudden death.

We contemplated the dead men and the Louisette in silence. Although the quiet was ours alone — Bicêtre was full of the despair of its patients.

The blade struck the neck of the first cadaver — the head leapt from the body, carried through the air several feet, and rolled over the stone slabs until it stopped at the courtyard wall. Similar details with the additional two corpses — the extended height, steel grooves, and angled blade allowed a clean cut.

Guillotin dabbed sweat and powder streaks from the edge of his wig. Antoine removed his own wig and scratched his scalp.

"There you have it," I said.

The Superintendent bowed slightly. Guillotin adjusted his lace cuffs.

We carted the Louisette back to my workshop for a few final alterations. I scrubbed the stains with wire brushes.

Sanson stood back and crossed his arms. "We'll need thicker restraints."

"A basket, maybe," I said.

He nodded. The watery smell of the cadavers clung to the dismantled wood. I gave up on the dark stains and tossed my brush to the wash pail.

"And," I added, "you should paint it red."

SPRING TO AUGUST, 1792. The summer air, that pottage of sewer and bodies, breads and coffee, and piss and wine. The Swiss Guard was massacred. The Revolutionary Tribunal began, the royal family hid in the Legislative Assembly. The Louisette took position at the Place du Carrousel.

August 27th, the heat. I stood beside Young Gabriel Sanson — you'll remember him as Headsman Charles-Henri Sanson's son and apprentice — on the scaffolding. Young Gabriel, in brown trousers and tri-colour cockade, rubbed lard into the Louisette's rope. Sanson, of course, wore his sweat-stained red. The square had its wilted hedgerows, green-grey with dust, but otherwise it was overly bright, bleached by the sun so that the cream walls of the Tuileries were painful to look at. A crowd, small for Paris, had gathered, and made way for the tumbril that carted three gentlemen: L'Abbé Sauvade, and Messieurs Guillot and Vimal, convicted of forging assignats.

I would have left the scaffold for the shade near the walls of the square, but Headsman Sanson put his hand on my shoulder and the moment to descend was gone. Young Gabriel grabbed the abbot by the upper arm and helped him step from tumbril to narrow stairs. We belted the abbot to the bascule and lowered the plank. The lunette closed over the man's neck. The abbot panicked as we locked the clamp, and thrashed against the restraints. Young Gabriel knelt at the front of the Louisette and pulled the abbot's ears to keep the man steady, but the abbot tugged out of Young Gabriel's grip. The blade fell; the head came off through the jaw. Young Gabriel lifted it. I stood next to Headsman Sanson, and we watched his son hold the head by the abbot's small tuft of hair—with the chin missing, the tongue hung down and got a few cheers. And then Young Gabriel mis-stepped in the blood slick that pooled from the open neck, slipped, and smashed in his own head on the corner of the scaffold.

CÉCILE—

The floating baths: the best development of the century. Not the maps or water pumps or the fortepiano—in the new Republic, who would need such an instrument?

I had the docks to myself—all of Paris wanted a

glimpse of Young Gabriel Sanson spitting blood, twitching into death beside his father's Louisette. I stripped and stood barefoot on wooden steps that led into the river. When I looked up, a man stepped onto the far end of the dock.

"Taskin?" I called. Only no, when he turned to me I realized it wasn't him. The man seemed too old, his face so gaunt his eyes bulged painfully from sunken sockets. (Since my expulsion from Blanchet's I'd "seen" Taskin everywhere.)

The man watched me, fiddled with his laces, and then overcame whatever battle raged in his head and untied his shirt and trousers. Open sores clustered his ears, and I couldn't make out the jawline from his swollen neck. I kept my distance. There was no way it was Taskin; every rib was visible. He eased himself into the water. I did the same, and with the length of the dock between us, we looped ropes around our wrists and floated.

"Brutal," I called to him. "The heat."

He stared at me, and then looked across the river at the lumberyard. Huge felled trees lay piled on each other on the shore: Italian spruce; ebony from black stands in the French African colonies; cypress flitches nearly forty years old that had aged to a warm, brownish hue—I remembered it from when I selected wood for the Louisette.

The sound of the city, the roar of Paris, carried over the river.

"Have you been to the executions?" I asked.

The man drew a breath and bobbed under the murky water, and his pale figure vanished in the muddy Seine.

I swam and tried to forget the oil—the waste that dribbled from cemeteries and animal yards and drained into the river—and picture the lakes I swam in as a boy.

At times I forget that you too, Cécile, came from the Low Country.

I DON'T KNOW how to describe the next six hours. That's a lie: between the river and my visit to your house that night I gambled and lost the rest of the purse I'd received for the Louisette.

You let me in. "You've had the news, then."

You stood under the chandelier in your townhouse. You played with a fan, opening and folding a swath of worn ostrich feathers. Your powdered hair was embellished with ribbons and faux topaz, and you'd painted bold eyebrows and enhanced your small lips.

"How did you hear already?" you said. "I just returned."

"What news?" I stepped inside. "There's news?"

"Oh." You touched a beauty mark on your chin. "Taskin's dead." The candles flickered in the cut and leaded crystal above. You ran a pale hand over the stomach panel of your gown and said, warmly: "There will be room for your instruments at the Conservatoire again. The palace."

"How did you hear? You saw him? Did he have anything, a letter, for me?"

"No," you said. "It's dark. And late—"

"He would have said something. A curse, if he didn't apologize."

"Tobias, I'm trying to be kind." You set down the fan and untied your cloak. "I don't think he thought about you at all."

I sat on the sofa and watched you shift your feet— the back of your brocaded gown and grey wig cleanly reflected in the mirrors along the wall.

"They found him in the river," you said. "But he had some wasting disease, and wouldn't have lasted long."

"No," I said—and I meant, Cécile, that I'd seen him at the river, watched him bob under and thought nothing of it. I should have told you; I didn't. But I was losing you, and I had to say something, so I tried: "I suppose, with the illness, it was the decent choice."

"Decent," you said. "You know they have imprisoned the Queen. The children." You looked like you wanted to say more, but bit your lip. You didn't ask me to leave, and I didn't offer.

Cécile—I woke that night in your bed. The room

was on the top floor of the townhouse and never quiet. The sounds of the city, coming from the streets and the neighbouring apartments, habitually slipped through the thin windowpanes. But that night it was silent. Paris held its breath. The curtains were drawn and you stood facing the mirror, naked, lit by the moon. You didn't see me, not from that angle, but I saw your body in the mirror, your skin so pale as to seem translucent. I could've mapped the blue veins that ran through your skin as Cassini de Thury mapped the rivers and topography of France. Your small hips, the red compression lines from your corset.

Cécile, I saw you take an inch of skin at the bottom of your left breast — the same breast you'd bared in front of Louis and Marie and the courtiers of Versailles all those years ago in that opera — and I saw you pinch the flesh until your knuckles turned white.

I left for Sanson's before you woke.

HE WAS SITTING on a bench in his garden with his cello and a bottle of wine next to him on the grass, and his bow on his lap. The sun hadn't hit, but the ground held the heat from the day before, and I could smell the herbs. *Mon dieu*, how the heat built on itself that summer —

"Sanson," I began. "I'm so sorry —"

"My wife says she will leave." Sanson lifted the bow from his lap and loosened the hair. "She will go to her sister's house in the country. Young Gabriel—she says at least he won't live this cursed life." He rested the bow on the cello and drank wine from the bottle. "I hear Taskin is dead."

I sat on a bench across from him. Black-beaked chiff-chaffs and a tiny goldcrest kinglet flitted in and out of the blackberry bushes.

He set the bottle aside. "Tell me about the Low Country."

The Low Country near the Rhine where I was a child—I can't bring myself to reminisce. Would I have been happy if I stayed? Is that something you ask yourself, Cécile?

FIVE MONTHS PASSED —a long five months—January 1793, a new year.

"There's always been blood." Sanson unbuttoned his vest and reclined in a high-backed chair in my workshop (still in the Cour du Commerce, rue Saint-André des Arts, Paris). "The sword on the block. Or standing. Last year there was time between executions. We'd clean the blade. Get a fresh noose."

I poured myself wine and offered him a glass—he declined. Shook rain from his hat. I drank my cup and drew another. The candle in the window guttered and flamed, throwing light over cattle bones, upended clavichord cases, shelves of scores, and the gold-leaf, ground-gypsum and rabbit-skin glue that I'd scraped together when I received a few elaborate commissions that'd turned out to be pranks.

"These days, we throw a bucket of water over the bascule," Sanson said. "When we run dry, the condemned lie in it. That muck." He pinched his nose and closed his wide-spaced eyes. "And they're about to increase the workload without compensation. Tobias, I'm underpaid. I make less. The costs of the extra jobs — we have to build three more carriages and a tumbril. Pay six hundred livres each for messengers to answer magistrates. And then there's the utensils — tongs and sulphur, you know. I'm expected to act as carpenter and repairman, and now, multiple executions in one day? I need help."

"The crowd seems keen," I said.

"The crowd, oh, they're riled. But they cross themselves if they fall under the scaffold's shadow. There's no willing extras." The rain on the windows turned to slush, and I found a fresh candle.

"Will you help?" he asked. "I move the guillotine tomorrow and I don't have the people."

"You go with the new name? Guillotine over Louisette?" I said. And to lighten the mood: "How would the King feel?"

Sanson leaned forward and cupped his face in his hands. "He'll feel relieved."

I CAME TO see you first, Cécile. No answer. Nothing. Not in the townhouse or the winter garden, where the bench and pathways were slick with freezing rain. At the pond, only the silver carp. A bedraggled mess of vines gripped the gazebo, and a few confused rose blossoms tried their best, but drooped under the weight of their own heavy petals. Finally, in your chamber—a sealed letter.

I sat on the sofa in the drawing room and read it. You'd left for London as Comtesse d'Antraigues. Married months ago. The jewellery caskets were gone—how had I missed that? What else had I missed? In daylight, with the curtains drawn, the striped upholstery had obvious wear. Candle wax pocked the carpet below the chandelier.

You are better off out of it, Tobias, you wrote. I returned the letter to its envelope and tucked it into my coat.

"I knew that years ago," I said aloud. At our last meeting, the beauty spot you wore probably covered a canker. Your eyes would have been strained by candlelit masquerades, hair thickened with wool, and the glow to your skin was mashed apple and lard. But—we were both pariahs.

"Remember?" I told the empty room. "You bared yourself on stage."

After I found your letter, I wrote the Montgolfier brothers and asked them how they had imagined their aerostat in the first place.

"It's as simple as this," they wrote back. "We burned scrap paper for years, and then we noticed what had been there all along: the ash caught on the gases and rose inside the chimney. It was time, anyone would have seen it."

An accident of time and place. You can believe that of the invention of the fortepiano, and you convinced yourself of it in your costume design. Could you give me as much with the guillotine?

JANUARY 21ST, 1793. You would have been in England.

Picture the Place de la Révolution from a position on the scaffold. A crowd so thick there is no sign of the cobblestones under the collage of red-capped cockades, bare heads and wigs, faces and elbows held at eye level—Parisians fill the flagstones from the pillars to the river, to the perimeter of red-and-blue uniformed guards that surround the scaffold in the centre of the square. The most-watched stage in Paris.

Drums, heard at first, and then seen. Cavalry with their swords drawn escort the green carriage. Sanson, in his burgundy tunic, stands out like a thumb, sweat-stained despite the January rain.

Louis xvi — that is, Citizen Capet — executed.

I SHOWED SANSON my letter to you, my explanation recorded here as far as this. We sat, blankets over our shoulders, in his garden. His wife was gone by then, unable to withstand the trial and execution of the Queen. Sanson finished reading and sniffed. "What of it?" he said.

"What do you think?"

"I think—" He handed me the letter. "You go into such detail over the fortepiano and the guillotine, only you leave out more recent years—you don't mention who continued to shore the guillotine's platforms and complete repairs, or who drove the condemned in the tumbril and cleared the corpses. Who helped lift the heads of the King and Queen."

"There is that," I admitted.

"Here's a question, then," he said. "Why should the hand feel shame for what the head commanded? I've never heard of one breakthrough so lamented, and another so riddled with covet."

"There's that, too."

I threw the letter to the fire and took up my quill yet again.

ONE MORE CHANCE, please: Cécile, I hope you will hear
what I'm saying. Let me try again: do you remember,
Cécile, the Aerostat Réveillon? You in yellow, Marie the
Queen in blue. The King in cream and ostrich feather.
The white and black marble wet with rain. The uneven
cobbles where Taskin and I set that first fortepiano.
Grey, mottled cloud behind the balloon—the taffeta
the colour of an idealized sky. The bleat of the sheep
Montauciel, the iridescent tail of the rooster and his
red pompadour comb, how the duck bobbed his head.
All faces followed them when the rope frayed, the balloon flew loose, and the Montgolfier brothers chased
its shadow over the grounds. Taskin and I carried our
instrument through Versailles into the opera house and
you, Cécile, sat and played. You ran your hand over the
fortepiano—white fingers against the ebony, porcelain
on the gold—and spoke: "A lily, Tobias."

Cécile, our Lord and Saviour was a carpenter.

ARGENTAVIS MAGNIFICENS

MORGAN AND I first met Howie at a dig. Or, I suppose, Howie met us—we didn't realize it was him at the time. Our roped excavation site sat two-thirds the way up a slope of the Milk River canyon, and the river, light brown with silt, sauntered below. Morgan and I had been at the site a number of days, and had the majority of the bones of a small false-saber *Dinictis felina* jacketed in parts and stored at the base of the canyon under the shade of a tarp-canopy, next to our tent and equipment—extra trowels, picks, and such. The last few pieces of the false-saber (head, front legs that bent back on themselves) were still in the dirt, balanced on pedestals of grey-brown consolidated ash and sediment. Morgan lay on his back in the sand beside the pedestals, chipping away at their undersides and holding plastered strips of burlap to the small cat's skull. I stirred a pail of water and plaster so it wouldn't set in the heat. Neither of us could see much above the striped lip of the canyon, but we noticed the trail of dust against the blue sky, and the intrusion of country radio and diesel rising from a one-ton. Then the slam of the truck door, a man backlit by the afternoon sun, and a minor rock slide where a black spaniel skidded down the cliff toward us.

"Must be lost," I said. The site was way off the highway at the Alberta–Montana border, surrounded only by the hoodoos that dotted the badlands.

Feet planted on the canyon's crest, the silhouette set his hands to his hips while the dog rattled stones ahead of itself, looking like it would run us over. Morgan sat up the best he could with one hand cementing the strip of burlap on the skull.

I left the stick in the plaster bucket and yelled, "Heel the dog, jackass."

The man's shape lifted a straw Galveston. I thought he'd yell back, but he whistled sharply and the dog stopped.

Morgan squinted, half-sitting in the ditch. "Who brings a dog to a dig?"

"An asshole."

"Some people, I tell you."

A second whistle and the spaniel backtracked — struggled its way up the loose side of the canyon and sat next to the man. The two of them, man and dog, watched us for a full hour. During that time Morgan and I sank plaster strips into the pail, removed excess paste between two squeezed fingers, and held each bandage while it dried around the fossilized cat. When the sun lowered we rinsed plaster and sand from our hands and faces, prepped dinner at a camp stove, and yelled again—this time about the man's radio. I wonder what he thought of us. Me, a tired, sweaty woman in a bandana shouting profanities from the base of the canyon. Morgan short and stocky, long dusty hair, and a face that he joked was a throwback to the Neanderthal. I don't know, maybe we were more amusing than I give us credit for. Still, Howie never descended the canyon to our level, or called to tell us who he was or what he wanted. After that hour of boring voyeurism he whistled the dog into the cab of the truck and drove elsewhere.

THE SECOND TIME we ran into Howie was weeks later at our university, when the Department of Geoscience where Morgan and I lectured hosted a memorial gala for a deceased donor. We were obligated to attend, but networking and small talk—that wasn't for me. I planned to catch the eye of the geoscience chair, down a free drink, and then sneak back to the lab where the false-saber sat on the table. (I had the hard plaster and burlap waiting under a wet cloth, and as soon as it softened would cut the jacket open with a utility knife and roll it back in sections.) Morgan intended to wave a picture of an in situ teratorn in front of the donors and see if he couldn't change the department's mind about sending us to the Andes. (The specimen, in the Bolivian altiplano, was our latest pipe-dream — the university had already told us no.)

We arrived late. Morgan and I edged around the auditorium to the bar at the side. While speeches droned on, I scanned the crowd. The department had paid a fortune — spared no cost in attracting wealth — and carted in temporary displays from the museum. Several ostrich-like ornithomimid fossils the university was famous for sat against a wall of windows overlooking the courtyard, and a replica of an *Apatosaurus* femur — a six-foot thigh bone from one of the largest-known sauropods — had a line of donors waiting for a photo op. Tablecloths, wine, gowns. Most people had pushed their seats back (dinner was long over) and were watching the stage, or chit-chatting amongst themselves. I spotted the geoscience chair talking to a group of black-clad mourners who crowded the exit. The mourners breathed together, and synchronously raised their cigarettes to their lips under the green light of the hall's exit sign — grief, I supposed, kept their motions in unison. I finished my drink and plotted a path through the tables, and then I saw a black spaniel curled at the feet of one of the attendees, a straw Galveston hung daintily on the corner of the chair back, and the man in the chair who, logic said, must own both the hat and the dog. The man was Howie Bring. Bring Petroleum, Bring Oil, Bring everything—he was the only donor with enough wealth to walk a dog into a reception. Even seated Howie was tall and lean, although I'd put him in his late sixties. He saw me and lifted his hand, gesturing Morgan and I toward his table.

"Constance," I introduced myself.

"Think we saw you at Milk River." Morgan sat beside him. I cringed, remembering the curses I'd shouted.

"That's right." Howie reached down and twisted his fingers in the black spaniel's curls. "I heard you got a chance for something big in the altiplano. Does it have hope?"

"It used to," I said. "The department vetoed it due to cost."

Morgan slipped the Polaroid from his pocket, straightened a bent corner, and set the photo on the table. "But if you're scouting—"

The photo, normally tacked to the corkboard in the lab, pictured a leather glove lying on a patch of dirt with the general location and year of the find pencilled underneath: *Bolivian altiplano, 22/01/83*. Red-and-grey rock surrounded a line of lighter, pinkish-tan vertebrae embedded in the tuff. The scale the glove provided, and the way the skeleton seemed situated, spoke of something huge and avian. *Argentavis magnificens* was our best estimate. A bird that pre-dated the mountain it fossilized in, and one of only two known specimens.

Howie turned the photo and leaned back in his chair, looking first at the line for the *Apatosaurus* femur, and then at us. He was either remembering, like I was, all the profanity we'd thrown at him from the hot canyon, or sizing us up—the over-bleached grin Morgan was proud of, and my denim and shitty blazer—versus the donor currently beside the femur: a woman, at most five feet tall; even standing on a chair her up-do didn't reach the top of the mounted thigh bone. She looked at the brown, polished head of the femur arcing above her and laughed, and then hiked her gown (black, beaded, vintage) above her ankles so that the camera captured her heels.

Howie touched the photo again, and with his other hand still resting on the spaniel, told us he'd made a fortune in oil and retired. He had an interest in the "black stuff's origins" and "just what the heck he'd cashed in for this life," did we understand that? He'd already explored subterranean bitumen leaks, those asphalt pools that "made up tar pits and whatnot." We'd dug on his land before, Howie claimed, though he didn't think we'd realized. That slip of dry mud he'd spotted us on, it'd been him who signed the permissions.

"My wife wants me to pour more money into her clinic." He nodded toward the woman in the black dress dismounting the chair beside the *Apatosaurus*. "She does plastic."

Of course she does, I thought, look at her — she was at least a decade and a half younger than Howie. Although, now that I did look, she didn't seem Botoxed. And if she'd had other work done, it must have been a reduction.

"But it occurs to me," Howie continued, "if you're confident in the reward, I've never toured the Andes."

"You're offering?" Morgan poured wine from a bottle that sat in the centre of the table.

"I'm offering." Howie raised his glass.

"Then we're confident." Morgan turned to me.

Before I could respond, applause broke from the tables closer to the stage and the tux-clad "mourners," returning from their smoke with the geoscience chair, picked up their cello and violins and filled the hall with fussy chamber music.

"Right, Constance?" Morgan pressed.

Having the photo come to life — to stand on the same patch of earth as *Argentavis magnificens* — would be prize enough for us. I wasn't sure that was what Howie meant by "reward," but the offer was too good to question. I raised my glass alongside theirs.

THE THIRD TIME we met Howie we had him tour the lab. We treated him to a dust mask and goggles, and for an hour or so he scraped calcite from the smooth, almost vitreous surface of the false-saber's ribs. That visit cascaded into a fourth, and so on — it seemed Howie had taken our invitation as a universal one. Or, I don't know, the six a.m. phone calls and unannounced drop-ins both at the university and my rental, all that could be commonplace for an oil baron.

Same time, Morgan left his boyfriend, and since it was July and we were set to leave for Bolivia early September, I let him sleep on my couch. For the next four weeks the three of us spent most evenings at my place, a one-bedroom bungalow on retired ranchland that edged the Kneehill badlands. The house had a veranda wrapped around three sides, an unkempt lawn, and a couple Saskatoon berry bushes the prairie dogs routinely stripped. The view, though, was what I paid for: farmland to the west and badlands parks to the east.

"The whole wide, flat world," Howie would say, and then lean his chair back, set his boots on the veranda railing, and raise his drink to the horizon. I bit my tongue when he pointed out which portion of the land was his, and as he waxed on about life "pressed book-like" while his spaniel dug apart gopher holes. It was hard not to mock him. Maybe because I'd been wrong about the musicians back at the gala, or maybe because

Howie'd brought his dog uninvited to both a dig and a memorial party, but I felt we couldn't get on the same track. Like although we'd met and travelled next to each other, I was tensed for him to pull away. Pull his funding away—he'd never *toured* the Andes, he'd said.

We entertained him. We walked the badlands and tested the backpack core-drill we had him purchase. Morgan listened to Howie recount his fights with his wife about her clinic, and I excused myself to analyze maps and core samples, and photographs of the dig site. We were set to leave in a month, and we knew nothing about where we were going besides the date of the flight. Thank god our guide-to-be, Julia, was on top of things at her end—she'd sent the samples, booked us a place in La Paz and a jeep and driver for the road from the city to the foot trail where she planned to meet us. She promised enough pack animals for our gear, which, with Howie's unchecked generosity, was growing. Besides the new drill we bought a portable computer (small as a briefcase), and a brand new '83 Magellan NAV that could pinpoint our latitude and longitude give or take a couple hundred metres. All stuff we truly didn't need, and had never used in the past.

Maybe the overspending added to our impatience. Summer felt both slower and more irritating than usual: Morgan's evolving collection of coffee cups side-lined the fossilized corals and crinoids I had displayed on the windowsill, Howie blasted a thumbhole single-shot at the prairie dogs, and me — I couldn't help but mention future digs. Places I wanted to go that would need Howie-level funding. We provoked each other and annoyed ourselves.

The night before we were scheduled to fly to La Paz — the only night Howie was actually supposed to join us for dinner and a chat — he was late. Morgan and I ate and turned off the grill. The evening cooled. We sat on the veranda and watched clouds — purple-blue, heavy — spit on the south. Our shadows stretched and then vanished with the sun, leaving the glow from the house behind us and a pair of headlights on the highway: Howie's maroon one-ton. The truck swerved, and then — about a hundred metres from my house — caught the soft shoulder and jerked from the road to the ditch where it smashed the wood and barbed-wire fence (a remnant from a time when the property had cattle). Howie opened the door and fell into the grass. The spaniel bolted over the road and ran between canola swaths in the neighbouring field.

"Jesus, Howie." I ran to the truck and pulled the keys from the ignition. "You hurt?"

"Violet." He stumbled up the ditch. Morgan slipped under his arm, steadying him. I picked up the straw Galveston and slapped the dirt from it.

"Let's get you inside," I said.

"Violet, heel," Howie yelled.

"Come on, Howie," I said. The dog, scared and running, wasn't going to stop. Or if she did, it would be so far into the field we wouldn't be able to see her.

He tripped on the porch steps and I ducked under his other arm, helping Morgan.

"My wife won't let me in my own house," Howie said.

"Don't worry about that now." To be honest—I didn't want to let him in either, but I did. I put fresh sheets on my bed for him since Morgan had the couch. When he passed out I staked a pup tent at the edge of the property for myself. It was too early to sleep. I sat on the front steps, worried and angry about the trip.

"So his wife cut him loose." Morgan handed me a pilsner and sat next to me. "I don't know what took her so long."

"What do you mean?"

"He pulled funding from her clinic."

"She does plastic," I said. "Who cares if someone doesn't get their lift and tuck?"

Morgan turned to me.

"Facial reconstruction, Constance," he said. "She does *that* sort of plastic. She's a surgeon."

I couldn't think of what to say, so I drank. We sat on the steps listening to the rock wrens and watched the storm flicker and boom miles south over the fields.

"Does that—" I began.

"Doesn't change anything."

Kneehill when it's wet — the long grass around the river turns green, and the plains, dead for most of the year, creep with small blue flowers. We stayed on the veranda well past dark. The spaniel running somewhere, Morgan beside me. In the black I couldn't see his face, and I assumed he couldn't see mine.

HOWIE PUSHED THE flight back to find the spaniel. I thought the dog was dead and told him as much, coyotes would have made a quick meal of her, but it was his call — if he wanted to re-book there wasn't anything Morgan or I could do. We watched him stride through the ranchland grasses toward the canyon, groaned, and packed a lunch to follow.

The path jackknifed to the base of the ravine, where it travelled alongside ribbons of brown water — what was left of a river that had worn the sandstone, exposing grey and tan stripes of consolidated sediment that dated to the late Cretaceous. I wondered what Howie saw when he looked at it (three hundred metres below us sat the coal zone, and a constant fight between preservationists and big oil), but I suppose he only had his eye out for the spaniel. He wasted three days trekking.

The fourth day I refused to search. Morgan and I let Howie comb the hoodoos alone and drove the highway with the windows down. We didn't have a set destination—anywhere to get away from the piercing whistles and the voice crying *Violet*. We ended up at the lab. It was a Sunday, and there was only one other person—a technician at the microfossil table, intent on his microscope. Morgan and I wheeled the sandbox containing the semi-jacketed false-saber (a wide, shallow Tupperware bin on a rollable island) to the centre of the room under the main fume hood and opened the lid. In planning the teratorn dig over the summer we'd lost interest in revealing the cat, and the jackets were only half-peeled from each section. I worked with an air scribe, much like a miniature jackhammer, and chipped away at the sandstone. Morgan started at the other end with brushes and a grinder. Because of our dust masks and the sound of the fume hood and the tools, I didn't notice that a guest had entered the lab until I set down the scribe and took up a syringe of epoxy.

"A moment." I finished with the consolidant (injected into a weak spot to help stabilize the fossil) and snapped a picture of the process, making a note of the action and time in the logbook. In the doorway—a black spaniel on a leash, the leash held by a short, well-dressed woman with thick brows and a wide mouth. The woman from the gala, Howie's wife.

I took off my safety glasses and cotton gloves, and squatted to greet the spaniel. The dog smelled of lavender soap and her soft coat had been clipped.

"Howie will be glad." Morgan shook the woman's hand.

"Constance," I greeted her, and added: "He's not here. He's searching the canyon. Where did you find the dog?"

"Near to our ranch." The woman unbuttoned her blazer and sat on a stool next to the false-saber's sandbox. "She was a black speck running the highway's shoulder. She wouldn't stop for me. I had to park up the road and grab her as she went by."

She twisted the spaniel's leash around her left hand and leaned for a better look at the false-saber. Three main jackets, and a couple buckets of smaller fragments where we might find missing pieces. In the first jacket, the pelvis and the right hind limb — thigh, shin bones, and foot — stretched half-uncovered in the matrix next to the part of the tail that had been preserved. The second contained the false-saber's ribcage, front limbs and neck; the third held the long-toothed skull. An array of brushes, air scribes, epoxy, syringes, safety glasses, and gloves lay beside the cat.

"He could fund us both if he wanted to," she said.

I straightened the row of scribes, and Morgan picked up his gloves.

"Thanks for dropping off the dog," he said.

"I also brought —" She passed me an envelope.

Howie's name was written in silver sharpie on the front.

"We'll give it to him," Morgan said. I agreed — I knew we wouldn't.

She looked at us like she knew it too, and unwound the spaniel's leash from her wrist. "You do that, then."

Morgan took the dog from her.

"It's a mistake," I said when she left. "Digging with him."

Morgan stepped back from the false-saber and spread his arms. Are you sure of that, his reach said. A bird with six-foot flight feathers. It tripped me up imagining it, and it was my living to un-puzzle the bits and pieces we found buried in the coulees. That giddiness behind the jigsaw — that was why I did it, I suppose. I tested the weight of the envelope Howie's wife had given me — photos, it seemed like — and I thought of her at the gala with her head tossed back, delighted at the absurdity of the huge femur. I opened it. It wasn't pictures of her, although it was photographs. Each image showed a face (I won't describe them) and underneath listed a procedure with a cash amount. I re-sealed it quickly. Morgan thrust his arms out a second time. The bright, overhead spotlight of the lab was unforgiving, and he looked old. Greying jaw-length hair, barrel chest, and thick brow. His boyfriend was gone, I remembered, and our lecture contracts were cancelled for the next year. We had the dog.

I trashed the envelope and began to pack the false-saber. We were stuck in this, whether we liked it or not.

HOWIE HAD MEAT on the grill when we brought the dog back and lied about her — we told him it was us who found her.

"She burned the pads of her feet on the highway," Morgan told him. "The only time I felt sorry for a dog."

"So you took her to a spa." Howie closed the barbecue and eased himself into a deck chair. We'd forgotten the dog was groomed, scented, and leashed.

"That's right," I said.

"Well, we washed her at the lab." Morgan unclipped the dog and looped the leash around the railing. The steak spit in the grill. The dog finished scouting the yard and clambered onto the veranda.

"It's pricy to buy last minute." Howie pinched the crown of his hat and set it on his lap. He was talking about our flights — we knew it, and backtracked. If we left tomorrow, Morgan reasoned, it would only cut short acclimatizing in La Paz and we could still make the other connections — the driver and such. I went so far as to tell Howie that if he wanted to trade the computer and NAV to make up the flight expense, that was all right with us. He took it quietly. Fanned himself with his Galveston, and agreed.

Then we were there: La Paz, Bolivia, where I tried to sleep. Morgan drank at the hotel bar, and Howie — Howie took us up on our offer and traded the tech for eighteen bottles of pisco. We barely had time to register the slap-down before all of us (spaniel included) were in the jeep headed to the high plateau and then dumped at the trailhead where our guide, Julia, met us with a string of alpacas.

Morgan dropped his bag. The landscape on the drive had been humid and flora-laden, but here at the higher elevation the plateau was characterized by aeolian erosion, and large rocks were worn away at the base by dirt and wind. The only plants were hardy grasses and mat-like cushion plants. We'd intended to camp, but Julia asked us to push on — she had an uncle on his deathbed. Or, she said, we could stay by ourselves and she would return in a few days. We were tired. Already the sky leached colour, darkening to the east. Howie, we saw when we turned to consult with him, looked like he'd taken a punch in the face, with dark brown bruises under his eyes.

"He should stay," Julia suggested. "Maybe even turn around."

"We're on Diamox, and we're doing this." Howie straightened his Galveston and whistled the spaniel to the foot trail.

"Or go on," she said. "Whatever." She wore her hair

braided on one side of her face, and combed it back with her fingers in frustration—I was startled to see a raised, crimson birthmark that began behind her left ear, held her eye slightly closed, and came to an abrupt stop in the centre of her cheek. She saw me looking, said something to herself in a language close to Spanish, and then turned to Morgan and me. "I thought you were professional."

"We are professional," I said. "And he is on Diamox. Four a day and fluids. But we haven't done altitude—I should have told you."

"Do you have headlamps?" she asked, and began to sort our equipment and ready the alpacas' panniers.

We hiked switchbacks in the dark. The gain in elevation didn't affect Morgan or the dog, but had me lightheaded and focused on breathing. Although when we reached the hamlet and I turned to Howie, I lost concern for myself. He'd drooled a sticky bib of saliva over his shirt, and his nailbeds (when he raised his hand to wipe his mouth) were purple.

"How long were you in La Paz?" Julia swore under her breath. "Never mind. He needs oxygen."

She went to get a tank. A couple kids unloaded the panniers from the alpacas in the dark, and Morgan and I assembled our wall tent. Both of us hurried the job, and with the spaniel underfoot it took twice as long as usual to get the fittings and rafters aligned and pitched. By the time we'd stashed the gear and set up our cots,

Julia'd helped Howie strap an oxygen mask over his nose and mouth. We stripped him of the wet shirt and wrapped a blanket around his shoulders.

"You should sleep." Julia balled Howie's shirt and tossed it to Morgan. She was right. But the tent canvas pulled and sagged in the wind like a lung, and Howie, who'd stopped wheezing and drifted off, woke choking on himself.

"We're not going to sleep." Morgan found the pisco bottles.

"No? Fine. Of course not. Then you can help." She zipped the tent screen behind us and we followed her to a fire pit, where the kids who'd unloaded our gear from the alpacas strummed a charango. Firelight flickered over pale-yellow and mint houses with aluminum or thatch roofs, and gardens. Only a single house had lights on, and Julia walked us toward the two open doors—a double-wide entryway and a kitchen where a number of women lifted five- and ten-gallon pots to the stove. Inside, a swept, packed dirt floor, a painting of Jesus on the wall, and colourful woven curtains. A wooden shelf held an open bottle and a line of shot glasses. Every bit of furniture—benches, two leather recliners, wooden stools, a couch—had been pushed against the exterior walls, and in the centre of the room a man in a faded green top and canvas shorts lay on a table under a bare lightbulb.

Behind the table another man (in a suit, his unbuttoned shirt loose around his huge gut) sat in the corner braiding palm fronds into a rope. A broad-chested senior chewed a cigar in one of the leather recliners, and on the couch a young man of about twenty leaned forward with his elbows on his knees. The door to the adjoining kitchen was open, and two or three women fanned the steaming copper pots. One of the women saw us and spoke to Julia, who in turn spoke to Morgan and me.

"This is a funeral," she said.

The man on the table—I hadn't realized. By "deathbed" she'd meant dead.

The youngest man rose from the couch behind the dead man and downed three shots from the glasses that lined the shelf. He raised his hands and spoke to the room in a dialect I again didn't catch, not exactly Spanish—I kicked myself for only researching the geology, not the language.

"Julia—" I said. Our intrusion felt tasteless at best. Moths battered the bare lightbulb above the body, their dusty wings casting flickered shadows in the haze of cigar smoke. She waved me quiet. The young man moved to the table, cupped the dead man's head, and slipped the braided palm fronds around the corpse's neck. Then he twisted the rope around his hand, braced against the dead man's throat, and began to strangle the body.

"His grandson," Julia said. "The cord seals the air-ways. For gases."

The grandson pulled tighter, so that the woven fronds dug into the dead man's neck, and then tied the rope off and turned to us. I put my hand to my face; Morgan lifted the pisco bottle. The men in the chairs nodded in unison—*Graçias*. Morgan carried it to the shelf and filled the row of shot glasses. The grandson downed three more shots ("For any smell," Julia explained) and he fell onto one of the chairs along the wall. The man with the prominent gut stood and cast a set of sheep knuckles to the dirt floor like dice. Morgan refilled their shots.

I stepped backwards into the night and closed my eyes. Maybe I could sleep—I should at the very least check on Howie. When I opened them there was no need. Howie stood at the edge of the fire, his oxygen tank hugging his bare chest and the spaniel close to his side. The green-and-blue blanket draped his shoulders and his straw Galveston sat on his head like it anointed him.

"Howie," I said. He passed me, stepping cautiously around the firepit and into the house as Julia carried a copper pot full of boiling water from the kitchen.

"It's a funeral," I called after him. "You sure you want to go in?" He groped his oxygen mask with one hand and lowered the other to the spaniel and her pink tongue.

Julia set the pot on the ground beside a box of cuy, and an older woman with a waist-length braid joined her. The woman lifted a jumpy cuy from the box and yanked its feet and head and it died. She handed it to Julia and took another. She handed the second dead cuy to me, and Julia and I dipped the animals into the boiling pot and then cold water, and we ripped the fur out with our fingers.

"You found the fossil?" I asked.

"I did." Julia rubbed a knife over the skin of the plucked cuy. She passed me the knife, picked up a razor, and ran the blade over any last fur. I used the knife, then took the razor from her and shaved the rodent.

"Is it close?" I asked.

"Very close." She passed me a bone fragment from her pocket.

"Shin," I said. Thin-walled and hollow. A bird, then. We were right.

She sliced the corners of her cuy's mouth and cut the testicles off, then she pricked the belly skin and pulled it open with two fingers and shook the guts into a bowl. She rinsed the carcass in a bucket. After all the cuy were prepared, we stuffed them with a mix of apple, cumin, and marigold, and set them on the stove with rocks on their backs to flatten the ribcages while they fried.

We rinsed our hands. Julia stood and stretched her legs. The entryway to the house was wide and the interior lit. Inside, men blew smoke around the corpse. The grandson poured alcohol on the door frame and spoke aloud to the house and the dirt. I saw Howie with a shot glass, watching Julia from one of the leather recliners—in the angled light of the doorway her birthmark was slightly shaded, and not as unattractive as unusual. Morgan left and returned with more pisco.

The night smelled of cigars, steeped coca leaves, and fried cuy, and wouldn't end. The body was stripped, washed with tea, and wrapped in white muslin. It looked—for all my unfamiliarity with everything else—like the bones we plastered and jacketed in the field. The dead man's grandson poured alcohol in the doorway and again said what sounded like a prayer to the house and dirt. Men blew more smoke on the door frame and windows and over the corpse. In the kitchen women lifted the rocks from the backs of the fried cuy and served bowls of meat and diced yams.

Julia poured Howie a mug of warm goat's milk and took away his shot glass. "Make sure your friend doesn't smoke," she told me.

We sat on the furniture pushed against the walls. I turned my dish, trying to find an approach to the cuy. Howie, the oxygen mask pressed to his face, pulled the spaniel off piles of food scraps and settled her beside his chair. Julia poured Morgan and me glasses of clear pomace brandy—her sleeve unrolled as she did, and she stopped to correct it. The bones of her wrist were wider than the forearm, and her hands, stained brown from peeling yams, were also wide-boned and thin.

Howie coughed into his mask and waved her toward him. She leaned close. When she was near enough that he could whisper, he reached out and set his fingers on her birthmark.

"If you came back with us," he said, "my wife could fix that."

"Jesus Christ." Morgan said.

I set aside my plate—the cuy were crunchy and fatty with not much meat.

Julia held Howie's gaze, then pulled her braid aside and showed him the mark went well behind the ear. "Too much scarring. Too painful."

"She could do it," Howie said. "But she's leaving—" He stopped abruptly, bent double, and puked a great fan of goat's milk onto the floor. Morgan and I stared at the mess. The spaniel lapped the vomit. Julia lit a cigar and took her turn with the sheep's knuckles.

"Thinking the dog will make it rich?" Howie wiped his mouth. And when we looked confused he reminded us of how we thought anything he touched turned to cash.

"I'm done for the night," I said.

"Take him with you when you go." Morgan pointed his fork at Howie. "Make him lie down."

Cigars, smoke. More wood on the bonfire. The sheep knuckles clattered on the packed dirt in a sort of game that, I suppose, wasn't a game.

In our tent I lit a lantern. Moths buffeted the screen door—there were so many, they must have bred in the loose shale of the mountains. Howie crawled into bed and touched the tubes at his chest. He reached for the water I offered him but closed his fist too early. I held the canteen and he drank. The pisco bottles shone in the corner with the knee pads, gloves, a sharpening stone—all the gear we'd hauled in.

"The NAV and the comp—why didn't you trade for something better than pisco?" I asked.

He sputtered, but managed some cynicism: "You think there's something better than toys and alcohol? You two, you and Morgan, you want what my wife wants—only money."

"It's not true," I said, although it felt like a half-truth.

"What's money anyway?" he asked.

I took the shin fragment from my pocket. Howie pinched the shard and turned it in the lamplight. The majority of the fragment was dark grey, with one end worn pink where—before Julia found it—it must have protruded from the rock and been exposed to rain and sun.

He seemed to drift, and I took the bone back thinking he would sleep, but he pushed his mask up and continued.

"Prospected and found," he said. "Oil. Years ago." His eyelid drooped and twitched. He raised his hand, palm forward. A surrender, I thought, but he held up three fingers. "My second wife," he said. "Third, with the common law. But I've the likes of you two pulling at me now."

"You really think that?" I remembered the envelope of photos, our lie about the dog, and I crossed the tent and uncorked a pisco. He waved the drink aside and twisted the tubes at his face.

He was afraid, I realized. The petroleum guru, Howie with the straw Galveston who'd rambled on under the hoodoos about how he built his fortune between layers of silt. He was terrified. And I thought of the spaniel, running the pads off her feet beside the highway before Howie's wife found her—the ridiculous stream of dust the lonely thing must have trailed in the heat. Howie brushed his nose and held his knuckles to the light. I could have laughed I was so surprised, only looking at his blue fingers clinging to the oxygen tubes, I was afraid too.

I started to stand and he grabbed my arm. His grip shocked me—the nails in my wrist. He didn't want me to leave. Or, rather, he didn't want to be left alone. Who I was had little to do with it. I set the pisco aside, wet a piece of burlap, and tried to clean the vomit from the stubble on his chin. He relaxed his hand a little, and I pried his fingers from my arm and moved them to the spaniel.

"We'll stay," I said, and he closed his eyes.

The moths buffeted their soft, meaty bodies against the screen. I lowered the gas on the lantern and crawled into my cot.

I WOKE TO Julia standing over me in the tent—her brown hair, the red stain on her cheek.

"Do you want to see this fossil?" she said. "Or do you want to take your friend back to La Paz?"

"How long will his oxygen last?" I asked. Howie's colour had improved—the mask covered his lower face, but the bags around his eyes had lost their swelling and the brown tint from last night. At least he slept.

"The tank is empty now," she said. "If you don't tell him, he could be all right."

She and I loaded a single alpaca with a pannier of the basics—backpack core-drill, marsh pick, trowels, plaster, burlap, gloves, water, etc.—and took a path between the houses. The hamlet looked different by day—more kids. Gardens. A single, visible power line. When we reached the edge of the houses we found the grandson, the man with his unbuttoned shirt, Morgan—his Neolithic profile, his arm around the man with the hairy gut—and a few others digging a grave on an open plot of land. Morgan peeled away from the gathering and joined me and Julia.

The trail led us up a slope, where we had a view of the hamlet's corral — alpacas and goats, tufts of wild millet. Beyond the corral, all those switchbacks we'd hiked in the dark. We stopped when we found loose float where Julia had found the shin bone, and she pointed to the source: a series of ledges a couple hundred metres above. I pinned a flag into the area. Morgan and I hiked, and she headed back to the hamlet. We were damp and breathing heavily when we reached the shelf. A curl of pinkish-tan vertebrae, lightened by the sun, stood out against the grey dirt and rock. Morgan ran his thumb over one, then tapped the surrounding ground with the marsh pick.

"Tight," I said. "Probably whole. Guess on the age?"

"Young," Morgan said. "Seven, eight million based on location."

I measured. From the first bone to the last visible — over three metres.

"Core sample," I suggested.

Morgan blew dust from the drive pins and aligned the extensions and secured the bit in place. We checked the water circulation and I placed my foot on the bit, notched the rock sideways, then eased the angle and drilled downward. The soft, layered sediment took barely fifteen minutes to breach. Morgan smoothed a square of burlap and I knocked the core sample loose, reaching the catcher in the hole to tong a couple snapped bits. We squatted and poked through the core. The consolidated ash was wiry — porous. A metre or so of light-grey, medium-grained tuff that was amply flecked with dark-brown and greenish-black mica. The base of the sample was full of shale and sandstone.

We pegged rope around the exposed bones, staked poles and cables into the rock, and secured a tarp to the poles for shade.

IT TOOK US a week to secure a dry stone wall above the specimen and clear the overburden. Soil samples had the tuff bed wavering around ten centimetres thick. Fine-grained. Grey to yellow, and sparkly with biotites where it was damp. The ash was interbedded with red sandstone and smaller maroon mudstones. Flakes of green-black mica stuck to our gloves and, working through the cotton, on our skin. Our clothes turned red with the dust, and then grey-black as we removed the sandstone and bared the tuff. Finally, we had more than a guess of what we were looking at.

We'd had to expand the dig marker to excavate the left wing, which had fossilized fully extended. The tissue and acetate glue painted on the weaker bones contrasted brightly against the soil, and gave us a visual hint at the full size — three point two one metres on the stretched wing. A jaw large enough to swallow a hare whole. Proportions said the primary feathers would have been as wide as a hand and as long as a man is tall.

We dug trenches into the tuff around the bones, and when enough of the skeleton was exposed Morgan used the humerus and tibiotarsus for calculation. The bird would have weighed eighty kilos and had a wingspan of six to eight metres. Morgan spread his arms — he was nowhere near the size. Wind flapped his shirt, torn and dusty, under the canopy.

Another few weeks and we'd finished trenching and started on the underburden, replacing supporting dirt with sandbags. Jacketing took longer than anticipated. We had to haul water in order to mix the plaster, and the cliffside wing required us to lie under the bones and hold the plastered burlap in place. Forty percent of the time the strips dried before we'd managed to get in position, and we ended up covered in plaster and dirt ourselves.

The afternoon humidity stayed consistent. Clouds rose, rain fell, and mist cleared as the sun set. Each night twilight gave the sky a yellow colour, like nothing I'd ever see again anywhere else, all of it pale and bright, then becoming translucent in a thin, breathless way.

No one told Howie about the oxygen tank, and since he wouldn't brave exertion, for the most part we forgot about him. He walked below, poking the ground before him with a stick, not yet counting on himself to make the ascent of barely a hundred metres. Always the empty tank hugging his chest, the straw Galveston and the spaniel. Kids kept him company in the corral, running Polaroids we took of the dig down the cliff so he could see.

"Do you think he'll fund us again?" I could hear Morgan from where I lay, half under the huge skull on its pedestal.

"No," I said. There was no way. "Almost done," I called. Still, thinking back to how long he'd watched us when we first met him on Milk River, that he'd passed over the clinic to bring us here, the way he searched for the dog— "Maybe," I changed my mind. The real answer. Look at what we found.

"It's ready," I said. "I'll push on this side. You got it?"

"On three," Morgan said.

We lifted. Turned the half-finished jacket onto its back. Morgan packed sand and damp tissue on the underside and I laid strips of burlap over that. When we were done I spat in the dirt and sat with my hands on my jeans. Across the dip of the valley: mountaintops, glaciers, volcanoes, and distant ricochets of crumbling rock. The bright sun washed the peaks and there was a headiness to the elevation.

I set down my trowel. "Howie," I called.

Morgan stood and yelled, "Howie — *Argentavis magnificens!*"

"Look here," I called. "Howie."

When Howie looked, I don't know if he understood. I can't describe how it felt. The kids in the field raised their arms, imitating us, caught in our excitement. We lifted the head of the huge teratorn, jacketed in white plaster and burlap, ready to be shipped home and uncovered. I threw my head back and laughed. "Howie," we shouted, and went on shouting.

THAT TINY LIFE

FINALLY, DATA TRANSMISSION from Corporate: a video file projects recent satellite footage of Saturn as a hologram above the galley table between Barry and me. The light of the little ringed planet casts a tan hue upwards onto the galley's overhead shielding and over the metal table where the two of us are seated, in the centre of TitanMineZero's Habitat Module waiting out the Megastorm.

The hologram starts with rotation; the satellite's long-range imager pulls away from Saturn and shifts focus to one of Saturn's moons—Titan is a hazy brown marble. Then the visual constricts to the moon's northern hemisphere and zooms in on a swirl of orange cloud where I approximate our outpost—and current location—to be. The glow from the holoprojection brightens the galley we've barricaded ourselves inside: four hundred square feet, absolute shielding. All hatches to the garden, equipment, and living modules double-sealed in case of a breach in thermal containment (it's *cold* out there, and the thunder, abated now, was so frequent it shook us like a train passing my living complex back home).

I laugh, I can't help it. We're both startled by the transmission popping into life, but holy 他妈的, that splash of colour above the table is a relief—it means telecommunications is chatting with the satellite again, and that Barry and I are back in touch with Earth. I know we're a couple billion kilometres from the home planet, that we're planted on Titan under the atmospheric mess flickering in the hologram, but we're no longer alone. I mean, I no longer feel alone.

And neither does Barry. He gives me a look through the moon that holds position over the table. Fingers crossed, his look says, and he touches a line of text that blinks in the air under the satellite footage of Titan. An audio file begins a voice-over of the looped video:

Earth to Titan CorporateHabitatZero:

Good news is we were able to run your stats and Habitat is cleared for safety — no leaks — so go ahead and unseal all junctions. More good news: the

Megastorm broke — check the satellite images and put together a report.

Now for the bad news — TitanMineZero is only intermittently responding to our ping and we need you to fix the connection or override manually and route through a second dish. Also a problem: a mudslide washed out the collection barrels and TitanMineZero's entire output for your term. There's no way you can make your HydrocarbonExtractionTarget, so there won't be any bonuses. We're sorry, we know you had this in the bag. Expect repairs from here forward, supervise clearing the landing pad, wait for materials to ship from the Belt Mines to rebuild or repair barrels, and set up for the next team's arrival in thirteen months.

Personal note: Nina and Barry — glad you two are alive. Stories to send home, hey? Speaking of which, it's been a while since we were able to forward the mail, so attached is a backlog of messages from family.

Barry waves his hand through the holo and the video loop pauses.

"Are they for real?" I wave the message back on. The Megastorm broke, actually finished and isn't a lull in the winds—that's a relief, but we *need* those bonuses. That cash goes to family on Earth. The extra chunk of pay is the reason we signed on — is the excuse I fed myself for leaving, anyway.

Barry enters the shield codes and presses his palm to the wall scanner. The overhead metal dome parts down the centre and retracts as two slabs, leaving the exterior window exposed. Clouds. Red-black and vicious, but tamer than when we sealed ourselves in here two months ago.

"Didn't you hear what I heard?" I ask. TitanMineZero is the biggest hydrocarbon extraction program Earth has, bigger than the various asteroid Belt Mines and way more efficient, since the automation is self-propelling, self-building, and self-evolving — when I was a kid, Corporate launched a rocket that dropped a couple million build-bots on Titan and let the place grow. Basically, Barry and I are a two-person checkpoint to an absurdly automated mine. They can afford our bonuses.

Barry waves the holo off again, and without the light from the projection we both notice personal files pop green on our private tablets.

"Backlog of mail." He pushes my tablet across the table toward me.

"There'll be an even nastier backlog of shit when we tell our families there's no payout." I glance at my files. There's a video from my older brother, Merven. I haven't heard from him in a few years, not since I

stopped replying to the messages from him, my sister
Rinella, and Gran.

"They have their own stuff going on. They'll be glad
we survived." Barry casts his files to the holoscreen.
Viable exoplanets replace the satellite footage above
the galley table; he waves past that to schematics of
breakthrough photon trajectory manipulation out of
Beijing, and past the floating text and diagrams to a
looped video of his sister's new kid—name and weight
in hanzi.

"A nephew. Congrats." Olive skin, black eyes, and
spiky hair. Fat beyond belief. Happy.

"Can't believe they're having babies while we're
gone," I say, at the same time thinking, what else would
they do? That's why we're here and they're there. So we
have something better to return to.

Barry circles the holo, watching his nephew stuff a
hand in his toothless mouth. "Blows the mind," Barry
says. Or something like that—I don't hear him properly
because I've tuned out, agitated by my communiqué.

The video Merven sent—my brother looks old.
Middle-aged, I mean, with thin hair, and his cheeks
have drooped below his jawbone like they've begun
to melt in the heat. The last file I saw was at least three
years back, which isn't a lot of time, but apparently
enough. He's wearing his junk-hauler's shirt under
a yellow raincoat with reflective stripes down the

sleeves—with the money I've sent back I thought he would have given up junk hauling. Merven stands in a hallway I don't recognize, and he doesn't speak right away. He stares into the camera while people go by in the background, a nurse it looks like, or some other professional who wears one of those mono-coloured medical uniforms. There's a doctor in a lab coat—so a hallway in a hospital, then. Merven turns his head and says something to someone standing off-camera, and then faces me.

"Gran died," he says. "She tripped stepping off the subway and hit her head on the platform. She was alone. Across town. Rinella's in the room now, with one of the dogs. Nina, I don't know if you'll watch this. I understand it's gotta be hard, but if you could write back—"

He pauses and looks off camera again.

"Well," he says. "It doesn't matter. She's gone." He reaches up and the video freezes, his thumb in the corner of the camera lens when the recording ends.

I replay the message, and then a third and fourth time.

Gran—what was she doing across the city without Rinella or Merven? I can't picture it. I can't even picture her unsteady. She always had five or so golden retrievers on leashes while she power-walked the complex. But, like Merven, she would be old now too. She'd been at least seventy-five when I left, so that would

put her near her nineties. I can't think of her that old.
What comes to mind instead is the day I told her I'd
signed on to the maintenance and observation position
at TitanMineZero. Gran tossed a crocheted dishcloth
into the sink, her sloppy golden retrievers fanned the
kitchen with their tails — three huge, panting beasts.
And I told her I was out of there. Vamoose. Twenty-four
years old, oblivious. What a prick I was.

"I can't stand myself," I say aloud, and then regret it.
Barry, less than a couple steps away, flips past a holo of
his brother-in-law lifting a net of flapping catfish, and
in the cramped space of the galley I know he heard.
"他妈的 everything, really. Why not."

"I shouldn't have taught you to swear." Barry zooms
the holoscreen in on the mouthy barbels of the catfish
that poke through the black netting.

"Probably not."

"Your pronunciation is shit."

That's his fault, but I don't get that far into the joke.
Out the window, orange evaporate rises from mud to
haze — an ethane/methane atmosphere, −179° C on a
beach day, and constantly twilight. Titan allows only
one percent of light through to the surface. A little ways
off, in the direction of the lake and the mine, three huge
rocks sit on the widespread umber mud. They're new,
and the mudslide must have carried them from the hill
behind us. Just outside the galley window, the ground

looks too bare—the Megastorm erased our footprints as well as the rover tracks that had criss-crossed the sand. A drift of brown silt covers the lower half of the rover bay doors. I guess we'll be walking the stairs up to the telecommunications tower.

There's a familiarity to the landscape. That could be because Barry and I have been on Titan in Habitat for almost four years, but I think it's more. When I was a kid, the dust storms that coated the city streets and the windows of Gran's apartment were the same shade of ochre. And if you took CityLineTrains from my old apartment complex (the DesertGreen) through the residential high-rises, past warehouses and parkades full of tents and squatters, and carried on to the final stop, you could catch glimpses of something similar. The distant, open desert, right there through the barbed wire, beyond the millet and sorghum fields and the automated combines.

"Final stop" is a misnomer—the trains curved back on themselves in a continuous loop—but Titan is its own similar "end of the line." Here, Barry and I are as far from Earth as you can work. Earth's Deep Solar Ferries swing around Saturn, picking up return crews and resources after dropping new teams. We were five years on the Ferry here, almost five years on Titan now, and soon we'll have five years on the Ferry home.

I replay Merven's video one more time, hoping I'll

catch a glimpse of who he's talking to when he looks away from the camera. The best I can guess is that it's the dogs Gran might have had with her; and then I remember Rinella had twin girls about four years ago, and I realize I don't have a clue.

The whole message is a blindside, but what can I do for her or them at a mining post a hefty five years' travel from home? Light a stick of incense and say a word at Barry's shrine? I suppose that would be a start.

"Take some time, Nina." Barry flicks his videos off the holo. "However much you need."

I archive Merven's file and throw my tablet to the galley table, annoyed that he read me so easily. "I'm good to go."

THE OVERHEAD WINDOW takes up twenty-five percent of Habitat's central dome, floor to ceiling. Opposite that, the dome has three main junctions that lead to different wings and allow for microclimates: the garden and protein farm modules; medical and fitness and sleep; rover bay and ExothermWearables and outdoor equipment. I grab the hatch wheel that leads to the garden modules and give it a spin.

"We should get to telecommunications first."

"I know." I do know. Titan is swinging around to the back of Saturn, where it'll stay for about a week.

That means no sunlight, and as the telecommunications array sits on the top of the hill behind Habitat, we need what little light we get. I'd hate to navigate the dark stairs with only the head- and hand-lamps on ExothermWearables. But I want to go to the garden module. For the fresh food—yes, we lived off nutrient paste during the storm—but more for the smell. The sulphur tang of the clouds hydrating plants, the plants themselves. The compost and the black soil in the worm bins. You can't get closer to home—couldn't be more *Earth Ideal*.

I'm half kidding. Back on Earth at Gran's, nothing smelled like nature. High-efficiency shower heads, faucets, urinals, and laundry, and still the city imposed water restrictions—the hallways of DesertGreenComplex were eternally bad with body odour, cheap lemon cleaner, and smog the filters hadn't scrubbed. The government-subsidized apartment blocks had been designed, like all low-income housing of the mid-twenty-first century, with a strict adherence to sustainable architecture: *waste wood converts into heating gas; biomass generation equals a carbon-neutral building; each complex treats its own sullage and blackwater; the roofs have solar panels and (you'll never believe it) gardens*—all perks advertised sixty years before Gran dragged us into the place with her dogs. There were three retrievers back then, I think, but that number altered drastically depending on breeding and whelping seasons—the dogs were her excuse of a livelihood.

"People will always want a dog," she explained to the neighbours. "It's like wearing your heart on a leash: safe."

She'd change the quote depending on who she was pitching to: hope on a leash, security on a leash, kids on a leash, etc. And for stores, she had the pedigrees and bloodlines. Dragging three kids and three golden retrievers into a one-room apartment, you'd think the neighbours would hate her, but by the time we arrived, the complex was well used. Ground-level ponds had transformed into teal, algae-ridden bogs, and the heat-regulating blinds adjusted on a timer instead of the original Intelligent Response to internal/external temp and sunlight. Bio-bins and recycling overflowed the courtyard and streets. Everything was trash— every summer I can recall, the patches of weeds that separated the vehicle and bicycle lanes burned to dirt with droughts and pet piss. Even Gran's prize-winning golden retrievers turned into garbage cans—their shit twenty percent compacted plastic fragments, dental floss, and Rinella's handmade beads.

Merven slept in his junker's truck, claiming that Gran, Rinella and I more than filled the apartment. Add to us the dogs—every doorway had a collapsible baby-gate for when we got sick of the swarms of puppies, but there weren't a lot of doorways. I slept in the living room on a Murphy bed, and Rinella crashed on the couch. Only Gran had her own room and I resented her the luxury. When they weren't in use, Gran's puppy crates took over our balcony, stored in stacks next to the rain barrel and the funnel collector. The kids in the apartment above us used to chuck rocks into our funnel, and when it was my turn to scoop pebbles from the barrel I'd take extra time and peer across the street.

Gran's apartment looked overtop of the monorail straight at another apartment complex, where occupants sat on their balconies in dust masks and goggles, taking in the exact view I was: other balconies full of barbecues, broken chairs and appliances, bicycles, dying houseplants, and, invariably, water collection barrels. The dark spread of the funnel collectors looked like a bloom of black flowers, all faced skyward and yearning for rain. Look to the ground and you got the monorail train, and under that, the cracked asphalt of the street. Back in the apartment — eau de hot pavement and dog. I thought it was normal. It was only after I'd left for Corporate training and returned home to visit that I realized the apartment's backhand of piss-paper, dog, and weed might have been part of the reason I'd never made close friends.

Was I an angry kid? Not really. Frustrated, sure, that Gran's main emotion seemed to be panic. The cost of water, we'd blown next week's food budget, et cetera. At the table with her breeding charts and puppy adverts, she was as useless as her worries. Patchwork finances and lifestyle Band-Aids — it was all *next litter of pups should cover a few months' rent*, or, *this dog show will raise our profile* — she never tried for an escape from that place.

So early mornings I'd smash the Murphy bed into the frame, stuff a training bra with toilet paper (and get reamed by Merven for that later — Did I want to wipe my ass with my hand? That shit cost money), and do the absolute minimum at school. When school ended I'd meet up with the true dropouts (I wasn't brave enough to quit attending classes) and steal neon coolers at BlackLightBowling. Evenings saw me stroll home buzzed, open a text, and giggle when I tried to tap the pictures bigger — it was normal that our district accept hand-me-down supplies from the richer ones, but that we were still using outdated, physical books?

Rinella had moved out, although no one could tell. She sat at the table in her embroidered kimono-style wrap and strung cheap jewellery or broke bud with her fingers. Merven would finish his weekly shower and yell at Rinella he couldn't go to work smelling like pot. Rinella would answer she didn't realize the junk-hauling business was that fucking fancy. Merven would counter, "Better than dropping night school to make ass-ugly necklaces," and Gran would beat Merven down with an oven mitt, yell at Rinella to shut up and be useful—clean the pup pen or wash the damn floor.

The oldest dog farted during fights—a round, fruity smell that in the heat made the stench of the apartment rival DesertGreen's sewage treatment. So I'd rescue both of us and take her for walks in the street where, if I looked up, I could watch the entire scene again through Gran's eighth-floor window, right next to the night clerk who never raised his blinds and a hundred other compartmentalized families.

On the walks—there's no comfortable way to say it—I'd take the dog to the top floor of a parkade and tie her leash to a rail so she didn't get lost. Then I'd bend over the railing, breathe as fast as possible with my head hanging over the spiral abyss of car ramps, and hyperventilate. The trick was, as soon as you felt a tingle—the start of the oxygen high—you swung upwards and choked yourself until you collapsed. *Speed Dream to Nirvana*—or at least to escape, to grab the blue-black static that chewed, gnawed, boiled the marrow from vision and sound. O_2 flashes were the closest I got, if not to God, then to a similar truth: there was more. Something else. Something we stood right at the edge of.

There had to be.

"HEY DREAMER, can we go now?" Barry turns the hatch wheel and opens the junction that leads to the ExothermWearables and the rovers. He's being cute, but I can hear the concern in his voice. We need to get to the telecommunications tower and check the status on the dish — hike all those stairs cut into the hillside — and there's under three hours of daylight left. I know I'm zoning out.

"Sure," I say. "Yeah, of course." I can't tell if "dreamer" is a dig, an endearment, or a nod to the past, and I don't want to get into it. I tap up a picture and stats of the rover bay doors.

"Nina." Barry shines a flashlight over the dark galley. Habitat has full power now, but lighting isn't essential and we don't want to push reserves until after we have a solid communications line to TitanMineZero as well as the satellite. You never know.

"At least let me check." If it's possible to drive up the hill, I'd like to. The stats from the rover bay, which we can see through the window is dented and blocked with silt, confirm the damage.

"We knew that," Barry says.

"Yeah." I don't like the Wearables. The combination of materials and tech, layers of interwoven heated insulation — it's hard to trust your life to a suit two inches thick. And the limited vision, despite all the rear-camera viewscreens in the faceplates, slows response time. It's not that I'm claustrophobic—I wouldn't have made it to Titan if that was the case—it's the lumbering around and the sense that every motion seems to take forever.

Barry ducks through the hatch and I follow his dark figure down the corridor. The air changes after a couple metres. It's not fresher than the galley, but on a separate filtration system than the one we've been breathing for two months, so, different. The smell of the suits, the cooler temperature. First junction is repair, maintenance, and ExothermWearable storage, and we head to the closet.

We pre-heat the Wearables. While those are warming, I get the WoolTech on. The leggings, torso, and hood of the under-suits are cobalt—a nice touch on a moon where everything is orange or brown—and the outer layer of the Wearables used to be a similar blue. The exoshells are unisex and older than us. I mean, they were here when we arrived. Model TitanGradeSix, which is warmer than what's used in the asteroid belt (where there's no atmosphere for thermal conduction) but has the bonus of being unpressurized (because of Titan's atmosphere) and less bulky. Previous teams have signed their names to the suits and doodled charms or blessings.

"Can you get my back?" Barry asks. I slide an O_2 tank into a sleeve inside his Wearable and secure the layers of WoolTech, Velcro, and ThermalRubber. He taps a test on his armscreen and then turns to zip me. We step over the lip of the airlock. Barry closes the hatch to the airlock behind us, I palm the final seal, and we sit and wait for acclimatization. The room cools.

"Nina, what is it?"

"It's nothing."

"It's not nothing."

The first time I met Barry he was in that suit—well, not that exact suit, but a training version. Corporate sent the two of us to Haughton Crater for isolation conditioning—six months in a cargo container on an Arctic island crater without radio contact. It was Earth, barely: the northern tip of Canada. Haughton Crater's actual crater—from the air you could see it for what it was: a twenty-three-kilometre pit blasted into the frozen dirt by an impact object thirty-nine million years ago. But on the ground we couldn't see the shape and there was nothing, no life but coin-sized patches of lichen waiting for rain. Arid, dusty-brown, fast-moving clouds. A landscape as close to Titan as Earth could get. It was lonely, and in isolation training and testing, I warmed to him. How could we not want connection in a place like that?

After Haughton Crater we trained together—I guess we'd passed the suitability match—and a year later we launched for Titan. Lifted-off from Earth, coupled with the orbiting Ferry Terminal, and then the two of us were alone on the Deep Solar Ferry burning to Titan.

The ferry's habitable section seemed small if you compared living space to cargo space, and big if you compared it to Gran's apartment — we shared the same expanse of windows as back home, only since Barry and I were weightless there was no sense of a floor or ceiling, and that opened things up. Barry could run on the treadmill while I floated above him watching the void. Unless we looked straight up (or down, whatever you'd like to call it) it was like we were in different rooms. Again, there wasn't much to do. Some tests and monitoring for the scientists — record vision alteration from fluid displacement, blood tests for immune system relaxation, vascular stiffening, and other, lesser-known effects of long-term space travel. All part of the deal.

Which is seeming like a raw deal now, without our bonus. Gran sells — sold — puppies. Barry's mother still fills her bathtub with eel-tailed catfish and ice and hawks beer-battered fish sticks under a false licence in Singapore. We both send money to family.

The drop in temperature in the airlock passes zero Celsius and across from me Barry's suit slowly frosts over.

"Oxygen loading as a kid, remember I told you about it?" I have to give him something. "Wake up with the dog licking my face."

Years of self-throttling, of hitting Cloud Nine. I kept choking, pressing on my own neck to cut off blood flow, to hover at the edge of sensory range before the whole world burned black.

And then the screens—I'm not sure how long I would have gone on choking without them. Probably forever. Thank god that when I was around thirteen, Corporate partnered with the city and billboard screens went up on warehouses and water towers. At first there were only pharmaceutical and education adverts, but after a month of LED pill bottles blinking into Gran's apartment, we got something else. Fifty-storey high-def images of space, of Earth from space, and of the Deep Solar Ferries. Gran's floor-to-ceiling windows, shit for privacy, gave us a prime view: the first deep-space cargo ships fired engines and left the construction dock in orbit, destined to *Further the Human Race via Titan—Affordable, Rapid Bootstrapping of the Solar System!* Open-pit mining of Saturn's moons, self-replicating build-bots—Industry that promises to *Revolutionize the Human Condition.* Below the screens, standing on the tacky asphalt, Merven was hauling some person's crap from his junk truck for resale.

My neck was sore from throttling, but that screen. Clear as if I were in orbit myself, a view of Earth rolling into the night. Flash of the storms, and so much water it made me thirsty.

"Nina." Rinella, sitting at the table behind me, stepped the dog into panties—the brood girl was in heat again and Rinella'd snipped a hole in a pair of Gran's floral underwear and stuck a pad at the rear so she wouldn't leave blood spots on the laminate.

"You need a scarf or something," she said.

I lifted my hands to my throat. It felt rough, and I knew it was red.

"I know how this place can feel." She pulled the dog's tail through the hole in the panties. "But you if you keep that up, you're going somewhere worse."

Merven slammed the door and dumped an armload of vintage necklaces on the table. "How much?" he asked.

"Bullshit, hand them over." Rinella bunched the panties at the dog's back and twisted the fabric into an elastic. She could repurpose the beads and Merven knew it, and the two of them started to yell. The dogs retreated to Gran on the couch under the wall of "Best of Show" ribbons. She pushed her reading glasses up her nose and ran her finger across her breeding charts.

That fight I locked myself in Gran's room and went through her closet. I read the letters she kept in her dresser and flipped through envelopes of photographs and magazine clippings: fields and trees and insane, impossible images like a colossal squid stretched over a rocky beach. Why did she have that stuff? Who had pictures *printed*?

I didn't notice the door open, and Gran caught me with the clippings spread on her quilt.

"Nina," she said. "Personal space."

I yelled, since everyone was yelling. "Personal space? If you cared about privacy you'd have us out of this hole. What do you do, anyway?" As far as I knew she'd never been outside the city. You couldn't leave on the trains. I'd tried—I'd taken transit as far as it would go: from DesertGreenComplex it rattled between tall buildings for hours, then through the richer part of the city with hardy palm trees, not just drought-tolerant grasses, then a glimpse of the ocean. Even there the city didn't stop; roadways disappeared under the waves and if you managed to whip around that section of transit at low tide you could see old park benches and fountains from way back when the oceans were lower. The trip took me eight hours and the train never left the city—it looped around, coiled back on itself, and eventually I got off where I'd started.

Gran sat next to me on the bed and gathered the pictures. Lifted her reading glasses from the strap on her neck. The dog in its rose-patterned panties whined and nosed at the closet—the latest batch of pups sold to the high-end shops that morning.

THERMAL EQUALIZATION FINISHES and the hatch between the airlock to the moon's surface opens with a loud crack—all the ice on the interior breaks off the weather-stripping.

"I'll never get used to that sound." Barry pushes the door fully open and we step onto Titan. Water ice—I make the distinction because this far from the sun it's methane that evaporates, rains, and freezes—pebbles, and brown silt. Past those three enormous boulders that sit on the plane toward the lake, the rise of the week-long night—a blacker horizon. Saturn, sliding between us and the sun. If we were able to see through the methane clouds the view would knock us over.

"They put us on prep," I say. "Prep and repair."

"Relax," Barry says. "It means we're retirees."

"Means we're maintenance staff and janitors with no extraction bonus. How's that better than hawking catfish sticks with your family?" Which is ridiculous, I know that. Our families get money, Corporate still cuts us cheques. The bonus, though, that was *compensation*—or, at least, it was solace.

It's hot in the suit, my boots are slippery with sweat, and we have an hour ahead of us hiking the stairs to the telecommunications tower.

"Barry." I put my hand on the hatch as he swings it closed. "Can the dish wait until tomorrow? Do we have to do this now?"

"Yeah, Nina, we do."

I know we do. I nod, but doubt he can see the "yes" through the bulk of my Wearable. Get it done.

The telecommunications dishes sit on top of the hill behind Habitat, and from the base of the stairs I count five visible bowls — that's all of them, but we can't tell if they're aimed correctly. The Megastorm could easily have swung anyone off target.

In the company's four decades of monitoring there hasn't been a weather pattern close to the Megastorm. Two months in Habitat's galley. Two months where Barry and I fixated on the atmospheric writhe against the overhead. When the view became an oppressive drum of hail and dirt, we closed the shields, sealed ourselves in, and turned to what Earth watched: satellite transmissions of a massive orange spiral — a whirlpool of cloud that enveloped our entire hemisphere. And then the transmissions stopped, and we went to minimum power usage and sat in the dark.

Nine years off Earth to date: four years at the outpost, five in transit on a route that, according to the math, added up to 3.5 billion kilometres of travel — the Deep Solar Ferry's trajectory slingshots the ships around asteroids and Jupiter to gain speed and arrive at the outpost on Titan within a lifespan. Extraction goals met or not, we deserve that bonus.

After the screens lit and the entire city — probably

the entire planet — watched the first Deep Solar Ferry leave dock, I buckled down: accelerated graduation, trade-school, tech, plumbing, Arctic and sub-arctic geology training to "recognize geomorphological markers that might constitute a valuable second (or third) mine," orbital conditioning/testing, the Ferry, Titan. All of the education was government-sponsored — scholarship — as long as you signed on to work after. The assignments were highly paid, time-consuming (not a joke, fifteen to twenty years including travel), and dangerous — of course it was poor urbanites who applied.

I told my family I'd joined up after I put my signature down. Merven paced in the craze of puppies, yelled, "Sellout," "Not your own person," and so on. How could I, he said, write off fifteen years my life? What was his problem, I countered. What did he think I'd been studying?

"Take a welding job for Corporate instead," Rinella pleaded. "Welders are only three-month terms. And you'd work at the station in orbit, right? Maybe we'd see you on the screens."

She was talking about the live feeds of construction of the Deep Solar Ferries. "You can't tell who's out there," I said.

"But we could talk," Merven said. "Instead of exchange recordings—"

"We don't even talk now." I was irritable and defensive. I felt like I was revisiting my childhood being there. That apartment, the smell, the sharp whine of seven newborn pups. Nothing was different, and I was hungover and jumpy from a combination of pills and alcohol. I hadn't planned on drinking, but when I arrived I'd stepped off the train and looked up. There they were, Gran, Merven, and Rinella lit in the frame of the apartment window, and I couldn't make myself go inside. What would I tell them? I bought the pills and mickey and walked back and forth staring at the apartment windows until it grew light enough that the old dog spotted me and started barking.

"Fifteen *years*. That's a jail term," Merven said. "A life sentence." He paced the apartment in his junker's coveralls and work boots. Gran herded the pups into dog crates and shut herself in her room. Rinella rubbed the old dog's ears and added, "How could you do this to yourself and not tell us?"

"Post-Scarcity Economy," I said, echoing Corporate's bullshit. The government's lines were embarrassing in the wealth of their promise: *Next Leap — Self Sufficiency in the Outer Solar System; Fulfill All Humanity's Dreams for Space!* Sure, the future might sparkle, but until we made it to stable off-world production and a guaranteed minimum income, until we had — God — *water* imports from the asteroid belt and a reduction in global

temperatures, then the paycheques were in long-term
outpost grunt work.

"I don't get you." I grabbed a leash and clipped it to
the old dog. "The pay for welders is nothing. Don't you
want something back?" That silenced them, mostly.

Outside the air was brothy and thick and stank of
hot bio-bin. I had to walk slowly to accommodate the
old dog's arthritis. I wandered dank, empty parkades
and the sunburnt weeds of DesertGreenComplex's
common grounds.

It was evening when the dog and I got home. Merven
had left, and Rinella lounged, vaping on the couch in
her robe. The pups slept in their kennels, the big dogs
on cushions. I knocked on Gran's door and sat across
from her on the bed. Took her hands. Through the wall
of window the sun christened the cityscape — towers
and apartments blackened sticks against its fiery pink.

"Gran," I said. "You know I respect you. But there's
no way —" Her worries were my own by that point,
the crummy water, nutrition, quality of life — I refused
to be as useless as she'd been.

I stayed with them that week, trying to find common ground before I left. The day prior to my shuttle
launch from Earth, Gran set her hidden photographs
on the table. I slid the stack closer to where I sat filling the last of my paperwork. She turned to scrub the
kitchen counter.

"I found these as a kid," I said. "I'd almost forgotten." I pulled a photo from the pile. A young Gran in stained white jeans and a maroon chemise held a naked, diapered infant, the kid's face and arms blurred with motion—me, I assumed. Merven and Rinella, looking about eleven and eight, flanked her. Both kids went shirtless in denim overalls. The three of them (with me in Gran's arms) stood in front of a lime-green taxi, expressions flat or tired, the taxi driver caught mid-lift loading plaid suitcases into the trunk. Three shaggy golden dogs (which generation, I couldn't tell) already filled the car.

"Go." Gran tossed the dishcloth into the sink and picked up a magazine clipping. Little blue-and-white houses on the blue-and-white ocean—Greece, or some other country that used to exist. "What's the point of staying?"

She was right. By that time all the high forests had blown away. The oceans choked on plankton, any glaciers vanished. Go, she told me. And she should know—her entire life in an apartment with a whirlwind of puppies and lazy-ass grandkids. I set the picture down. I would reroute the cheques to her, enough currency to black-market some eggs. Beans. Protein that wasn't a powdered supplement. Savings. Maybe soon she'd be able to—

I handed her the photo. "The modules will be state-of-the-art," I said. Those robotics improved generationally, and the off-Earth habitats were advertised as luxury. So many resources and discoveries coming in. Pretty soon we'd have opportunities beyond our wildest—

She pushed the clippings aside and grabbed my arm, pulling me into a hug. "Nina."

THE FLIGHT TO the Saturn system: five years shitting into a vacuum cleaner. Advanced resistive exercise. Monotony punctuated by shock: seeing the return Ferry through the window, passing back the way we came, taking a previous outpost pair with them. Barry and I cheered—raised apple juice in sippy bags over the radio. "乾杯—Gān bēi!" A toast to Earth's expats. And the back-glance of Jupiter: foreign swirls of gas, soft-edged in the dark.

Then a few more years of boredom before rolling into the Saturn system—its gallery of cratered moons. Barry next to me in the observatory. The walls behind us covered with clips and paper and Velcro.

A gap in the bright rings below, Saturn's silent roll to our left. A moon blazed with light—I gasped, suddenly dizzy, directionless. We were falling, not floating, and falling endlessly—there was nothing to hit. I grabbed for a wall.

Barry let go and spun weightless. "Afraid of a collision?"

"Tell me this tub knows where it's headed."

Out the portal, the rings looped shadows over the pastel giant. Barry unclipped an ancestral placard from its shrine and hung it in the air in front of the window. He lit a stick of incense and set it to float alongside.

"There," he said. "Let them have a view."

What a view: those rings—at first a solid and uniform white, but as we grew closer we saw ridges and shadows. Closer still, aggregates of icy particles—a compilation that continually formed and dispersed.

Barry pointed to the orange-and-brown haze that was Titan, our outpost-to-be. "That'll be us, Nina." The moon minuscule next to the planet, next to the teal shadows stretched across the giant's tan and green gases.

I groped for the wall again. Barry's placard floating in front of Saturn didn't help, it just bared the universe: a struggle to grasp—to retain perspective—and an overwhelming veneration that science couldn't hold at bay. The fire on the incense burned spherical and purple then snuffed itself—filled the Ferry with faux jasmine.

Five years Barry and I had floated in the Deep Solar Ferry. We took down pictures and personals—the photos at the shrine, drawings, holiday decor, Sudoku— before packing ourselves into the lander. Point the cameras toward the ground and launch. Control the burn during descent, parachutes, then Titan.

We first saw the moon's surface through the fish-eye cam in our lander. Orange cloud rushed the windows, thinned, and gave way to a continent of ochre ridges and flats. The craft burned closer, eastern plains filled the screen, dunes to the south slipped from view, and we were right on top of the site: a monumental, maze-like system of pipes drew oil from the lake, automation continuously scratched methane and water ice from the regolith, and behind the mine the shiny speck of Habitat's dome and a meandering staircase cut into the hill. At the top of the stairs, circles that we realized were huge telecommunications dishes—it all said civilization, humanity, *Earth Was Here*.

Faster, closer, the jolt of landing—the cam full of brown ice pebbles and mud—and holy 他妈的, the weight of our bodies, the crush of the gravity of even that small moon after years of zero-g, of having to lift your tongue to talk.

On the surface, Titan seemed so much like Earth: atmosphere, ground—even if the air was unbreathable and the moon only a brown, muddy basin, Titan had creeks, rivers, steam. The rain was methane and the lakes liquid hydrocarbons, but the fact it had any form of precipitation at all brought back the memory of home, true home: the city hunkered under deep purple cloud, a white-blue flash of lightning, the whimper of Gran's dogs, and the scurry of neighbours adjusting the angle of funnel collectors and setting any canister that could catch water on their balconies.

Inside Habitat, Barry and I hauled our atrophied asses through procedure—acclimatized to humidity and changes in air and temperature from the Deep Solar Ferry—and collapsed in the galley. To be *sitting* again, feeling our own weight, while the clouds darkened above us in the overhead dome. That *above* was a direction, and the smell from the garden module: wet dirt.

The previous team had left us a seasoned cast-iron pan we could barely lift. We managed, instead of cooking, to rehydrate a package of nutrient gruel and drink it from mugs at the galley table. Barry hooked his portable to Habitat's telecommunications system and tapped messages to Corporate and to home: *Made it.*

Sending the message woke the Habitat console, and brought to life the holoscreen. Images of what the last team had been researching appeared over the table.

"Enceladus," I said. Titan's sister moon, her white pole tinted lilac and cracked with turquoise. Next, a shot with the moon blackened, and the ice jets' fine mist against the black. "Water vapour, salt crystals, ice particles." Overlaying the moon, a network of lines showed blueprints for a mining expansion. Ice, for water and oxygen.

"Looks like Titan will gain neighbours—go Corporate." There was energy to Barry's voice. I don't know how he summoned so much excitement for Corporate. More ships, faster ships, asteroid mines, now Enceladus, and off in the future at the edge of nullity, the ludicrous fantasy of exoplanet colonies—he was more of a dreamer than I was that way. I was too tired, too sore to care, and I wanted home. I slid my chair under the galley overhead and tilted back under the deep brown haze. Titan sat midway through its day cycle (fifteen point nine Earth days), careening behind Saturn into dark.

"Open a pic of Earth," I said.

Barry brought up an image—a dot, a speck at the edge of Saturn's rings.

"Something closer."

He looked at me, took his legs off the table, and pulled up a photo from the Ferry trip. Two hundred and fifty miles above Europe, a satellite hung over scattered white clouds, solar panels glinting copper, spread like some mechanical dragon. Next pic: Eastern North America pale with winter storms. Then Southeast Asia at night, lit electrically, playing at its own night sky. More photos—a pebbled mosaic of land, atmosphere, oceans.

Barry set his mug in the air and we were both shocked when it smashed to the ground.

NEXT MONTHS, us versus gravity. Next years—

Transmissions: Merven posed with a hand on the cab of his new junk truck. The family cheered "Hellooooo Nina!" from an apartment with forty percent more square footage. Gran did a hand-held tour of her garden—container-grown peanuts on the shiny glass balcony. Rinella, officially back home in the second bedroom ("A second bedroom, can you believe it?"), held twins on her lap. And the puppies—that wriggle of yellow that came and went while Gran, or Merven with his sweat-stained shirts and greying hair, filmed their greetings.

The more videos they sent, the less I found to say. How many times could I describe a moon with constant cloud cover? Barry and I—we visited each other at night. During the day, we bled time with cards and Sudoku, gardening, exercises, maintenance checks in ExothermWearables, and updating mine reports. Slowly, Merven's "News Reels" started to sound more like jabs—a close-up of a picture on the wall: me, surrounded by sketches of the retired or deceased brood dogs, pressed flowers, and incense sticks.

It's me, not them, I reminded myself, and scattered food to the crickets. Untangled fine red worms from soil and separated them to new bins in the garden module. Inflated cryoballoons and monitored weather patterns in the south. But I watched fewer videos, then quit entirely, and eventually the transmissions stopped coming. We'd always been moving on, I told myself, gaining distance over time until we faded from each other's view. If we'd even been looking toward each other to start.

BARRY AND I reach the lookout and telecommunications tower on the summit of the hill. The main dish for the mine hangs at an odd angle, and must have been knocked off target by the storm. That it hasn't righted itself will be an automation issue, and as soon as we've caught our breath from the hike we'll check that the system has begun self-repair. Barry leans against the wall that rings the lookout.

From our vantage point, Habitat's domed exterior shines orange and silver in the haze. The greenhouses, connected to the central galley by junctions and corridors, spread from it like the start of something—a web of mould, or the blind taproots of the soilless plants in aeroponics. Past the modules, but only about half a kilometre south, there's a new river where the hydrocarbon storage barrels should be. Sometime over the last couple months, while Barry and I hunkered under Habitat's shielding, the Megastorm peeled the land. Mud slid by us like it was nothing—like we were nothing—and took everything we'd scraped together.

That river, it could have taken us, too. Such a close call.

But if I'm honest, what isn't? Suddenly I'm worried about sinkholes, about a trip and a chaotic skid down the hill, a cracked face-plate in our Wearables, and all the other unpredictable 拉屎. How can I take a step without risking everything—myself, Barry, family? Those jobs—the welder jobs that Rinella pushed me to get—I wish I'd taken one now.

"Remember losing sight of Earth?" I ask.

Barry grabs my hands. "Nina." Both our Wearables are coated in red soot, none of the blessings or charms visible. "Whatever you're kicking yourself over—"

"Okay." I raise a hand. "Yield."

But I can't. I can't let it go, not truly. I still see Gran, or, I remember her, and I can't stop.

"I have to sit." Gran at our Earth launch, her light cotton dress flattened against her knees by the wind, the three dogs on the leash lying like lions on the dirt patch beyond the orange plastic barrier fence. Barry and I—as we carted to the shuttle that sunny morning I stood, punched a fist into the blue air and held it, trying to catch her eye.

It's hard to breathe. Barry kneels in front of me on a patch of brown rocks, smooth like river stone or cobbles, half-embedded in the wet sand. Not sand, really; organic soot, hydrocarbon polymers that clump and rain to the surface year after year.

"You gonna tell me what was in your transmission?" he asks.

"I'll be fine," I say, knowing he's worried. And, seated in the mud with my head between my knees, I will be. Of course I will. But—

Gran throwing that dishcloth in the sink, her expression as I listed my reasons, wrote her off as use-less—convinced myself I'd made it. The apartment. Merven and Rinella. Those luminous, sunlit dogs. That tiny life.

THE WHITE

—

(A NOVELLA)

I

—

MELANIE

WHAT IS WORSE than rubbing bag balm onto chaffed udders — suddenly worse than home and chores at home — is that right at this instant on the bus to school the other kids keep two seats back from her. These rural kids of which she is now fabulously one. These losers who, when they boarded, she was desperate to do any, seriously any after-school activity with — community service, even detention — these assholes hold their mittens next to their mouths and their mouths to each other's ears and spread dirt on her. Even after a full year of sucking up to these jerks — these idiots she called her friends until now — they scan her head, run their eyes over the left side of her scalp where a patch of hair is cropped down to a blonde inch, and know—with her father in the town's drunk tank three times this summer, of course they know—that her father pulled her out of bed in the middle of last night and shaved half her head.

The bus lurches to a stop in the parking lot. She sits with her eyes closed in the funk of wet winter-wear, vinyl seats, and exhaust. The other students leave first. Let them. She waits until the bus empties, then stomps down the high, wet stairs, dragging her empty pack through the snow, not toward the school, but back to the highway. There's no way she's spending another day in that tiny human bullpen where a "clarinet" might as well be an exotic farm tool, and where the newbie teacher herds them all out to tour farms where they live and not a kid pipes up because, well, field trip. The bell jangles behind her. The thought of class with those traitors—she could puke.

At the highway she pulls off a glove and rubs the skin under her glasses between her cheekbone and eye. Her eye sockets are soft and puffed. She straightens her glasses then thumbs a passing car. When the car doesn't stop, she jerks her hand down.

Her friends. Another car passes with a wet hiss. Those bullshits. She kicks a lump of snow off the shoulder of the road onto the highway toward the disappearing vehicle. "Those bull-fucks," she yells. She kicks a second lump of hard-packed snow onto the lane.

Her friends deserve something more violently gross than names, though. She'll eat a rock. And right before she swallows the rock, she will stick a pin through her tongue. Or worse: pick up a red-brown tampon from the field at lunch, swing it round her head by the string, and let it fly. She rubs her thumb across her fist. Her head is freezing—colder than her ungloved hand.

She blows on her fingers and creates a damp warmth that will soon be a more miserable cold than before. She presses her fingertips to the side of her head, gently, slowly, as if reaching to pet a strange dog. Across the highway and along the valley basin the grey river, buoyant with broken slabs of ice, flows quietly. Naked aspen, mingled with mountain ash and their orange, ice-crusted berries, stand pencilled along the near bank. The road too is grey, the sky the colour of a coffee filter rinsed and dried for reuse. She hawks a loogie, wipes a thread of spit from her lip with the back of her hand, then wipes her hand on her coat. The snow she's kicked is strewn across both lanes of the highway. It would be chancy for a car to dodge all of them. She pulls her glove back on, walks to the centre line, and kicks the lumps off the highway.

The neighbour's rusted blue hatchback finally pulls over, spitting salty slush onto the shoulder. Melanie steps into the snow to give it room. Axel's driving, Kendra in the front beside him with her camera, and in the backseat, this boy about fourteen, her age, slides to the middle and crams his side against a tower of deep, grey trays, the trays used to bus tables in cafeterias. The trays are loaded with baby birds and are piled, alternating width to length, to within an inch of the roof. In the rear, the plastic containers are stacked double-wide and padded around the base with old towels—even Axel's driving won't shake them. She gets in the car. There's the smell from the trays, and this boy in a black kilt whose hip bone or belt—hard to tell—jabs into her side. He's blushing, this kid, or wearing makeup, or was recently slapped. Looking at the boy—who the hell wears a *kilt?*—and knowing Axel, all these options seem valid. No way she'll ask. No need to start a conversation that will force her to explain why she's not in class, what she's doing hitchhiking, and why half her hair is gone.

"Shut the door or get out." Axel rattles the gearshift. Melanie swings the door closed and hits the lock. If Axel even noticed her head, he doesn't care. Kendra probably guesses. But the kid, the boy, he doesn't know anything—he could surmise whatever, even the truth. Her cheeks flush and she pulls off her gloves and presses the backs of her hands to her face, then her hair. Damn her for wearing all her secrets on the outside.

CODY

There's no buckle, or the buckle's trapped under the cushion, down the crack behind the seat where the blonde girl's sitting, so he holds the seatbelt strap across himself with the metal clip in his hand, faking it, and riding, for the first time ever, gloriously unrestrained.

The car rounds a curve and he tenses to avoid tilting further into the girl. Axel drives fast, and the car rides low, heavy with all four passengers. The torque is different than that of the Greyhound, and it pulls at his stomach when the corner ends and the car picks up even more speed. He squeezes the metal, and the head of his seatbelt heats in his hand. He thought Axel would be dull and, you know, old. Wrong. Axel's way past old, he's old enough to be interesting: he's ancient. And then there's Axel's fake leg, and Kendra who was introduced as Axel's apprentice, and this crazy car full of birds. For over twenty-four hours in the aisle seat of the Greyhound, trapped in the licorice stink of the washroom's automatic flush and the armpits and cologne of the man next to him, Cody had imagined what this year would be like with Great-Uncle Old: farm-ish, boring, lonely. Wrong. Being in a speeding car with an ancient one-legged uncle, leaning against a girl's wet lumberjack coat, surrounded by the barny scent of so many baby chickens—this is a thousand times better than he could have hoped. This is incredible.

He rests his elbow on the curved rim of a tray and dips his fingers into the chicks. The one he cups cheeps—the sound could scratch glass. And from such a tiny bird. He can feel the wiggly warm breath in its rib cage. He runs his palm above the backs of the chicks. So many. The movement arouses the flock and chirps fill the car. Truly loud.

They're so soft. He should fill a room with chicks, like those ball rooms in malls for toddlers. And he could be covered with the chirpers. They probably don't weigh much. How many chicks would it take to fill a room? The car is full, how many are here?

"How many birds?" Cody leans forward so that his head is in the space between Axel and Kendra in the front. "How many?"

Axel presses the gas and rounds a corner. Kendra uncrosses her arms and cracks open the window. She's old too, not too old, but definitely adult. Over twenty, or even his mother's age, thirty-something. She has a pale spray of freckles over her face, ears, and neck that look like they might carry on down her skin. Her dark hair, pulled into a tight braid, hangs over her shoulder. Despite the almost wet smoothness of the braid itself, the ends below the elastic are kinked. Cody's best friend back home had hair like that—she couldn't keep it out of her mouth.

He sits back and pulls the seatbelt tighter. Pale blue-grey eyelids blink at him from the trays, like clouds in the chicks' sunny, fluffy bodies. The beaks, open and chirping, are too many to count. Holy hockey, they are loud.

And numerous. The trays are stacked so high on his right he can't see out that window and has to look left, past the girl, to see the pastures, snow, and under the snow weird purple bulges that he's just now figured out are, delightfully, cabbages. Fields of cabbage, of cows — not milk-carton cows, but tan and chestnut things with low-slung pale, peachy-white udders — that stand in the pastures with snow on their backs.

Uncle Ancient-Axel pulls off the highway onto a gravel road, a long driveway really, and finally — finally — Cody's feet are on ground, his canvas sneakers wet and muddy. He stretches, stuffs his hands into the pockets of his hoodie, and breathes deeply. A zest hangs in the air under the clouds and over the snow, mingles with the smell of the girl who's now standing beside him: cow and wet felt and hay. The girl looks maybe fourteen, hopefully fourteen, his age, or at least thirteen. Or fifteen is fine, too.

He pushes back the hood of his sweater. The car is parked between a small black pickup and a low, one-storey building. A barn, or workshop maybe, with an outdoor sink and shower beside the entryway. Then there's a cedar-shake house with a porch. Beyond the house, further up the drive, rows of skinny sheds. He tugs his backpack from the car, walks to the porch, and sets the bag out of the snow under the eaves. The sheds are clustered under netting that's tented over their entire area. They look cheap — plywood structures with two doors each. The outer door is a chicken-wire cage about two feet deep. The inner door is part plywood and part old-style Western prison bars.

The plywood is streaked with what look like splashes of white paint, and the fibreglass roofs seem bleached, but the bars gleam. Cody rubs his ear. If this were a horror movie, Axel's farm would be the place to avoid. To the left, across a barbed-wire fence, cows meander around a red barn and house. A dairy farm? Past the two properties, trees and treed mountains. He brushes his bangs out of his eyes. No chickens, but they would be penned in this weather, wouldn't they?

"Where's the chickens?" Cody calls. The girl, standing by the car, straightens her glasses and snorts.

Axel slams the driver's door and limps around to the back of the car. He pops the hatchback. Cody walks back to the drive and follows. His sneakers have no grip, and he skids on the slush and gravel. Axel lifts the top tray from the stack in the rear of the car. Cody leans over the chicks in the tray underneath. They're silent, maybe dead. But no. They blink, twitch their stumpy wings, and start to chirp.

"Pick it up." Axel tilts his head toward the trays with a fast, impatient jerk. Kendra has already fetched a shop-vac, and Melanie, the girl, stacks the trays from the back seat beside the car.

Cody tugs the sleeves of his hoodie down over his fingers and grabs both sides of a tray from the trunk. He lifts, hoisting it higher than he intended—the chicks are so light, they are nothing but fluff and sound. He looks around again for a pen or chicken house.

Axel crosses the drive to the workshop/barn and manages the stairs, hopping each step on his good leg and swinging the fake up after. Cody follows gingerly, testing the grip of his sneakers on the wood steps. The entry is a hallway with two doors in the left wall, and an outside sink and shower built into the right. The sink is deep, square, and stands on thin steel legs. The shower is a sheet of plastic pushed back from a nozzle, a square of rimmed plastic flooring with a drain, and the whole nudie stage opens on a sightline to the driveway and the world.

Axel throws open the second door on the left, the one further along the hall, and drops his tray of chicks onto the patched linoleum floor inside. He shoves the tray into the room with his foot and holds the door open waiting for Cody. Cody bends, sets his tray of chicks on the ground, and slides them into the room. Axel slams the door. When it doesn't latch, he bumps it into place with his shoulder. Cody follows Axel back outside, heads to the car and picks up another tray of birds. Kendra leans into the car and the vacuum pitches higher. Melanie tugs out a floor mat. Cody's legs below the knees are freezing. Stupid to have worn the kilt without jeans or leggings, but this cold is not the cold he's used to. A leaching cold, like the cold that hangs out in the low corners of swimming pools, or the murky sand at the bottom of lakes. His kilt, okay, is maybe unusual—his aunt shook her head when she dropped him at the bus stop—but here even his sneakers are out of place.

AXEL

Twenty trays stacked by the floor-drain in the centre of the feed room. Two hundred peeping chicks per tray at twenty trays. Makes four thousand chicks. Sets up this week's feed. Now to get the feeders stored—stockpiled along the back wall next to the old cement mixer—and then come the fun chores, the rounds. The walk-by of fifteen hawks and all ninety pretty gyrfalcons, but especially the white. That bird. Not a grey barb or vein. Not a fracture. And tomorrow he'll fly her. First time out. The breach of that bird's wing—he shakes *think-ing* about it. Thirty years of tinkering and he's done it. Bred falcons to perfection.

Only he can't keep his excitement fired as he considers the boy's weak ankles, the—what's the kid wearing, a skirt? He looks at the kid, and damn it he has doubt. Doubt that the white will be flawless. And this irritation despite the three decades of breeding gyrfalcons—fifty-plus years' flying and capture—when no other falconer could coax a gyr to drop an egg. Pah. Axel bends and slides two five-gallon pails out from beside the deep-freeze.

"Take one." He shakes a pail at the boy, rattling the metal handle. The kid, hesitation from the top down, reaches and backs off. Does he have to coax him? "Take it." The boy finally takes the bucket. Axel lifts a tray of chicks and dumps them into his own pail. He gestures for the boy to do the same, but the kid just stands there, holding the bucket by the lip. "Get on it." Axel drops the tray and waits. The kid sets the bucket down and tilts a tray, easing the peepers into his pail. Axel grabs two wooden plugs—circles of plywood cut to fit inside the pails—and tosses one to the boy so that the kid will catch it or be hit. The plug bounces off the boy's palm and whacks the ground. He rubs his hand down his skirt. Axel fits his own board over the chicks inside the pail, plants his fists in the centre of the board, and presses down. If the kid does not do this. But the kid does, remarkably. Axel counts out one hundred and twenty seconds—the boy staring at his shoes the whole time—then lifts the wood and dumps the dead chicks back into the tray. The kid lifts his own pail and upturns it over the empty tray. The plug clunks out. Chicks tumble after it.

Axel paws through Cody's tray. At his touch a few birds twitch. He sorts the dead from the merely limp. Twenty or so still cheeping.

"Hold out your hand." Axel grabs the kid's hand and tucks the feet of a chick between his fingers. "Watch." He takes three chicks himself, grips the legs, whacks their heads on the edge of the freezer, and tosses them back into the tray.

The boy opens his mouth, then closes it and pinches his earlobe.

Axel takes three more chicks and busts their heads on the deep-freeze. Again. Through all twenty or so chicks the kid stands there. "Ever been fishing? Haven't you conked a trout?" What kid hasn't bludgeoned a fish?

The kid shakes his head. One jerk, to the left, so that the boy could have meant no, or it could have been the kid not listening and tilting toward the question, asking, Huh? Whichever, seems the kid's already tiring. He's holding his arm up all right, but the chick dangles from his hand like he has no control over his wrist.

What's the boy done today? Nothing. No, the kid's pale in the sickly fragile way of not enough scuffling. When Axel was a boy kids were non-stop action. Ha, he remembers when he hopped, goddamn hopped, all the way up a mountainside creek and back—having unstrapped his leg for swimming—and he thought nothing of it. Granted he was older, maybe twenty, and had already hopped freight ships and travelled everywhere there were birds, but the point is when he took off, he was only a year or two older than the boy. The point is, the kid should be ready to break his own neck and care even less about a pail of feeder chicks.

"Don't piss yourself." No time for this. Axel takes the chick from the boy and hits it on the freezer. He refills both pails, picks up the plug, and tosses it over. The kid pushes on the wood properly this time. Better.

After ten trays each, the kid is wiping his hands constantly on, yes definitely, a fucking skirt. Yellow fluffs all over him.

"Get used to it." Sooner the better. Hundred-fifteen birds, the farm at capacity, and each falcon or hawk needs feeding. Axel stacks the trays of dead chicks in the corner by the freezer. He limps from the room, the kid already ahead of him washing at the sink.

Axel braces himself in the entranceway, grabbing either side of the hall, and calls. Kendra gives him a thumbs-up. She's almost finished vacuuming the car.

The neighbour girl is shaking the floor mats over the frozen driveway. And his boy at the sink, the nail brush rough and reddening the kid's soapy skin, goddamn scrubbing his hands.

KENDRA

The shop-vac shut down and the chicks stored in the feed room. The highway currently car-free, the paddock empty, the cows far-off and still. Axel done yelling instructions at the boy. Blessed silence. The type of quiet that lets her hear distance: crows hidden in the cloud-covered hills. The white noise of the river. Kendra sits in the driver's seat and coils the shop-vac's hose. Across the paddock, at the dairy house, the creak and slap of the front door as the neighbour Milo — sweater, no coat — steps onto the porch. He leans on the rail, raises his hand to his eyes, then lifts it further in recognition. Kendra raises her arm in reply.

"He said I could take the day off." Melanie tugs the passenger-seat floor mat into place.

From the way Melanie cleaned the car, hoovering rock and hay and fluff from the foot-wells like their presence offended her, Kendra expected sarcasm, a vocal bite, or at least a tense tone, but the girl's words are a flat-out lie. Too obvious a lie. What's she thinking? That

Kendra hasn't seen Milo senseless on the deck chair the whole summer? Granted, Milo's polite enough when he hands over the home-brewed spirits he trades her and Axel for clearing the pasture of rabbits, and Milo was decent enough — decent being maybe too strong a word — *person* enough to have been guilted back to the dairy farm after his old man's stroke. But Milo definitely hasn't been up to giving permission for what looks like years. Probably since way before Melanie was born. She doubts the girl has ever asked for permission for anything. The way he's leaning, like he relies on the porch rail to keep him upright — she can almost smell the stale booze across the distance. So why lie? The lie is so obvious it's rude. Why's the girl challenging her?

"Don't have to cover for him." Kendra lowers her hand.

Melanie slams the passenger door and leans against it. "Who's covering?"

"So we didn't pick you up off the side of the highway?" Kendra snaps the vacuum hose in place and reels in the cord.

Melanie rolls her eyes and stretches her arms out along the top of the vehicle. She looks ridiculous, like Jesus on the cross, or like she's trying to sell the car. "What's next?" she says. With her attitude, it's possible she buzzed her own hair. Though the style seems more in character with the boy at the sink. His coif — it's almost a mohawk, only the top stripe isn't gelled and hangs limply over his brow and eyes. The shorter hair at the back and sides is clipped to about an inch in length. Dark brown with a touch of curl. Cute.

The boy — what to do but laugh? — his thin legs, pale and weak. Like sprouts in early spring, or, during a sudden winter warmth, like the translucent, purple-white of January crocuses. His fingers are also violet, but a deeper purple, almost blue, from the icy water he's washing his hands in. Axel should have looked the boy over before dragging him to kill chicks. The way the kid grinned and rubbed his hands in the bird bins the whole ride here.

And that kilt. He doesn't have the knees for the kilt. Bud-like, bulgy things, brashly white below the hem of the black pleated wool. To think that Axel'd bragged about his nephew coming. He'd been so excited he'd gone on about how "staunch a farm hand" the kid would be, and no need to pay a boy, a relative. No need, he'd said, not even trying to be sly, to give the kid a bird.

She almost left right then and there. Plenty of places she could go. Sanders with the red-tail hawks down in Texas, or work with Verlyn at his peregrine rehab centre Alberta way. Falconers she hunted chukar with outside Alamosa at her first meet years ago. Neither Sanders nor Verlyn are breeders, but she wouldn't have to fight them to have her own damn bird. Her own bird was part of her and Axel's gentleman's work contract. She should have made Axel spit on it. For the last three years she's waited through his excuses: the sale prices too high, the gyrfalcons oversold—though they've only sold six in the last season—and that brilliantly plumed female? Needed for the following year's breeding. She almost took her truck and flaked. But she didn't. Maybe it was all that Zen patience she picked up losing the community meat draw every third Sunday. Whatever made her stay, it turned out to be worth it. Axel will give her a bird this year, finally, that ass, because otherwise she *will* leave, and Axel needs her. This kid he's been ranting about—her potential replacement—is, well, a pansy.

There's just no chance. The boy is so fresh he's hopeless. Even the girl would be a better stand-in if Kendra took off. Melanie's a liar and a fake, but reliable enough to set up the milking every dawn before school. Kendra climbs the stairs and shuts off the tap. The kid shakes out his hands, hitting the side of the sink, winces, and tucks his fingers under his armpits.

It's because of this kid's ineptitude that Kendra relaxes. She's relaxed enough to find the kid's discomfort funny. In fact, she's carelessly lazy about the whole situation now that she sees what's coming: bird, money, and a So Take That, Axel.

"What next?" Melanie asks.

Above the farms, the clouds are thick and slate

coloured and sag, weighted, over the mountain ridge. "What's next?" Kendra repeats. Up the yard Axel, carrying the white gyrfalcon on his glove, surveys the breeding pens. A pact: let the bird know they will give it what it wants. The first step in training. It's not rage or hunger, as people assume, that inspires the birds to kill, it's play. Kendra's watched a falcon carry a feather a hundred metres up, release it, then smack it out of the air before it hit the ground. That's the energy, the spirit of alert, high excitement, that she and Axel hone.

Axel bends at the knee to peer in a pen and, doing so, drops his arm. The white spreads her wing to regain balance and falters. Axel twists his forearm in response. The bird regains footing. "That" — Kendra slaps her hands together — "is next." Let that grab her fist, that white chunk she helped hatch. And as she trudges through the snow she actually feels a burst of joy aimed at the future, at what she's finally putting a leash on here, in this moment — life.

MILO

Across the paddock, beyond the slurry lagoon of cow dung and melted snow, over the fence, he squints at his daughter. His girl, absolutely. He recognizes the oversized red-and-black toggle coat, its plaid, felted wool that's too big for her at the shoulders, the arms, and the waist—his coat. She drapes her pack on the fence between the properties and, as Kendra and a kid walk the trail to where Axel's birds are, she sneaks up the stairs into the hatchling barn. He scratches his chin—beard—too much hair now to be called stubble. He woke her up drunk last night, he remembers that. Has a vague recollection of shaking her out of bed for help with his father, her grandfather. Too bad the memory isn't gone entirely. Well, too bad he woke her.

But she should be in school. He crosses the snow and mud-slicked paddock. The cows blink at him. They seem disinterested and not at all distressed. She must have milked them again. His job. Shit, be honest, milking's practically her job now. He skirts the lagoon holding his breath and picks up the pace. This year on the dairy, a whole childhood on the dairy, and he still can't handle the smell of the dung pit. Of course that's partly the hangover, which hasn't even begun to hit properly—he's still drunk. Unfocused and dizzy behind the eyes.

He ducks the barbed-wire fence. Axel's place. Netting's in good shape despite the age, or maybe it's new. Some of the fibreglass roofs've been replaced on the bird boxes. Mewses are same-old, though. When he was nine—that'd be over thirty years ago, when Axel first moved here—he peeked through one of the feed slots in the breeding pens. The mewses had barely been built, and though the wood was dry, it smelled of paint enough for him check his fingers after touching the wall. The interior was dim. A triple-stripped oil drum, red and white with a hole cut in the side, had been settled into a corner. Hay, feathers, smell of bird shit like old cream and cashews. And the birds — two speckled gyrfalcons perched yellow-footed on dowels screwed into the walls. By the time he spotted them they already had their black eyes on him. That was it — he took off. Not sure what freaked him out so badly, the birds being there, or that they'd seen him, or the spooky thought that Axel might somehow know. Whichever, it kept him off Axel's property as a teen, and his friends, well, if they had wanted to snoop their curiosity was beaten when he brought his father's garage distillery into the conversation.

He climbs the stairs and hesitates at the door his daughter disappeared into. He should turn around and let her be. Last night might have been bad. How bad? He grabs the doorknob. He's in the same clothes as yesterday, well, as all this week. Gumboots, jogging pants, one of his old man's old sweaters, scarf. But how bad could last night have really been? Not like Melanie hasn't already seen it all.

The room inside smells of pine, hay, and dust, and is washed in low red light — lit like a darkroom or brothel. What would Melanie be doing developing film? He thinks porn, then, no way. Heat lamps. Heat lamps are clamped to the counter that circles the room. Okay. That's why the red. He closes the door behind him, tugging hard to compress the rubber flap against the insulation taped over the door jamb. The middle of the room is a makeshift wall of bookshelves. Seems like Axel's picked up every loose piece of furniture he's found on the roadside. Cords and extension cords from electric heaters loop half-buried in hay over the unfinished floor. He steps over the mess and runs his hand down the shelves of photo albums.

Around the room plastic sheeting is stretched taut over fibreglass insulation and stapled to bare studs. There must be over fifty lamps clamped to the counter that frames the room, and their filaments—painful to look at—reflect pink and red off the plastic. Cut-down cardboard boxes, each with a lip four to six inches, are stacked on the left. Beside them, haphazard pillars of aluminum tins.

He leans against the nearest bookcase and dusts through photo albums. The collections on the middle shelf date back ten years or more. He tugs out a thick green compilation and cracks it halfway. Infant birds. Falcons. No idea how old. White fluff barely covers their bodies. Each bird has a dot inked onto its forehead. Typewritten cue cards are sealed into the album under each photo. Date, name, and what looks like breed stock. He replaces the collection and selects another. Older. Adult birds this time. Photos have places— "Quebec," "Tuktoyaktuk"—and dates. A third collection. This one old enough to have small plastic pockets, not the stiff, peel-back pages of the previous two. Axel as a young man—his hair pale brown or dirty blonde, difficult to tell with the camera filter— seated on a brick wall. He wears shorts, his bare legs are crossed at the ankles, and he salutes the photographer with a beer. Behind him, hills and mountains uphol- stered with short trees and brush that could be alpine. Blue sky above the peaks. Another photo: a young girl in a cap, no, a wimple and bandeau—a nun?—holds a hawk on a glove. She wears boots under her skirt and stands in a garden, or on the path between gardens. Flowers, no idea what type, tall-stemmed with weighty, petalled heads. The girl's eyebrows and eyes and skin are dark—Spanish?

There's recent photos, too, unlabelled and still in an envelope on the bottom shelf. He thumbs out the top print—Axel perched on a stool, bent over an incubator. Axel sits with his jumpsuit open and pulled half off, the arms tied around his waist. His chest is a mess of white hair but, admittedly, even at his age, he's in enviable shape. His pant-leg is rolled up over his knee and shows off his stump. The incubator's plastic lid is raised, and ten or so speckled eggs lie on the rods. Kendra must have taken these. Melanie isn't in any of them. Milo puts the photos back. Enough, get on with it. He steps around the furniture.

Melanie stands at the far end of the room with her back to him. To the front of her sits an empty steel-rod contact incubator—the same incubator Axel sat beside in the photo. The rods are covered with a clear plastic lid, and dials—presumably temperature and humidity gauges—line the lower panel. With the plastic cover and metal rods it looks both like a record player and a gas-station hotdog roller, only larger. Enough room for three or four dozen eggs, normal eggs—he's not sure about the size of falcon eggs. In the picture they seemed smaller. On the counter beside the incubator is a blue metal box with a pinhole—a candler.

Melanie leans over the counter. Her coat—his old coat—rises from the back of her knees. Way too big on her. So are the cut-off boots. She clicks on the candler and is lightly backlit—tufts of wool and dust. She turns sideways and kneels. The beam of light, meant to pierce eggs, is fierce, but doesn't change the illumination of the room and she doesn't look his way. A flash of red—the heat lamps again—shoots across the wire frame of her glasses. She raises her hand to the candler.

She looks different. Her jaw is relaxed—first time he's seen it unclenched in years. Maybe ever. But that's not it. In the beam her palm becomes a radiant orange, rosy with bones. Like a flashlight tucked in the mouth for a ghost story—how the beam shadows the sinuses. That's not it either.

What is it? What's different? Her usual glasses, the same frames for the last three years, but he can see more of her face than he's used to. Her cheekbones— too wide now, but possibly pretty when she grows. Her face—her hair is cut, that's what's weird.

Her hair. Right. He held her. He did that.

Leave now, he tells himself. He shouldn't be here. He's still drunk. He should leave her alone and go. Now. Only there's footsteps in the hall.

Melanie jerks her hand out of the light and stumbles up. The door opens. Axel scans them both. Shit.

"Wait." Milo steadies himself on a bookcase. Melanie gives him a look—disgust? Contempt? Both. He deserves both.

Axel sucks in his cheeks and strides into the room. He seizes Melanie under the armpit. With his free arm he points to the wall and waves his finger at charts and breeding plans taped on the plastic sheeting. He sucks his cheeks again then slaps Melanie across the jaw and lets her drop. "Out."

Milo steps toward them and stops. Do something. Do what? He coughs—Axel's kicked up a wake of dust and hay particles. Her hair, he did that.

Melanie, one hand to her ear and chin, scrambles through the hay and cords toward the exit.

Milo raises his arms and gives her space. "You're missing school," he says. Well, she is.

Melanie rushes by him, shoves Kendra and some kid at the door.

Milo coughs again and wipes his mouth. Her footsteps boom down the hall and front stairs.

Kendra picks at the back of her hand. "What are you waiting for?"

She either means "Get lost" or "Why the hell is he not helping his daughter?" Why is he waiting? He runs after his kid. Down the stairs and across the drive. "Melanie." He grabs her backpack from the fence and skids into the snowy paddock. "Melanie, wait." He stops jogging and leans over, planting his hands on the rickety slurry fence as his daughter runs away from him, over the paddock toward their house. As much as the field lets her run: the mud's suction on her boots half-trips her every third step, until she does trip on the porch stairs—the stairs he hasn't shovelled—and crawls into the house.

He straightens up. His feet sink further into the mud. "Kiddo." The front door shuts behind her, but the screen door hasn't latched and it creaks open again. The house is not that far off, maybe a hundred metres, but the thought of following her inside makes him tired.

It's an effort to even think of crossing the damn paddock. And if he did go after her, well, what he's done is, again, past apology. He rubs a hand over his chapped skin, fingering the cracks at the corners of his lips. Too dehydrated to even spit. Too sore — suddenly too stiff from passing out at the kitchen table — to move.

Across the field the bathroom light switches on then off. Melanie should be in class. Bent over a desk doing long division. Or, what's the math grade eight covers? Tries to cover, in that school. The graffitied tables are probably the same tables from when he was a kid. Some of the carved "fucks" are probably his. His old textbooks — they're probably still in use. Students are likely still allowed in the lab supplies. Well, not allowed per se, but there was no lock on the chemical cupboard when he was in eighth grade. Hell, that time he convinced the loner kid to coat his hand in water and ethanol and light it on fire. The alcohol had pooled between the boy's fingers and the kid's skin had bubbled. Smokies on a campfire. Barbaric.

The light's faded, and dark blue-grey has collected at the base of the clouds. An hour or two must have passed. Time does that lately, skip him over when his mind's elsewhere. It means, at least, that he doesn't have to think, so that's good. So is feeling sick — it's deserved.

In front of him, the poles around the slurry tilt like the wind has forced them over. Not that there's wind.

He's still holding her pack. He unzips it. Crumpled paper. That's it, nothing else. No real reason for her to even bring the pack to school. Except to fake having it together, "it" being her life. His fault. Seven years with him. Since she was six. And almost a whole year doing his chores here at the dairy. Christ.

What's her life actually like? Her school and friends. What are the names or looks of any of her teachers? It's like dredging, trying to pull these thoughts out of his brain. Does she have friends? Memory. It's like having dropped his keys in the pasture.

II

—

MELANIE

THE JOB IS QUICK, an hour or two, each barn stall rigged to electronically read the ear chip of each cow and dispense feed with the correct antibiotic or hormone. All she has to do is attach the milkers, and those vacuum on automatically when she brings them close enough to the teats. Then there is the consistent chug of the milk machines, and the chewing, and the comforting way the cows lean on the metal rails in their stalls so that their sides touch. She works her way between two of their great boney asses and lays her cheek on a back.

"Hey, cow." Her jaw's tender, and the cow hot and full of pulse. The hair she has left falls into her face. She closes her eyes and rubs her hand over the cow's short hide. Her fingers are soft from napping in the bath all day, and small tan hairs stick to her fingertips. One of her first memories is of cows. In it she is standing with her back against her father's legs and looking up at big, wet, bovine noses. Their pink tongues lick their own pink nostrils. Could it have been this farm? She can't think of a time when her father had driven her anywhere, or taken her on any sort of trip. Maybe, and this thought is a shock, she's lived here before? But no, there's only the one memory.

Everything else takes place in the city. The same city where Candice, her bestie, still gets to live and spend her school year reading fortunes at lunch hour and inventing quizzes for boys — Circle Five: cupcake, banana, melon, left, right, hand, feet, puppies, dinosaur, neon, black, kiss, sex. They never know how to answer, boys. She rubs her nose on the heifer. The warmth of the cow radiates through its hair against her lower lip. She cozies up and kisses it.

She and Candice spent all of grade seven lunching in the art room around the Ouija board. The mood of the art room — with its batik and dusty papier mâché — wasn't voodoo enough for the board, but the point wasn't exactly Ouija anyway, the point was the boys they hung out with around the board, so they forgave the lack of spook. The room, at least, was private.

Melanie's hand, partly covered by Rowan's, moved with the dial.

"B. J. You know what that means." Candice buffed her nails on her jeans and the boys laughed. "Blow job?"

She hadn't. She let go of the dial and tugged the back of her pants. They were too loose to hold properly to her hips, but the smaller size at the store had left two inches of ankle bone visible.

"Don't you get anything?" Candice stood and packed the board back into the box. "I mean, you should. It's not like your head's full."

Rowan's friend feigned a stretch and slipped his arm around Candice.

"Enough perv," Candice said. She tugged Melanie's wrist and walked her into the bathroom. "Look." Candice leaned into the mirror. "You should at least know what it means." She twisted her mouth and wiped the corner of her eyes. "This eyeliner is the worst."

"Now I do."

"You what?"

"Know what it means." Melanie turned the bathroom taps on full and shut herself in a stall.

"Your place after school?" Candice grabbed the stall and hoisted her head and shoulders over the door. "He likes you, you know. Rowan."

"Don't look."

"You're not peeing or anything." Candice switched off the lights and left the bathroom.

Later they did end up at Melanie's apartment—

Candice liked that Milo was always out. "Got any bananas? Cucumber?" Candice opened the fridge.

"Let's go to your house." Candice's mom would make iced tea and dump them at the University, where Candice was supposed to practise piano in a music room.

"Come on," Candice said. "Call Rowan. When's your dad back? Oh right, he's never back." She surfaced with a zucchini. "This is what you do." She lifted the veggie to her lips. "You circle around, and then lick the length and put your mouth on it."

"Let's go out, then," Melanie said.

Candice nibbled the zucchini's skin. "Okay, but you should change."

"Why?"

"Whatever." Candice tossed the vegetable to Melanie. "I wish I had pants cool enough to wear every day."

But that was when she was thirteen. About a year and a half ago. None of that seems real anymore. Except for the pants, and they're still not cool. Who cares? Who gives a crap? She's stuck here now. She lifts her head off the cow. Hay and grain dust hangs in the cloud of animal humidity. What would Candice say about this place? You got your wish. Your lame-ass comfy farm. And family.

She misses wandering the basement at the Uni, trying to find unlocked doors to practice rooms. Fooling around with the insides of the pianos while her father mopped up barf or blood at his hospital job. She'd scratch the felt blocks or run her nails over the thick wires. There was so much going on inside the instruments, little joints and hinges that sat and waited for, for what? Something to do. She even misses her father's awkward stories when he came home from work, when he'd sit across from her at the table, reeking of bourbon and piss, and try to talk.

She scratches the bristly hairs along the cow's spine. The cow lifts its nose from the feed trough and flicks its ears. She'll have to get supper. But that's later. Right now there's perfect contentment in leaning on the cow and waiting for the reliable, automatic shutdown of the milkers. There's the lovely, boring pulse of fifty chewing cows, the warmth she's retained from the bath, and the loosening effect the steam had on her lungs. Here, things are easy.

The milkers shut down. She pops the machines from each cow, grabs the tin of bag balm, and squeezes the udders for heat and hardness. All good—supple and flabby after milking. A rough patch on an older cow. She drags her fingers through the salve and works it into and around the teat. Then she turns off the lights and shuts the barn door behind herself.

Outside, the snow is spread like a sodden blanket over the pasture. She can't see her father, if he's still out there in the night. He might have trudged home. The lights in their house are off, but that means nothing. He sits in the dark so often. He doesn't take care of himself. And when he tries to—that nasty stuff last night. She crosses to the house, picks up the shovel from beside the porch stairs, and chips at the iced steps. After a while the blade works between the ice and the wood and it all pries off in one satisfying slab.

She props the shovel against the rail and opens the door. Her father sits at the kitchen table—no tablecloth, the surface sticky with cup rings and piled with dishes. His hair, overgrown, hangs over his stupid tubular neck scarf and brushes the top of a faded wool sweater that's Austin's, her grandfather's. She steps out of her boots, walks to the stove, and, keeping the shaved side of her head away from Milo and toward the clock and kitchen window, crosses her arms. He jerks his gaze down and bites the hair that hangs over his top lip and looks back up. Puckered forehead and watered eyes. His cheeks, no, the entire bottom of his face seems swollen, but that could be the beard. He should trim it—too much orange when his skin already looks sandpapered. He runs his fingers over the rim of a Mason jar—his home-stilled spirits—on the table beside a stack of bowls.

"I quit school."

He pushes the jar aside and pulls a tarnished sugar dish and a lighter out of the mess of plates and cups.

"Okay." He flips over the dish.

"What do you mean, okay?" She uncrosses her arms. His lanky fingers leave streaks on the oxidized silver. The tarnish is deeper—charred mauve—around the patterned rim and three ornate feet. At some point it was polished half-heartedly. "I quit school."

Milo tilts his head and tenses his shoulders, like he's both acknowledging that he heard her, and asking her why she's upset—what did she expect? Why is she upset? What did she think he'd say? From the room down the hall her grandfather starts to moan. Her father picks up the sugar dish, blows in it, and sets it upright. He flicks the lighter. The creamer, tea, and coffee pot that the dish belongs to sit on top of a cupboard. A little dent in the coffee pot, but otherwise similar to ones she's seen in pawn shops. Surprising Milo hasn't hocked it. The house is all her grandfather's stuff, and he hasn't touched any of it. Maybe with the still he doesn't need to. He spins the lid off the Mason jar.

She switches on the gas stove and heats up leftover porridge. Her grandfather moans again, a sound from the throat not the voice. The old man doesn't talk since his stroke. She's never heard him talk. She spoons the porridge into the bowl and adds brown sugar and fresh whole milk before walking it down the hall.

The smell from the old man's room is not quite rank, but bad: unwashed laundry, dried crap and baby powder, mouth. She raises the porridge to her nose before she steps through the doorway. The room is carpeted, it's the only room in the house that is, and the thick padding is pappy and gross. Who knows what's soaked through? She's yet to find a vacuum.

She sits on the bed beside her grandfather and spoons him the porridge. The old man's skin is flaky around the mouth, and the outer corner of his eyes crusted. She leans over him and wipes his lips with her sleeve. For a moment he's quiet—relieved?—then he turns his head to the side and begins punching the bed with shaky, weak taps.

"What is it, Gramp?" She lifts the quilt to change his posture. "What can I do?" Then she smells it. His diaper needs changing. Oh, old man. She brings the porridge bowl back out and sets it in the sink. She can't believe she was ever jealous of friends with grandparents, yards, pets, music lessons. Now she has it all: an old man she doesn't know, his house. The kitchen with painted plates hanging on the walls. The locked piano that takes up the parlour—it is a parlour, "living room" is too modern a word—the piano has been there so long the wheels have sunk a half-inch into the wood floor. The bathroom is the only room she likes, the tub dead-centre with a curtain and no plastic tub-surround to mould over.

Water fills the porridge bowl and spills over the oats still crusted around the sides from this morning. She shuts off the tap and touches her cheekbone where Axel slapped her. This whole day. No, the entire year — she feels like grinding rocks into her gramp's porridge. Or at least salt.

Hitting — she thought hitting was the limit. Milo never hit her. Even last night, what happened was more an accident than an incident: Milo — drunk, that goes without saying — pulled her out of bed to trim his hair, and when she wouldn't, he cut a tuft off her head. He didn't even yell when Axel struck her. She should yell now. Something horrible. She mouths the word "cunt" — soundlessly so Milo can't hear — exploring the brush of her tongue first at the back of her throat and then the tip of it against her palate.

When she turns, her father has lit the home-still. The blue flame, like that of the gas stove idling on low, flickers in the sugar dish. Different from the light of the candler through her hand this afternoon. That's the light that should be in her house, should welcome her when she comes home from school or from a friend's or from the barn — that ruddy orange glow, that warmth.

The moan starts up again, this time punctuated with cough. She bites her lip, then lifts a bucket from under the sink and fills it with warm water and dish soap.

CODY

The couch is upholstered in stiff, woven synthetic so old it's broken or melted in place, and itchy even through the sheets Kendra gave him. He rolls onto his side. It's impossible to sleep. Every time he does drift off, his breath catches on the confusing scent of dirt or manure that who knows how long ago seeped into everything, and he gasps awake. Also, across from his bed on the couch, in front of the living room window — worse because he can't see it — the table: jars of dye, leather, wire, the sawed-off handle of a broom, a four-foot strip of snakeskin, knives, and curved hide needles. No point in watching because there is no light, but when he stares at the general area of the table hard enough, the dark comes together, like he's summoned something in the quiet, the quiet that's so quiet and black he might as well be buried alive.

Little pieces of the couch's weave break off under his nails through the sheet. He should stop picking Axel's furniture, but it distracts him from the thick night. His blankets are wet. At home he never sleeps with enough covers to sweat, but the room is too invisible to throw back the quilt.

Don't think about the room. Think about the cabbages. Cows. The blonde girl. No, that leads to the chicks and the bus ride. Think of home. Summer. Last summer his mom got so skinny she was hospitalized, and he spent as much time with her as he could. Nights, school hours, weekends.

"You should go to class." His mom let Aunt Jen raise the hospital bed and prop her pillows.

Cody flipped a page of his math book. "How about home-school?"

"Home-school?" she said. "Are you kidding? You won't survive. They'll roast you."

"Home-school kids only get picked on if they go to school," he said. Over the previous month, her skin had dulled, blue veins showed on either side of her forehead, and her legs—when she slipped and let him see them—were a violet-grey grid of bruised veins. He flipped to the answer key. "Am I right?" He was afraid to leave her—she was only eating ice chips. She laughed, her gums and tongue pale enough to make him lightheaded.

"He's not wrong." Aunt Jen finished with the bed and sat next to his mom. "Where's lunch today?"

He can't remember how she replied to his aunt's question, but he remembers that she waved it off, citing a joke about her hunger strike for the greater good.

Aunt Jen put her hands to the sides of her head. "Holy. Holy—did you just say what I think you said? Because you can't have said what I heard you say."

"Jenny." His mom lay back on the pillows.

"She's great with jokes," he said before he thought.

His mom smiled. Aunt Jen ran her hand over her head and went, "You're not getting off that easy."

"I know, Jenny."

His aunt kicked him out to the cafeteria. He shouldn't have said it. He should have let Aunt Jen force sense into her. But he joked, like she does, like they always do.

Now he's here, sweating it out in Uncle Ancient's house, T-minus who knows how long left to the night, and there's no cars, no footsteps, no low television or yells or laughter from a family in an apartment above or below, no cussing from the sidewalk—no sidewalk. Not even ticking clocks like old people are supposed to keep around. If he told this to his mother, she'd be all, You're complaining about silence? The running gag being that he never gives her any. But he already used Axel's phone once to leave a message saying that he'd arrived and was safe and all the other stuff she'd like to hear. Only the stuff she'd like to hear. She's got to know he's homesick. Lying—a skill he needs to work on. Good at being smart-mouth dumb, though. Got stupid mastered. But lying? Still needs practice.

What he'd like to say to her, to sass at her, is how many chicks he'll kill if she leaves him here. Two thousand today. Does she think she's protecting him, sending him away when she's sick again, only telling him on a stupid postcard he found stashed in his school work? By summer he'll be the biggest chicken serial killer of all time. Next to Axel, of course, but Axel sort've gets an out because he's missing a leg. Where did that logic come from, Cody can hear his mom saying. She'd probably follow it up with the joke she's proud of, like she did in the note she left him: You think labs are fun? You think I'm having such a great time with my labs you want to join me? Labs are not only puppies, kiddo. Some involve needles.

A stupid crack. Why couldn't — why can't — she just say what she means? He pinches the couch fibre through the damp sheet. But, leaving a phone message before bed, he didn't complain, not even jokingly, because this time something is really wrong. It must be. Why else would she send him here? To kill chickens? She's lying again, she must be sicker than she said, or worse. She didn't even pack an outline for his school work.

He rolls onto his side. He must have slept, because after a while a pale glow grows around the edge of the curtains. The light appears far away, the sort of light that doesn't seem real, and it disappears when he looks directly at it. He sees it best when he gives up — when he catches it accidentally out the corner of his eye, or if he stares past where he thinks the curtains end and doesn't squint.

Then there's enough light to see shapes. The counter that separates the living room from the kitchen. Bar stools. The table across from him under the window, chairs, and next to the chairs the front entrance. Rows of coats and coveralls hanging on pegs. His correspondence courses in a stack on the floor. He pushes back his covers and goes to the window. Behind the curtain, frost creeps along the glass, and the centre of the windowpane is clouded with moisture. He cups his hands and peers through, but the moisture is too opaque. The house is chilly. He gets dressed—both jeans and kilt since it's cold—then opens the front door and steps out on the frosty porch. Snow has come down and is still coming down. Thick, wet flakes, like pulp clearing out of juice, so fabulously flat and heavy, and yet unbelievably, unnervingly, quiet.

AXEL

There's Kendra, finally, with one hand splayed on the grill of her truck, the other up behind her neck as she stands at the turnoff to the highway. The front of her Nissan points skyward. The back end is buried in his ditch. Looks like she pushed the truck there, how she's standing, but he saw her float off the icy highway and spin on the shoulder. Her clothes are frosted white from wading her way out. And snow is still falling, patting her on the head like it wants her to stay down.

"Late," he calls from the breeding pens. "Already took care of the feeding." Filled a bucket—her job—with feeder chicks and did the rounds. Slid yellow tufts into each pen. Walked the yard. Made sure the chicks were eaten. Removed leftover bits so the meat didn't lie there and rot. All that, and he didn't even force Cody, who's loitering on the front porch—skirt and all—to help him. Would have been a headache. Not a doubt.

He sets down the bucket of chick scraps. "Took more than two hours to get through feeding without you." The last time he made the rounds alone was late spring, when Kendra broke contract and attended the falconry meet, and without having to dig the pen doors out of the snow the work took a third the time. Broke contract—ha! The trip might as well be chiselled into her contract since she absconds every year.

"I'm fine," she calls back. "Thanks for asking." She clasps her hands behind her head.

Cody makes his way down the porch and hangs his fingers in the netting around the yard. Lately, Axel's left the taming and fist-training to Kendra, and instead sketched breeding plans for March. Predicted projected offspring's plumage based on the female—the white—and different males. This is the year his reputation rides on. He breeds this trait, she takes that to the meet, see what they say then. Can't deny what he's built after eyeing that white bird.

And Kendra's late on the day he'd planned to start flying that first, flawless gyr. Late, after her nattering all year about the definition of apprentice. The month before Cody arrived she refused to do anything that didn't deal with birds—no electrical repairs, no painting, no shovelling—though he pays her for eight-hour days year-round.

"No way you'll get that truck out." The engine ticks cool under a growing mask of snow. "Doubt anyone's towing today."

"Shit." She slaps the hood and walks down the drive. "Yeah, I know." She fishes her keys from her pocket and unlocks the door to the yard. Cody tugs his hood up and hooks his fingers back in the net.

"At least I didn't hit the river." She paws through the scraps of gristle in Axel's bucket, picks out the larger bits, and fills the pockets of her vest. "Training the white today?"

She stands there in front of him, her refurbished fishing vest packed with feed like they can carry on. Like it doesn't matter to her she's late. Like her affronts have been nothing. "The weather's too bad," he says. It isn't. Not with the netting as a filter for the snowfall.

"The weather's too bad," she repeats. "Unbelievable."

She Velcroes the flaps down over her pockets of chicks and tightens her ponytail.

"Did you see the snow?" Cody says. Is he joking? He doesn't say it like he's siding against Kendra, he says it like he hasn't seen anyone in years, he's got that much energy. Kendra exhales.

"See the snow? Did I fucking see the snow?" She gestures to her hair—the ends evolving icily at her back—and her clothes. "You're not flying her, then. Christ." She pushes past Axel's shoulder and takes a shovel from the equipment shed. The netting that forms the roof has collected a layer of heavy snow overnight.

"Drove out just for that?" he says.

"What did you expect?" She prods the roof with the handle. She does it gingerly, trying to keep out of the way as clumps of snow plop through the nets onto the ground. Why is she so difficult? Like she doesn't understand that he wants her here. If he didn't want her here, would he have let her follow him home like a puppy? Apprentice the last three years? If he didn't want her here, he wouldn't be pissed off.

"Might as well have stayed in town," he says.

"Bitch to yourself." She walks the yard prodding the mesh until the roof of snow is down and she's breathing audibly into the clouded sky. "I was late, that's all."

"Might as well take off, then, now that your work's done." He nods to the truck. "Good luck with that."

"Because of the goddamn snow. My truck's in the ditch because I was on my way here. Fuck it, Axel." She stabs the shovel into the snow. "Give me my bird and I'll go."

Three years ago Kendra had been grateful to be in the vicinity of his birds. She'd looked him up after, she said, she'd found out ninety percent of the gyrfalcons flown at the meet—all the gyrs bred in captivity— came from him. She'd seen him swinging a training lure in the pasture one summer morning and left her Nissan door hanging wide to the wind. She stepped off the highway with a stride like she was used to walking fields and she stayed on. He thought the nephew would be as enamoured as she had been. But the kid, clinging to the netting, seems on the verge of hysterics. He can't deal with this now. He turns to the house.

Kendra calls after him. "Going to take it to the grave. I should have known."

If Kendra is going to bridle he's not going to give her the satisfaction of giving in. He steps inside.

"It's in your will, then?" Kendra calls as he shuts the door.

He sits at the table and pulls the jars of leather dyes toward himself. Their coloured shadows stain the wood: green, red, deep blue.

They're his falcons. They'd be hers too if she backed off. She's young, serious about birds. The time the hawk grabbed her neck she stayed calm. He hasn't marked a bird out for her, the bird he wants her to fly is not an heirloom he'd put in his will, he wants to hand it over with honour. Why can't she see the act is, how can he put it? — not religious, but holy. And now, because of the boy, she thinks she has sway. Damn her. He's always counted her vote.

He pulls the snakeskin into the shadow of the leather dye. The kid's quilt and sheet are folded on the couch. A mess of papers on the floor beside the table. Momentary guilt about the kid. He rubs his thumb over a spot of dye on the table and tosses the leather aside.

On the mantel and bookshelf beside the table are over thirty hoods. Small, jewel-hued, snakeskin-crested, feather-topped, one entirely of rabbit fur that looks like a pom-pom. Dainty things, and an art the boy might like.

The front room has been empty all morning and still the air around the couch smells of his brother's daughter's son's minty hair soap, or, loath to think, the boy's perfume. A comfort in the scent, regardless.

KENDRA

The freshness in the air — the snow has brought down all the exhaust and dirt of the highway. Crows are

about. A teed-off school of them alights in the poplars
by the road and suddenly it's as if the trees have leaves,
there's that many birds. They'll need to piss off. They
create too much distraction. Them, and Milo tearing
down the fence around the slurry in the dairy yard—
there's a bad idea if she ever saw one.

"You know who else bred falcons?" she says. "Hitler.
Bred them to kill Allied carrier pigeons. Nazis gave it
up after bringing down their own doves." She tucks her
thumbs in the armpits of her vest. "Fuck him. We're
training the white." Cody reaches his hand through
the net wall and unlatches the door's lock from outside.
Hilarious. "Don't let Axel catch you breaking in."

He blushes and backs out. She grabs his sleeve.
"God—I was kidding. Come in." His jeans are wet and
dark from the shin down. She'd send him back in for
boots but doubts the kid has enough nerve left to ask
Axel to loan a pair. Anyway, it looks like he's wearing
his entire wardrobe—jeans, kilt, hoodie, orange fleece
under the hoodie. He's probably layered enough socks
in his sneakers to keep his feet dry.

"Go on. Grab a glove."

He brushes his bangs out of his face, takes a step to
the equipment shed, and pauses to bite a hangnail. His
cheeks are still red, as well as his nose—he looks like
he's been scrubbed. His eyelashes—they're long enough
to paint with. What a sorry kid. Maybe she shouldn't

have mentioned the Nazis to him. Germans would have been better. She should cut back on swearing, too. But, damn it, today she deserves her cuss words. Her poor truck. Fishtailed every tap to the brakes. The way she lifted off the slippery lick of driveway was plain spooky. Somewhere under the ice there should have been gravel, but the rear end spun and floated and, whoops, she was looking up at snow syphoning down from the clouds. And it's still falling.

There's a good, weighty, foot and a half of drift in front of the wood door to the flight pen. So Axel shovelled the screen door clear and fed the birds, but hasn't handled them today. Nice. The white should still be hungry enough for a few short flights in the training yard. Nothing tricky. Post to fist. She shovels the snow from the pen and opens it.

The white sits neat on a low perch. Kendra pulls her glove out of her belt and flexes stiffness from the fingers — dried blood, cold leather, and yolk-sack. "Good girl," she says. "Come see this." She shoulder-checks. Cody's picked up two gauntlet-cut gloves.

"They're both lefts." He holds the gloves toward her.

She reaches into a vest pocket and fiddles out a feed chick. "You just need one." She rips a bit off and tucks it into her glove. "Hup, hup!"

The bird shifts on its perch but doesn't make the jump to her arm. Only six inches. Come on. Black eyes—the only colour on it. White feet, white nails. Not even the usual faint turquoise dusting the root of the beak. And a female, a big girl. She calls again. The bird tilts her head but stays put. Okay. She rubs the chick against the white's beak, then lets the bird step rather than hop. "Why're you not jumping?" The grip on her glove—no lack of strength there. "Hey girl? Being lazy?" Wings spread around her fist in a feathery tent. Lovely. Just lovely.

She carries the bird to the centre post in the training tent and tucks another ripped chick into her glove.

What's wrong? "Hup." The bird does nothing. Not overfed. Axel was planning on training her today, so he wouldn't have given enough to make her fat.

Cody tucks the wrist of his sweater under his glove. "What's it doing?"

The wrong thing, to be honest. A bird sees the meat, it jumps to the meat. Especially after a taste. Natural. The second step in training after carting it around on the fist for a day, and Axel did that yesterday.

"She's not doing much." Could be the crows. Every so often a flock sights the farm and gets pissy. It was worse when she car-hawked—drove around tossing a red-tail out her window at ducks in sloughs off the highway. The crows had learned to recognize her truck, and the vehicle was always covered in turd. "Hold out your hand." She lifts the white from the post and passes her to Cody.

"Wait." Cody stretches back from his arm, like he's trying to leave it.

"Don't let go." She wraps the jesses around his fist and thumb.

"Wait, please?"

"Hang on." She unearths the pellet gun from the shed. The crows, attracted by her earlier collapse of the snow roof and by the falcon, have flocked over. Falcons from the other pens shriek and jingle. The white doesn't seem to notice. She sits, imposing but docile, on Cody's fist. The kid holds the bird out from his body like flames. Like a firework or a sparkler. Like it might go for the eyes.

"How'd you like the couch?" She got him set up last night before she left. He'd said, "You're leaving?" And she'd replied, "What, you think I live here?" Not that the prospect of staying at Axel's was disturbing; she's stayed on the couch in other winters when the roads were bad. Fuck. She'll have to stay today if she doesn't get that truck out of the ditch. Huge piss-off. She loads the pellet gun and scopes a parked crow. Misses.

"All right," he says.

"Survived the night, I suppose." She lines up another shot. Shoots. The crows scatter from the netting and batter around the barn and house. "We can clean out that room." The jerk birds land on the roof again and she takes a shot through the netting.

The boy's bird arm sags and rises. He grabs the arm with his right hand and tries to keep the bird stable.

"Axel—I know he seems tough." Is tough. "How long you here?"

The kid cringes—bends a bit at the knees—and says, "Well." He lets go of his arm and tries to reach into his hoodie pocket.

"Just a minute." She takes the white and sets it on the post. Then takes the postcard Cody offers and hands him the pellet gun. "Line up the notch with the groove." The postcard hasn't been through the mail, doesn't even have a stamp. Golden lab puppies sit in a basket on the front of the card. Big yellow ribbons tied in bows round their necks. Corny, but cute. She flips it over.

Hey Cody, my best lad,

Hope you're loving that farm! I want to be honest with you, but don't worry, okay? I can feel your worry from here. Now here goes: my holiday is not a fun one. Can you believe it but there is more than one meaning of "lab?" Turns out I mixed up Labrador retriever with laboratory testing. I need to be in the hospital. I know you're sick of that joke. It's for me. Your Aunt Jen is here.

I love you,
    Mom.

P.S. I'm glad you're doing your school work.

The writing is tight and blue, cramped by the end, and the postscript is written around the edge of the card like a frame. Kendra flips the card back over. The puppies are all ears and oversized fluffy feet. The kid hasn't taken a shot yet. "You won't hit one. Go on."

He raises the gun and cracks off a pellet. The crows aren't small, but they're mobile and hard to focus on in the snow.

"Kind of fun, hey?" Out past the pens where the falcons are tinkling their ankle bells, along the edge of the pastures where the forest starts to spread over the hills and mountains, the cedars stand so deeply green they're black. Wintergreen. The whole morning might be minty, actually, if she were free of Axel's mood. She should try to salvage the day. She bends the card and lets it snap straight. The boy is silly, but also — doleful? She feels the sudden need to be honest with him.

"The white." She takes the bird from the post. When she tilts her arm up the bird stretches its wings and shifts its talons to keep balance. "This girl. I think she might be a dud." She wasn't sure before she said it, but coming out it feels right. She waves her hand by the bird's right eye. No reaction.

The kid lowers the gun. He might shoot his foot how he's holding it, but what the hell. It's pellets. Who knows, might cheer him up? "Fat birds — overfed birds — they don't fly. So it could be that, but she didn't eat much. Doesn't make sense that she's fat anyway, because she devoured the chick I gave her."

The boy squints at the white. He looks different now that she's read the card. Not so much awkward as uneasy. "Maybe she's not into food," he says.

"She likes the food. But check it out." She reaches into her pocket and pulls out a feeder. "Okay, watch." She lets go of the bird's jesses then tosses the chick into the snow a couple metres ahead. The white wobbles forward and back like her hand is a rodeo pony, but doesn't leap. She tosses her up and forward. The bird flaps, kind of flies aimlessly and hits the snow two feet from the chick with her left wing still spread. "She can't seem to see where it's at."

They give it another go. This time the white gets her claws tangled in the netting wall. "No depth perception."

"What'll you tell Axel?"

Good question. Maybe nothing. What a revelation. There's no way he will breed from her if he knows. He could take her impairment to mean her whole line will be duds. And they might be fine. "The thing is, they don't fly the birds where we sell anyway. Too hot."

Kendra works the netting off the bird's talons. "She looks beautiful, doesn't she." Somehow, this is shocking. Kendra throws the bird again, toward the direction of the feed. "And down she goes." She lifts the white from snow. Its wings, tail, and feet leave an impression, finger-like, like someone scooped up a snowball barehanded. "Let's take out a real bird."

She settles the white back into the flight pen and lets a hawk hop skilfully on her hand. Cocoa and orange. A Harris—nothing fancy, but a hawk can manage the trees. Large, as all the female raptors are, but not as big as the white. Maybe the white's size affects her slowness too. But let that go for now. Get hold of the rest of the day. "Lola, meet Cody." Lola bends forward then back and fans her deeply brown, white-dipped tail and gains balance on Kendra's fist. "Let's hunt for real."

MILO

The fence post wobbles easily under his push—back and forth, loose in the dirt—and breaks off at the rotten base under the ground. He lies down and, reaching into the hole, pulls pulpy chunks of wood from the soil. Face to the dirt is good. A nod of penitence. He's

relieved—ashamed about that relief but still relieved—
that he didn't drink last night. Even though he spent
the night at his father's still. Checked the boiler, loaded
the wash mixed the day before (basic grain mash, turbo
yeast) and started the fire. Steamed off the heads. Might
as well do it right if he's going to do it—as a test to
himself. And so far he passed. Didn't drink.

The first night in eleven months, and though his
recovery prior to this latest binge was insignificant
(twenty-four long days) this time the abstinence feels
real. He's finally quit.

He stands and brushes the snow from the replacement pole. Mid-winter is possibly the worst time to be
fixing the fence around the slurry. He's been planning
to do it since the summer. Well, not planning, but that's
when it was obvious the fence needed to be fixed. The
whole side slanted inward. If someone leaned on it, the
fence would collapse and he or she'd be in a crusty mess
of feces and hay scraped from the barn and mixed with
runoff from the pastures. He hadn't been able to handle
the job's smell in the summer, and if he's honest with
himself, he didn't know how to start. Doesn't, actually,
but he can't make a broken fence worse, can he? And
right now the watery cow patties in the lagoon are covered with two feet of insulating snow and don't smell.
Digging into the half-frozen ground to replace rotten
poles is giving him the workout and sweat he needs.

He's already feeling antsy and ill, got to do something to pass the time.

It would be nice if the cows were here in the pasture instead of the barn so it wouldn't look like he was talking to himself, throwing his head back and saying, "Remember the time she was eight and you didn't make her lunches for a year?" The whole year, that same year, he day-drank on the job with Gary, and stole a rat. Random stories. He'd forgotten. The job with Gary, bio-waste crew, was the type of job where booze and weed were okay. As long as you could mop and scrape the morgue boxes and surgical floor, you were good. He'd been cleaning animal cages in the research wing of the hospital, saw the rat, and he tucked it in his shirt pocket for Melanie.

A research rat. What can he do but laugh? Especially now that the first step is made: he stopped drinking. Second step—how to get her back to school. Maybe she'll go by herself—there's still a chance.

He jostles the new pole in the frozen hole. The metal's sturdier than the wood was but the pole tilts. The hole is too big. Maybe cement when the weather gets better. Way off in spring. Shit. The edge is wearing off his motivation. That's the last replacement for today.

He dusts the snow from his toque and looks at what he's done so far—taken down the fence but not put it back up. Propped a couple poles in the dirt. Anyone could walk through and step into the slurry. Right now, with the pristine snow covering, they wouldn't even know it was there. The only structure is the ramp with its metal gate. He should have left the fence alone. Now it'll have to wait. Anyway, they probably need a whole new pit. From the notes and supplies Austin has lying around, it looks like his father planned to replace the lagoon with a more modern cement structure, complete with a pump and an agitator in the base. Starting mid-winter is ridiculous for that much work. He'll do it, but in the summer. It can wait.

He pulls a tarp over the pile of dismantled posts and rails. The clouds, white with a wash of steel, dropped down the mountainside this morning and boxed the farm in.

"Hey, Dairy," Kendra calls from the fence between properties. The snowfall interrupts the view even from the pit to the fence, and he squints to see her clearly as she heads over from the mewses across the pasture. The boy from yesterday follows her. Maybe fourteen? Melanie's age, if he's right. He carries a hawk on his arm. With a kilt and a bird and dark hair slicked wet over his head the boy looks like he's ready for a photo shoot — one of those ones from the TV make-over and modelling shows Melanie watches — until they get closer and it's apparent the boy is, if not miserable, ninety-percent apprehensive.

"Fixing the fence?" She has her SLR camera in a clear plastic bag slung over her shoulder. Her vest stuffed with dead chicks and what look like sandwiches.

"Good day." He says it staring at the hawk the kid's holding. Good day? Sounds like he's chatting up the bird.

"Not even close." She points to the highway. "Trucked it into the ditch."

"Didn't expect you." He crams a corner of the tarp under a pole. "Thought, after Melanie yesterday . . ."

"Not my business," she answers.

What she's really saying, what she must be saying, is, Not my problem. He swallows the urge to tell her he's stopped drinking.

"Your tractor up and running?" She heads to his garage. He follows her and opens the door. The garage shares a wall with the barn and is an expansion built by his father for the tractor and for his father's baby, the still. The still isn't massive — eight feet high including the copper boiler, pipes, and chambers — but it's a good size, and imported. Blessedly simple to use, as he found when he and Melanie arrived: day before, blend a neutral grain spirit, purified water, botanicals if he's being fancy, and let it steep overnight. Next day take the wash and get the still boiling — fired by sawdust bricks. Takes a couple hours, then boil the alcohol off through different chambers and the condenser. That's it—spirits flow. Monitor heads, hearts, tails. His father used a bottler, but that's too much effort. Mason jars and jugs from last night's distillation sit on the floor between the still and the tractor.

"I'd have to search out the keys. Clear the snow. I don't know, with this weather—" he steps over the Mason jars and flicks dried hay and manure off the back tire. Allis-Chalmers 185 with a three-point hitch, orange. Fifteen or twenty years old, but an upgrade from the tank that his old man had before. Some dings, all his. He rubs a dent in the hood.

"Shit," she says.

"Tomorrow." He kicks hay off the floor drain. The boy, holding the bird, stands on his toes and peers in the still's boiler window. "Don't touch that." The boy jerks back. Kid shouldn't even be here—should see this. Hellsake both of them smell of wet feathers, the boy of feather and wool. The kid's face is pink, no, wait, red now after that reprimand.

"Tomorrow," he says.

"Shit. Fine. Yes." She pinches her chin and adds, "Since I'm here."

Since she's here. "How much do you want?"

"How much can you spare?"

"Look, I quit yesterday." Sounds stupid once he says it. Kendra tucks her hands into the back pockets of her jeans. She doesn't believe him. He clenches his jaw.

Why would she believe him? She's had a great view of his escapades all year. Every time he passed out on the porch or in the field. Chasing cows, whatever gave the tractor the dent—who knows what else. He rubs his hands down his coat. "I quit."

"You want me to take it all, then?" She says it too quickly, like she was waiting for him to tell her he quit. Like she suspected after yesterday he'd at least try, and like it's hopeless. Like he's so hopeless there's no point berating him.

The jars are scattered over the entire garage—shelves and floor. "Well, I don't think you can carry it all."

"Fine." Kendra smirks and loops her fingers through her camera strap—she better not be taking a picture. She untwists the strap at her neck. "I'll pick up two on our way back."

"Fine." She's always so damn sarcastic. Or maybe it's her look: high-bridged nose, closely spaced, narrowed eyes, and those freckles—they seem more like a blemish she's looking past, or pissily ignoring, than part of her skin. He steps outside with them as Melanie steals from the house. "Look, I'm keeping the farm. You know. After." After the old man dies. Hadn't been planning to but, hey, he hadn't been planning anything.

"Whatever. Tractor tomorrow?"

"Yeah." As they cross the pasture toward the forest

he can feel his energy deflate. Why did he say anything? That shit about the farm, that he quit. Shouldn't have. A horn sounds, and on the highway the school bus slows, but doesn't stop, and continues on past. Melanie turns and follows Kendra and the boy through the pasture at a distance. So much for returning to school.

He heads to the house, and makes it to the kitchen in time to grab the phone. Melanie's school. "I know she missed yesterday," he says. "And she'll miss today, too." He drops his scarf and coat. "I was supposed to call, yes I realize that." He fumbles his boots off. "Sick? Not exactly." He pulls on the cord. "I think she's sad." Was that too much? There's silence on the other end of the line. "With her grandfather and all. Yes. Austin. Thank-you."

After the platitudes the teacher suggests, "Why don't we come out? The class."

"Come out?" He lifts a stack of plates. There's no room left in the sink. The counter beside it is overrun with cups waiting to be washed.

"You're on a dairy farm, right? Your home property? Why don't we bring the class, her friends, and come for a tour?"

Not sure he sees the logic in this. They *live* on farms, right? "Well." He sets the plates back on the table and opens a cupboard. Full, even though there's a tray of clean dishes waiting to be shelved.

"Well, she could come back to school with us after that."

He works through this proposition. There's something not right about it. Melanie didn't run toward school, she left it. But the teacher is offering to solve the problem for him, and that's a good thing. "All right."

How did the cups ever fit in the cupboard in the first place? How do two people go through so many cups? *Three* people, Christ. And mostly his cups. All the mess in this place is from him. All the unfinished shit lying around the farm is his. His father completes everything—the garage, the still—the old man would never start something without knowing he could beat it. He made sure that he had the time and resources. As a kid, if Milo wanted a trip, a potato gun, a car, his excitement got stunted by his father. The old man would ask, What would you do with it afterwards? Have you calculated the cost? How are you going to care for it? And Milo never carried through. He lost steam in planning.

He sits at the table and stares over the dishes, through the living room window to the snowy pasture. He rests his head on the table, sicker now. All morning he's been lightheaded and dizzy. Now he's sweating. Not puking or shitting, yet, but that's how it'll go.

Down the hall his father moans. Milo's arms ache from demolishing the fence. He hasn't done any physical labour since the hospital, but he's handled mess for years. Was that what made him come back after the old man's stroke? Was that what made him think he could handle his father's crap? He leans back in his chair and smacks his thighs. "Well, you'll handle it now, won't you." You'll handle it too, old man.

III

—

MELANIE

SHE'S ALREADY BUZZED the rest of her hair (left it on the bathroom floor) and milked the cows by the time her father sees her. He kicked around the field for hours, knocking the slurry pit's rail down. Shouting at himself the way that, back home at the apartment, the homeless guys on the street did. People-watching is different here. There, she and Milo lived across from a Liquor Mart, and a group of homeless set up camp under the eaves beside it. Always something to see in the street, as long as they didn't catch you spying. One guy gave her the two fingers to the eyes—I'm Watching You—every time she left the apartment, until after a month she got tired of the hassle and did the gesture back and he laughed. Like it was the best joke. On the farm, everyone can see everyone and no one thinks it's funny. Kendra and that boy — Milo followed them into the dairy's garage only a moment ago. And Axel in his house, he opens and closes the blinds a crack, like he's trying not to care about what Kendra is up to.

She's seen Axel and Kendra train the birds — hup a bird from a post to their gloves, fly it back and forth like a game of catch, swing a fur tube into the air and let the bird chase it. The kite is her favourite — they tie a fake duck to the kite string, send it up, and let the falcons dive and drag it down like they're jet-fuelled. If the weather were clear, that's what they might be doing now.

She pulls down the back of her toque. Her neck is freezing. Who knew hair kept you warm? The snow is falling faster, the flakes becoming almost watery. It's difficult to look through them into the distance, there are so many. Kendra comes out of the dairy barn with that boy, all bony hips and kilt. He's got a brown bird on his fist. Milo follows them from the garage — he must be showing off the still. No rent and all the home-brew he can brew — How much brew could a home-still brew if a home-still would still brew? Too much.

He sees her watching. She tugs her toque down and he looks away first, and then toward the highway, where the school bus slows but doesn't stop. They all watch its cautious chug through the weather: Axel from his hiding place behind the blinds, Milo from the barn, and Kendra and the boy in the pasture. Even the bird cranes its head in the direction of the highway. The boy stops, but Kendra only takes a few paces backwards to snap a photo. The bus rounds the corner toward town and disappears. Then they carry on to the forest, as if nothing occurred. Like nothing's wrong.

Kendra and the boy don't stop at the edge of the pasture. That's where Kendra usually turns — she'll walk the pasture and flush rabbits from the brush while the bird sits on the railing waiting for an opportunity. Instead, Kendra and the boy with the bird walk until they reach the forest.

A flicker of motion at Axel's window again. With those two gone, and if Axel is inside, she could sneak back over there. The hatchling room is probably locked, but what if it isn't? She could flip through the photos. The crap-washed cliffs in Iceland, Mexico, and Argentina — wherever that is. Maybe Axel would explain the pictures. The places. She reaches for a strand of hair to bite, then blushes. Reckless, dumb. It's not like Axel likes her.

Kendra and the boy disappear into the trees. The boy — why couldn't Kendra train her? Melanie pulls her toque lower — she can't get it right, it catches on her trimmed hair and flattens it in uncomfortable dir-ections — and follows their tracks across the field. At the edge of the pasture the snow mounds, then slants to nothing after the first few trees.

She walks through the high drift, sinking up to her waist in air pockets that surround the low branches. Snow and needles tip into her boots. From the trees comes the smell of wet cedar and rotting wood. The winter so far is mild, and the moss, soaked with melted snow, is green even through the filtered light.

She stops at the edge and stares into the clouds. Trace the flakes to their origin and she can see the height. There's no end to the sky or the snowfall. Only white above her. She scoops a glove of snow and compresses it. The snow clings to itself, not like that sugary powder of really cold days. More like a handshake, the way the thick flakes come down, touch each other, and spiral into the pasture.

Kendra and the boy aren't here.

What will she do now that she quit school? Keep going, she guesses. Follow them, since they've gone further, somewhere she can't see.

CODY

A woods. That's what this place is, not a forest, a woods. Trees, so many trees, thrust skyward and disappear above their branches. And if these trees are huge, remnants of even bigger trees — stumps the size of dinner tables — crumble back into the soil. Ferns, thin saplings, and a low moss that sprouts brown-green beads on threads. The forest floor is soft and damp, but not unfirm — it bends under his sneakers, as if, below the layer of needles and rotting wood, the ground might be hollow. Low brush hangs with bits of cobweb and old berries. Lola, on his hand, flashes glances into the boughs and swivels her head in a way that makes it look loose. She fans and tucks her tail to adjust balance.

"She can't fall, right?" Dumb question. Lola has monster grip. His thumb and fingers are stuck half-curled under her feet. Well, the tightness is either Lola's bird toes, or the stiff leather of the glove, or the cold, or it might be the jesses — leather straps slip-knotted to the brilliantly yellow legs and wound around his fingers — or possibly panic. He told Kendra about his mom. Not really told, but he gave her the card and she read it. Plus she went and told him about the white gyrfalcon. So now he's got another secret to keep: Axel's favourite bird is defective.

His foot slides off a root and he flails his arm. Lola spreads her wings and tugs on the jesses. The feathers around her throat raise and her beak opens and she shrieks — all he can think is, Get It Off. She flaps and jumps, but the jesses catch and she swings down and hangs from his fist.

"What do I do," he calls. Lola thrashes. "What should I do?" Being this close, closer than close — actually holding a falcon — should be Fun Incorporated, but Lola is blurry brown feathers and yellow-fanged beak and she's kind of horrible. She twists, and her wingbeats bring her high enough that she clips his cheekbone. He grabs his cheek with his free hand and throws his bird-arm out, stretching Lola as far away as he can get her. "Am I okay?" Doesn't feel like blood, but — what if there's blood? "Is there a wound?"

Kendra plants her walking stick in a cushion of snow and reaches over and jerks his arm down. The jesses momentarily slacken. Lola grabs his glove and rights herself. "A bit of feather in the face, that's it. No wound." Kendra purses her lips then turns her face away from him. She's trying not to smile — he knows it.

"She was so light." Cody bites his lip. Don't cry. Don't cry, lame-ass. "Heavier upside down." The bird folds her wings like nothing happened and all's good. Sleek, burgundy feathers at the shoulder.

Kendra unwraps the leather from around his thumb and tosses Lola into the bushes. The trees impede any real flight; Lola bumps her wings and body through the brush to a stump. "Not the best spot." Kendra jerks her walking stick from the ground. "Branches, limited sight. We probably won't catch anything. But it's snowing too heavily in the pasture." She digs out another stick. "Here."

Kendra stabs thickets and whistles the bird along. Cody whacks underbrush a few metres to her left and hikes the slope behind her. She should talk more. She doesn't have to wisecrack, but she could say, like, how fun the postcard was, or how she had a dog as a kid. Loosen the mood. Why did he even show her? Because she asked him how long he was staying and he panicked—he realized he doesn't know. The bird follows them in the branches overhead.

"Quiet." Kendra stops. So does he.

"What is it?"

"I can see your coat," Kendra yells into the forest. And then Cody can too. The girl from yesterday, down the slope of the hill.

"Are you going to join us or just stalk us?" Kendra calls.

The girl stands there, a splash of red in the blacks and browns of the trees.

"We're going to keep going, then." Kendra continues up the slope. She stabs her stick into bushes as she goes.

"Doesn't she go to school?" he asks.

"Don't you?" Kendra veers south.

The trees break and a half-frozen creek spills down the mountain on his right. Along the edge water-sodden foliage conceals rocks and pits. Some places his leg sinks as deeply in the moss as it did in the snow in the pasture.

"This is a mountain?" He's never hiked a mountain before and his thighs burn like crazy. The creek gurgles tea-coloured over the rocks, bending the light and jumping off the ground into an almost vertical stream.

"It's a mountain." Kendra nods her head. She keeps her pace over the moss and rotting logs.

Cody stops. "You gonna tell Axel about the white?"

"He'll find out."

Cody stares at her. How can she stand having this horrible secret, this pit in her, and not act? She has no plan to hide or tell the secret. It's like his mom planting the postcard—she sent him off to the Greyhound station assuming he'd find it, but she didn't know. For him there's two choices: confess or cover. And if he waits too long to tell, quicksand happens. The confession gets sucked internal and then there's no option but to lie. Like when he caught his mom, after she'd run out of ice, scraping the frost out of the freezer. He knew her pica picked up with low iron, anemia from not eating. He could have told Aunt Jen.

"Wait," he calls. The ground shouldn't be this steep. Shouldn't be sideways. He's going to tip down the mountainside and his skull will crack on the rocks. He collapses into a squat and tucks his head between his knees.

Kendra turns and walks back down. The bird screeches in a tree. "The creek gave you vertigo?" She stabs her walking stick into a patch of dirty snow and crouches. "Deep breaths through your nose. Have you eaten anything?"

Deep breaths. Almost creepy how much air gets into his lungs, and how it no longer feels cold in his chest like it did this morning. He's a fish in a new bowl: bit of a shocker, then acclimatization. "It was like snorkelling."

"Snorkelling?" Kendra looks at him like he's the defective one instead of the white. Like he's the most confused person in the world.

"My mom took me to Hawaii," he says. "We went out on a boat to the reef and when I put my face in it was all, horrible." How to describe it? He couldn't feel his body, let alone control it. Had no idea how big or small he was; his arms and legs felt like they went on forever, past the end of the world. And the fish were way too close. Little shards of colour darted about, far, near, too near—near enough it was like someone had upended a change jar and pelted him with nickels. But that was nothing compared to his panic when the school broke below him and the reef dropped away into opaque, empty blue. He couldn't see with the tears in his mask, and lost a flipper trying to get back in the boat before the current drifted him away from everything. "I suck at swimming," he tells her.

"Keep breathing." Kendra sits beside him. She takes off her glove, pulls two plastic-wrapped sandwiches from her vest and passes one over. "Made them at six a.m. and they're squashed," she says. He sets his glove beside hers and opens the wrapping. The bread smells of plastic and the mustard is canary yellow, but it's not so bad. He didn't realize how hungry he was. The bird eyes the glove from the tree, hungry as well. Kendra too, from the size of the bite she's taken.

He's never seen a woman take such a big bite. His mom is more of a crumb person—she licks her finger and dabs crumbs off the plate from around the bread. Or sips broth. She boils down beef knuckles, onions, and carrots until the house is wet. Then she says, "Can you feel that?" while she scrapes the congealed fat from the surface of the cold broth and taps it into a soup can. "There's a layer of fat on everything," she'll say, and shower. Which, to him, makes the apartment damper than the soup had, but has her feeling better and joking again.

Kendra rests her sandwich on her knee and unscrews the lid from the Thermos. Before she swallows, Lola drops from her branch and hits the ground halfway between the two of them and the girl, barely visible down the slope. Kendra tosses her plastic wrap at Cody, swallows the butt of her sandwich, and jogs down to where the bird is tented around a kicking rabbit. She lifts her camera, pulls back the plastic bag and snaps a picture, and then bends over and swaps the rabbit for a chick from her vest. Holding the rabbit by the neck, she lifts it and it goes still.

Cody works his way down, one hand on the rocks and snow beside the stream. His kilt drags over the wet moss and collects twigs, and because of the kilt and the slope he can't see where he steps. Way down the hill—the girl again, standing in the trees. He stops next to Kendra and blows into his hands. He means to ask Kendra about her, it's nice that there is someone his age here, but his feet are numb and his palm throbs where he planted it on a rock, and there's a rabbit dangling from Kendra's grip. Brown, furry ears lie flat over the back of her hand. Its eyes are half-shut, but it curls its legs and kicks.

"Looks like you were useful anyway, stalker," Kendra yells to the girl. "Flushed us a hare." Kendra runs two fingers over the rabbit's ears then does a little twist at its spine, and then a bigger twist that rips the head from the neck. She tosses the head to Lola and turns, so that she's squatting between the body and the falcon, and lays the rabbit on the ground.

She flips out a pocket knife and cuts a horizontal line through the belly skin. Laying the knife aside, she grips the skin with her fingers and peels it up from the cut so that the fur folds back on itself and the hide tears off the body inside out. Without the skin the body is mottled and bloody. Scrawny—he'd never have guessed a rabbit. It looks cold, but that must be him projecting because it steams. She bags the skin and body separately.

The falcon rips fur and meat from the open neck of the head. Kendra grabs a chunk of snow and scrubs her fingers, then rinses her hands in the creek. "Lucky catch," she says.

Looking at her, bent over the stream beside a rabbit she decapitated—he was stupid to tell her about the snorkelling. Kendra shakes the creek water off her hands. She hikes to where they'd been sitting and gets the Thermos and their gloves, then down again and pulls Lola off the rabbit.

The bird has needles stuck to its breast, and the bulge of its swollen crop is visible under the wet feathers. Kendra pulls strings of flesh off its beak. "Okay, take her."

He doesn't want to. He so doesn't want to. But down at the trees he can see the girl watching them. He eases his hand into the glove and holds out his arm. Kendra transfers the bird and wraps the jesses. The hawk's wet, clumpy, and sits with its wings untucked and half-limp at its sides. The gold-black eyes take over most of the head. His arm seems too close, and, at the same time, as if it reaches into another space. It's his and not his—like the bird's claimed it. If it wasn't obvious that he was in too deep when he shut himself in that car with four thousand baby chicks on their death ride, it's obvious now. Not only is he in too deep, he's in the wrong pond completely. The white bird, his uncle, Kendra's lies, the trees and snow — deep breaths.

AXEL

The curtain catches on the rod and refuses to slide. He jerks it with his right hand, his left hand planted against the cedar wall-panelling for balance, since his leg's in the middle of the room. Too hot for the leg. Too hot for anything but skivvies because today, the first day this winter he's spent inside sewing hoods, he lit the stove and overestimated the wood. Small pieces. Burned too fast. That's fine. Clothes needed a wash — his jumper and long johns are soaking in the tub.

He gets the curtain across as the porch sensor light flicks on. Kendra and the kid. If she hasn't got her truck towed she'll have to ask for a room. After this morning he's not offering. He lifts his leg and sets it next to his chair at the table.

The boy enters, red-cheeked and queasy, like he's survived a carnival ride. His hair slick on his scalp with melted snow, and bird shit down that skirt. Does the kid even notice? Kendra kicks dirt and snow off her boots on the door frame. Bagged fur sprouts from her vest pocket and she carries a jar of Milo's home-still in each hand. Her camera across her chest. Cold air wafts off both her and the boy. Behind them light shines from the dairy barn. He can't tell who's milking but it's probably the granddaughter.

Kendra shoulders the door closed and hoists the jars on the table next to his dyes and today's work. He's only finished two hoods, but they're quality. The first has a polished brown leather crest and snakeskin side panels. A bead and plume on top. The second is dyed royal blue, no trimmings. The boy sits across from him and pulls the hoods across the table. Axel sweeps loose snake scales into a pile. "Get your truck out?"

She looks at him like she's sizing up the challenge. "That falcon was shit today."

The kid sets down the hoods.

"What falcon?"

Kendra seals the rabbit in Tupperware. "The white." She washes her hands. "What else?"

"You took her out?"

"Nah." She opens a cupboard and pinches three jiggers. "Only in the training yard."

"Well?" She's stringing him on. Get on with it. He grips the edge of the table. "They're always shit the first time out."

"Shit like couldn't hit a fist? Couldn't find the fist."

She sets the jiggers down and picks up the blue hood. "Nice stitches."

"First time out. Should've stayed in the pen."

"Told you we did. Kept landing sideways in the snow. Lost the mark with the chick in full sight, then got tangled in the netting." She pulls up a chair and tilts it back on two legs. She wipes her palms over her hair—a darkened, wet auburn—and squeezes drips out of her braid onto the carpet. "Fine, not tangled. Flew into it. Flew being generous. Flapped."

Axel takes the blue hood from next to the jiggers and sets it back beside the brown. "How'd it hit a rabbit then?"

"Am I on trial here? Lola did that."

Why is she saying this? There is no way that bird is bad. All the photos and records in the hatchling barn back him.

"Course she still might breed well." Kendra tilts a jar of Milo's home-still. She says that out of spite. She knows— she knows—that if there was a wrong bristle on the bird, which there is not, of course he wouldn't breed it.

He slams his hands down on the table, rattling the dye jars. The boy jerks back. "You listen." He grabs Kendra's arm.

"You want me to listen?" Kendra leans in and scans him. "You listen. That bird is overlarge. And some recessive pigment. It's off. Fly it yourself."

He lets go of her and reaches for his prosthetic. He will fly the white, he'll take her out now.

"What?" Kendra spreads her arms and gestures to the leg he's holding by the knee. "What? You gonna hit me with that? Slap me like you slapped that girl?"

Axel sets the leg across his lap. That hit bothered her? Hadn't thought it would bother her. Hadn't thought about it at all.

She drops her gaze and pushes her fingers into her eyes. "You know, there's bottles everywhere. And he claims he's quit." She pours all three of them a shot. "Like that's possible."

He hasn't given a thought to what's going on at the dairy either. Would rather not think of Austin. Saw him once after the stroke. Swaying mess carted into the house. Once was enough. He turns his jigger. The quality of the home-still dropped when Milo took over, that's certain.

He downs his home-still the same time the power cuts.

"The lights are out," the kid says.

"Snow's heavy." Axel slides the kid's shot to him. "Gonna need more than a thimble."

The kid doesn't touch the jigger. "When will the power come back on?" He tugs the sleeves of his hoodie over his hands.

"Not tonight." Kendra pushes her chair back and

goes to the spare room. She comes back with a deck of cards, a crib board, and a candle. "Game?"

"Why not?" Pours another jigger.

"That sure you'll win?" She deals.

Look at her. She bates—tugs at her jesses—she's restless. But it's more than that; her discomfort is muscular. He has what she wants, a bird, and she can't see how to get it. What she thinks she needs. She scratches her neck and tugs her braid to her lips. By her age—no, younger, he'd been younger than her—he'd already travelled south through Chile, then Argentina, and been hired on at a convent to hawk pigeons off the church. He sorts his cards. Jack of diamonds and eight of spades to her crib. Cut is a two of diamonds. He opens the play. "Three."

Kendra lays her card. "Six for two." She pegs.

The way mountains bit the sky. The flock of dove-grey nuns that crossed by him daily on the stone garden path. The coos and strutted challenges from the pigeons up the steeple. Orange trees. Sugarcane—he chewed a stick like a child until the gardener christened him Sweetie. *Dulce*, Sweetie, dig the yams. Sweetie, over here, help tie up flowers.

"Taking your sweet time." Kendra tops their jiggers. Snow whisks the window and sticks.

"Nine for six."

"Fifteen for two."

"Nineteen." He'd been too spirited to stay put, despite the draw that country had, how it urged one to settle. Girls there married Christ as fledglings, and even the glaciers deemed the mountain crevices home-worthy. After a year he jumped a freight ship and pitched up the Atlantic to Greenland, to Iceland, where he first saw gyrfalcons, and hurried back to the north of North America and the nesting grounds.

"Twenty-nine." Kendra lays a king. She hasn't been anywhere. She comes from an hour's drive away from this place, from a town of semi drivers whose highlight is racing a rig on logging roads after coyotes. Sure she's been to falconry meets, but what does that mean? Everyone there has a purchased bird. Not the same if you buy it.

"Go." The rim of the candle melts and wax spills down to the holder. The wick curls and the flame lengthens. He found the birds nesting in the cliffs and climbed. Dried mute came loose under his fingers, crumbled over his back, and dusted away behind him. After half a day he reached into a hole in the rock and lifted a pin-feathered eyas. He held the falcon to his chest and descended single-handed until his foot slipped on the dusty rock and his leg broke badly. Still he managed to kayak back with a splintered calf.

"One for the last. Nine." She pegs.

"Fourteen. One for last." He paddled into camp with

the bird in his shirt keeping him awake—its flurried heartbeat racing faster than his own. After that, hospitalization, where the doctor took his leg. Immobile, he begged them to bring the bird in and prove it was fine. Hired a kid to keep it in a toolshed. Trained the child to catch mice and rats to feed the falcon. His first apprentice, he supposes.

Kendra pegs for him. "Show already."

Cody fiddles with the damper and sits between them at the table. He pushes his jigger Kendra's way.

Axel lifts his leg off his lap and hands it to the boy. "Your mother's father, my brother, drove to the hospital when it first came off. A self-proclaimed priest. Not a real priest. An asshole. Don't know how he found a woman who could stand him. Always beating on everyone. Including himself." Not beating, berating. He remembers the visit as a film, as if it wasn't him it happened to, as if he'd been the bird the child held in the corner as his brother shook his head, disgusted at the stump—disgusted by the waste—and by the joy of the man in the hospital bed.

He spreads his cards. "Fifteen two, plus two runs plus a pair. Twelve."

The kid clutches the leg at the top and lets the foot dangle. His face is round and his hair, dried in the heat of the fire, fans with a slight curl over his forehead into his eyes.

Kendra rubs her neck and lays her hand. Three, six, nine, king, all diamond. Flush. He could have seen that coming during the play.

"Look," Kendra says. "Maybe I'm wrong."

KENDRA

There's no way she's wrong about that bird. But it's possible she shouldn't have told Axel. And maybe she shouldn't have poured the boy a shot, as he's still staring at it like it's the gateway to hell. Between that postcard and the leg Axel handed him, he's not doing badly — given himself a job tossing logs to the woodstove every hour, although it was way too hot to start.

Kendra crosses and uncrosses her legs beneath the table, pushes her sleeves over her elbows, then peels off her layered tops till she's down to her undershirt. She deals. Behind her, the woodstove blazes.

Goddamn Axel though, spying through the window this afternoon, being pissy about her truck — he pushed her too far.

Let it go and relax. Count to ten, or meditate on, on what? That she feels sorry for Axel despite the last three years of building rage?

Both of them next to naked and failing at cribbage. She's distracted during the plays, Axel is frustrated.

And trying to teach the kid is pointless. He doesn't understand suits, and talks the whole time, breaking the quiet with awkward little laughs, and she's worried that Axel — with the mood he's in — will either hit the boy, or say something else weird about their family.

"Here." Kendra downs the kid's home-still that's been there all evening. Better for both of them. "Axel, we should feed him."

"You want me to feed him?" He hops to the counter. The rabbit is still on the counter in the bag and he picks it up.

"Are we —" Cody says. "Is that dinner?"

Kendra says "no" at the same time Axel says "yes" and she follows up with "Give the boy a break."

Axel tosses the bag to the freezer.

"The power's off, outside would be a better storage place."

He ignores her. Grabs a Tupperware full of frozen empanadas and hops to the porch, slams a half-dozen on the barbecue.

"Jesus, it's freezing, put some clothes on." How does she always end up with this role? She holds out a coat. He accepts. All three of them stand in the dark on the porch. Cody's brought the fake leg, but she doesn't point it out. The cold is a welcome break from the heat inside.

"Argentina," Axel says. "The nuns put us to work

and I learned food. Not just these"—he taps the empanadas with the barbecue tongs—"the birds we flew, they
ate snake."

The home-still is working and the moment feels
almost good. The kid is oddly interested in food, like
the sandwich this morning, and she might get a story
from Axel that hopefully won't end on him eating a
raw fish—head and all—after catching it swimming,
or some other ridiculous exaggeration about his youth.
Actually, even if he gets into how he started that would
be good. He could use a reminder right now that when
the falcon population dropped and the wild capture
ban went through, he was the first to breed gyrs with
any success. The respect he has at the meets—it would
be good for Cody to see that side of him. Rather than
whatever this is—Axel barbecuing, single-legged, in
his underwear in a snowstorm.

"The nuns?" the kid says. She's glad he does because
she's curious too, and she snaps a picture of the two of
them before anyone can object.

"Argentina?" she prods. But they miss their chance—
cutting through the thick, windswept snowfall, the
chug of the tractor. And when they look to the sound,
they see Melanie peering through the slats of the porch.
The girl runs.

"Hey," Kendra calls. "Join us." She shouldn't be
out in the storm. They're protected from the wind on

the porch, but past the lip of the roof the snow whips through the blackout.

"You're siding with the girl?" Axel squeezes the tongs.

Siding—? She's going to call again but she sees a beam of light bouncing across the pasture. Melanie has a flashlight, she'll be okay.

"Was she with you, when you flew the white?" Axel.

Of all the petty shit—what was she hoping to get from this man again?

MILO

The yard, half-melted and wet all day, is crusted and glassy. Snow falls, sharp and small, and in gusts that cut through his flashlight's swath and make it difficult to focus on the outline of the buildings. He shuts off the flashlight and lets a burst of queasiness past. The barn becomes a void in the flurry. The lights are out, as is the motion sensor that should flicker reliably across the field from Axel's place. The power's failed—start the generator. This job he can manage.

Earlier, a moment ago when he went to change the old man, there was no way. He knew it as soon as he entered the room and saw Austin. An invalid, his blankets shoved to his waist, in greying pyjamas. Austin who, before the stroke, Christ. Starting when Milo was seven, Austin had him heat water and bring soap and towels to the field or barn—wherever Austin'd wrestled a calf from a pelvis. Austin wiped the birth sac and fluid from the calf with hay, then soaped his arms and chest and washed in the bucket. Delivered and doctored all his own cattle. Had even managed the bull—harnessed the beast, penned it, settled the teaser, then come alongside the animal and hupped him. Terrifying, even poled. The bull was massive. Got scary height on its hind legs, with chest and shoulders rested on the teaser's ass. He'd refused to hold the harness rope or be near the pen during semen collection. Milo sold the bull with the market calves first thing after moving back with Melanie. Artificial insemination from purchased straws is so much easier—even Melanie can do that. But when he was a kid, there was Austin next to seventeen hundred pounds of horny meat, directing its unwieldy pink shlong into a fake vagina.

He circles to the generator under the lean-to around the back of the barn. The dull red metal is fused with patches of snow. He keys it, but it won't catch. Try again. Eight-gallon tank so fourteen hours run time. The genset—if it ever starts—should boast enough watts to run the house as well as a portion of the milkers and the milk bin. He tries the dipstick. Dry. Okay.

Such discrepancy—Austin's collapsed chest, arms

curled like the tendons have shrunk, even the facial fat
has faded away and left this emaciated human—it's
almost easy to dismiss what remains of his father. Well,
no. If that were true, he'd be able to clean the old man.
He wouldn't be hung up on embarrassment. The old
man clenching his fist and pawing the blankets—goddamn. Thought he'd way outlived embarrassment.

There's too much of a drift at the side door to the
garage so he opens the main barn door and fumbles
through to the garage that way. Tractor grease, machine
oil, cut-gas, warmed by the smell of compressed sawdust bricks, and by body heat from the cows beyond
the wall. He sets a hand on the tractor and spits in the
floor drain. The smell of the diesel is no good. Get it
outside. He clears a few bottles out of the main door—
might as well, since he has to rescue Kendra's truck
tomorrow—and opens the garage. Probably shouldn't
syphon in the garage anyway, he's got that much sense.
He steps on the running board, grabs the canopy support, and swings into the seat. He bends over the wheel
and drives into the snow and wind, ducks at the door
even though the plastic canopy above has clearance.

In the drive, he parks the tractor and dismounts. He
walks back to the garage and crawls behind the boiler
and finds a length of tubing. He blows the dust out of it
and lets it uncoil. Long enough. Grab the jerry can and
back outside. The wind blows his coat against his back

and he leans into the square-nosed body of the tractor.
He's got this. He pulls his glove off with his teeth and
twists the cap off the gas tank and sets it on the seat of
the tractor. Glove back on. Tubing slid into the tank.
He readies the jerry can and sucks on the loose end of
the tube. As he sucks, a beam of light bounces over him
in the drive — a flashlight. Melanie runs up to him; her
glasses are crooked and she's holding her toque on with
one hand. She doesn't see him and almost collides, but
at the last minute veers away. The tubing spits diesel
over his teeth.

He pukes. The gas spills over the snow. He yanks
the tube out of the tractor and pukes again. Bile and
whatever he ate last. When did he eat last? He kneels
in the snow and dry-retches. Burns his throat and nose.
She'll think he's drunk. He can't tell if that's better than
him saying he quit and her thinking it a lie.

IV

—

MELANIE

THE PASTURE IS covered in snow and soft underfoot, and she almost steps on the tarp and poles — almost topples into the slurry because Milo took the rails down — as she runs away from Axel's place toward home.

The replacement pole wobbles, but she holds it anyway and catches her breath and laughs. It's a bit funny — when Kendra develops that photo, there's going to be Axel naked flipping some sort of huge perogies on the barbecue, that boy with the bird shit down his black kilt holding Axel's prosthetic, and — at the back and the bottom of the image — Melanie, red-eyed from the flash, peeking through the rails at the edge of the porch.

She shakes the pole and clicks on her flashlight. What

was she thinking, peeking in their window? She followed Kendra and the boy from their hike—or hunt, whatever it was—to the barn, where Kendra disappeared into the garage and emerged with Milo's home-still. Milked the cows—good thing that happened before the power cut, it would take too long to do it by hand—and then grabbed a flashlight and scoped the hatchling barn because what else was she supposed to do, go home? No one was outside, and the hatchling barn was locked. The outdoor shower had an icicle from the shower head, and Kendra's Nissan balanced a cushion of snow on the nose and windshield in the ditch. When the lights cut, she thought she might brave knocking on Axel's door. They might invite her in, let her play cards or swap stories. Tell her they knew about Austin and would talk to Milo for her. Get him into a home. For now, they'd say, here's a huge perogy. Hope you like it!

She's an idiot. When they stepped onto the porch Kendra was drinking Milo's hootch. Axel had clearly had a few, or maybe he always stripped down and barbecued in the dark. She assumed because she watched them all summer—loitered by the fence when they trained falcons, took shots at crows, hunted her pasture—she assumed that they'd seen her. She thought, she realizes, they'd rescue her. Take her in. But then they stepped onto the porch and barbecued like the storm was just a storm.

Why doesn't it feel that way to her? She aims the flashlight toward her house and begins to run again. It's like this winter, it's a darker winter. She can't run fast enough in the rubber boots, in the snow and the freezing mud beneath the snow. She almost tramples Milo, barfing in the snow beside the tractor, and she veers toward the house. Inside, she slams the door behind her. Lets her coat fall on the ground, wet. And the boots, they can stay in the kitchen. She pulls a blanket around her shoulders. Snow rustles the window. The wind drags high-pitched above the roof. Through the walls, the old man's wet cough.

Why always her? And not even time to catch her breath. She feels her way across the hall to the old man's bed and finds his hand — softening calluses, knuckles and skin. His arm, too. She works her fingers behind his shoulder, then raises his head and adjusts the pillows so his neck is supported. The cough stops. Then a loud, filmy breath — almost a gag — that triggers a round of wheezing. He stinks.

Why can't Milo do this? It looks like he started to — there's a pail of soapy water next to the bed. She bites her lip. She peels back the blankets. She hasn't put the old man's pyjama bottoms on him for months to make cleaning easier. She holds the flashlight in her mouth and unpins the cloth at his hip. The flashlight tastes of eraser and rubber bands, and its beam focuses directly on him. He doesn't look as old as he feels—yes, his skin is dry, and thin, and the purple bruise on top of his hand has stayed for over a month, but there's no wrinkles outside of his face. His skin's like hers. Well, paler, puddlier, but without the light it feels like he's about to lose his thighs, like his flesh will drop from the bone. She closes the safety pin and flicks her eyes—flashlight still in her mouth—to the dark where his face is. It's hard to touch him not knowing if he's in there or if he's gone. Out of sight. Incommunicado. She gets the diaper off.

He sniffs as the cloth touches his groin—the water's a bit cool. Under the light, his penis is a drip of flesh, extra dough that sloughs from his frame. Like a sad pet. Poor little guy. She rinses the cloth and rolls the flashlight in her teeth. She could touch it. Run her fingers over it. That seance at her old place, the one the boys crashed, where Rowan tried to stuff her hand down his pants—his hip bones peaked as high as the old man's in front of her, but Rowan's skin, tanned, warm and firm, smelled of bread. The pressure of Rowan's hand splayed over the back of her head.

The hard plastic of the flashlight pushes aside her tongue. She spits it out. What if—what if she really is that kid? The girl who walks from the high-school bathroom carrying her own stool. Real solid shit, not the energy bars that idiot boys melt into turd shapes and leave in the water fountains. What if she's the kid the counsellors encourage other kids to avoid? She's here staring at her grandfather's wiener thinking about blow jobs.

She can't even finish wiping the old man down. She fastens the diaper and covers him. Then undoes the diaper and makes herself finish.

CODY

He's holding the leg because, after Axel handed it to him and he'd carried it to the porch, he'd had to carry it back in and wasn't sure where to put it. For all the world it feels like vacuuming—heavy at the base and light at the top. He expected it to be more solid, wooden and chipped, but the leg is closer to a bicycle: a metal rod with a plastic foot, and a cup at the top with a corset cinch and fastener.

Kendra takes a deep What's With Him? breath and spreads out her cards. What is with Axel? They're fed, so he can't use hunger as an excuse, and back inside and with the fire there is no way anyone could even pretend to be cold. Cody pictures his gramps—the man who stood unsmiling in the photos behind his family—self-flagellating his back with a belt beside a potato patch during a dry, dusty mid-afternoon, under a prairie sun that casts and coats the scene sepia, like the filter in the antique family photo. Axel doesn't know what he's talking about. From what Cody's mom told him, his gramps never hit her or Aunt Jen. He was a serious, super-old dad they didn't get to know much before he died. Car accident. Or maybe lung cancer. He collected, his mom said, proverbs. Sayings — "Living is licking honey off a thorn" — that sort of style. She said he had a line for every family issue and it drove her mad. But who knows? It's not like she doesn't lie.

Cody tries not to look at Axel's stump, but the only things to do are: 1) Wander the house. He did that. Every spare drawer — forget room — is wacky with ankle bells, leather ribbons, feathers, photo albums, books on tanning hides and taxidermy, folders of type-written breeding observations, and boxes. He could 2) Watch the crib game — what's crib? — or 3) Load the stove. The room's way too hot already. Kendra's down to an undershirt and jeans, and Axel's way past underdressed.

The stump, pale and small, comes to a finish above the knee, and doesn't quite look like the leg is bent — that's how they do the effect in movies. A scar curls along the side and back of the thigh where the skin must have been folded. The scar is waxy, white, and raised — like the flesh was soldered rather than stitched — and he has an overwhelming urge to pick it off in one long strip. Axel adjusts the elastic of his briefs and meets

Cody's eyes. Cody jerks his gaze to his lap and brushes at a stain.

Axel swipes the cards and shuffles. Cody bites his thumbnail, then stands and moves from the chair to the couch. He leans back and tilts the prosthetic so that it rests like a pet against his own leg. Axel glances his way. He straightens the leg and sits forward again. He shouldn't have looked at the stump. Why does he always stare? Though that girl stared too, through the porch without any excuse at all. And Axel is stare-worthy. In the candlelight Uncle Old has gone from ancient to prehistoric in a way that's freaking scary. He's topless—bottomless too except for his undies—and hair sprouts from the collarbone down. Almost his entire body is crazy with wiry white fuzz—he's hairy like the fluffy baby falcons in the picture albums. His foot is Tendon City, his skin stretched over the liga-ments and scooped under the ankle bone in a dip that could hold water. The calf is astounding—larger than Cody's thigh, and a vein wanders it like an underground river. Axel's eyes are blue, the skin around them leath-ery brown, as his eyelids probably are too, though Cody can't tell—Axel's staring Kendra down like she's about to bolt, like he dares her to make the first move. Like he crawled out of some cracked avian fossil bed as a revision of raptors himself.

He fingers the buckle of the prosthetic. Axel's leg,

which is nothing when it's on him, has become its own thing when off. What should he do with it? His mom, when she was tired in the hospital, jokingly said, "I wish you could take my bladder and go to the bathroom for me." Aunt Jen closed her book and said, "I wish I could take your stomach and eat the damn food for you."

Cody lets Axel's foot stand for itself and lies down on the couch with his head close to the woodstove. He tucks his legs under the kilt. Cards flip across the table. There's the whirr and thunk of the shuffled deck and Kendra says, "You can sleep in the room."

"Yeah, maybe," he answers. But really, yeah right. The pictures are bad enough, he doesn't want to imagine what's in the boxes.

He rubs his mouth and sits up. He must have slept, because Kendra has stripped down further in the heat. Her pants are folded on the floor. She slaps her last card on the table and throws her arm over the back of her chair. She has last season's tan, and in the sleeveless undershirt it looks like she's wearing long, almond-coloured dinner gloves that cut high on her biceps. Where the tan is, her freckles are numerous, but half-blended into the darker tone. Her face, too: over her clenched chin, her cheeks, her nose, under her eyebrows and up her arched forehead into her hairline — copper speckles. The rest of her skin, whatever isn't sun-beat, is pale. The candle has burnt low, but the stove is hot, and her upper lip and chest—the start of her breasts—are gold with sweat and light. She crosses her legs and the skin of her thigh peels audibly from the leather seat.

The prosthetic stands next to Axel. The room smells of coffee and body odour. He's thirsty.

"I'm going outside," he says. Kendra sweeps and shuffles.

Cody steps into an extra pair of boots and out onto the deck. He eats a fistful of snow off the rail and another off the steps where the stuff has piled and quit. What did the hospital do with Axel's old leg? Burn it? Burial would be odd—a miniature graveyard on the side of the main site. Toss it? They couldn't have put it in the garbage. What do they do with a bit of you that dies before the rest?

The clouds have gone. New ones start to roll in over the valley, but at this moment stars are out, even in the rising light. How can it be night and day? Dark and light at the same time? Snow melts under his boots. The sky above the eastern mountain is pale grey, like the night has been wrung out of it.

Across the paddock, a slab of snow falls from the eaves of the dairy house. The shift gives him the willies, like his presence has woken everything up. "Sorry," he says.

Axel calls, "Is it light?"

Kendra adds, "Has it stopped fucking snowing?"

No, he wants to say. Don't come out. It's still so early. Don't come out here. Let me be here alone. Inside they shuffle clothing and coats.

A cow lifts its head in the yard. In the yard. In front of him. How did he miss it?

KENDRA

It's barely light, way too early — it would still be too early if she had slept — and cows are all over the place. There's a cow in Axel's yard, a few on the road, a number dispersed in the pasture. Like someone dropped a bag of marbles, they've scattered over the landscape. Milo, out on the highway, waves and yells, trying to herd them off the road. He flags a car and it slows as it passes the dairy. Her truck in the ditch is a white pyramid.

The big tan in the yard shies away from Axel as he breaks trail through the snow toward the training yard. Leaving the morning work to her, of course.

"Help me with the feed." She hands Cody his hoodie and treks a path from the house to the hatchling barn. He follows her to the building and up the stairs. She unlocks the hatchling room. Cody lingers at the door and pulls on his sweater.

"You should see this place in the spring." At the

moment there's no hatchlings and the room is dark, but in March, if the boy's still here — and by the sound of that postcard he'll be here a while — he'll see the falcons start to lay. Axel has rearing timed to the second. Each pair lay three or four eggs per batch, and she or Axel remove them from the oil-drum nests in the breeding pens. They bring the eggs here, rows and rows of eggs — up to fifty, though there's usually only fifteen or so at a time — and turn on the automatic rolling metal rods of the contact incubator. The eggs are weighed, and the humidity of the incubator adjusted accordingly. After ten days the candler will show half-shading — a network of capillaries and veins — and each heartbeat is monitored through the stethoscope. Thirty-one days and the first batch of hatchlings peep in tins under the red heat lamps. New life, that fast. "Yeah." She finds the box of vitamin powder on a shelf and pushes it into Cody's chest. "Other room for now."

The feed room's clammy with the damp, feathery scent of the feeder chicks stacked in trays in the corner. She wheels the cement mixer out from beside the deep-freeze and quarts of purified water. A small grey Kobalt, who knows why Axel got it originally, but it works to stir the vitamins into the dead birds. She lifts the top tray and tumbles the feeders into the mixer. "Add some of the powder." The chicks fill three-quarters of the mixer.

Cody examines the label on the box.

"Parrot powder. Vitamins for the falcons. Axel's scratched that off, of course. One of his trade secrets."

He sprinkles a tablespoon of green powder on the chicks.

"It's not sugar." She gestures and he dumps more. "Good." She picks up a gallon of distilled water and adds a slosh. "Then you turn the crank." She starts right away. No point waiting for the kid to do it.

The kid backs off and leans on the freezer. "I'm okay to watch." He plants his hands on the lid, hops on, and pulls his kilt over his knees. "You do this every day?"

"Course." One of the rituals. "There's more to it when there's hatchlings." She turns the crank at the back. The chicks toss over each other and the powder and water work into their down and form a paste. "Pass me a bucket." Cody slides off the freezer and passes her one of the five-gallon chick-crushing pails. She tilts the mixer and the birds fall into the bucket in clumps, stuck together with the vitamin coating.

She carries the bucket down the stairs and across the drive to the training yard. No need for keys — Axel left the door open behind him. "Hey," she calls. "Where you at?" He must have gone straight for the white. It would be so much easier if she hadn't said anything. If she hadn't taken the white out and not known anything. She trudges past the breeding pens and toward the back of the yard. The kid, behind her, uses her as a breakwater from the melting snow and cows and Axel. She sets down the bucket. "What gives?" Between flight pens, Axel paces and tugs on his glove. Snow grinds unevenly under his steps, his limp accentuated as his right foot doesn't clear the snow. He flexes the glove and opens the pen. He lifts out the white.

Axel with a bird, it's like seeing him with his leg on. Like it's another appendage. Like the bird's sitting in for something. Hop it on and it not only co-operates, it belongs. And Christ, the size of the white. Three years since it hatched, reached adult plumage, and it's now ready to mate. This circle, this rearing, is why she's here. Maybe she didn't give the bird enough of a chance. Axel strides through the snow to the pasture and the bird tips sideways; its right wing beats the air while the left stays folded. He twists the jesses around his fist to help it keep hold. Enough of a chance? She's full of wistful crap. Axel exits the netting, the lure — duck wing attached to a leather ball attached to a rope — over his shoulder.

"Starting off big," she calls. "Maybe keep her in the yard?"

He raises the back of his hand to her as he strides away.

"I'm serious." Fuck. "Wait." She pushes by Cody and follows Axel over the drive and paddock, skirting the slurry lagoon. Milo's property's a mess. The tractor sits in his driveway between puddles of frozen sick and holes in the ice where, by the looks of it, gas spilled out of the syphon. Have to admire him, though—a night like that and there he is, out on the road herding heads, his shoulder pushed against a heifer.

Axel legs it through the snow, following the cow trails through the open gate to just inside of the pasture. He's barely on the far side of the pole and wire fence when he unwinds the white's jesses.

"Why're all the cows out?" Cody asks.

"Gate's open." That should be obvious. The cows on the highway are likely licking salt. "Hitching a ride," she jokes. "Who knows?"

Axel pulls the bird in to his chest and murmurs to the top of its head. He raises his arm. "Stand back."

The bird lifts. Kendra raises her fist to her mouth. Let it fly. Let it fly and, let it not fly—it's not trained to come back. The bird flutters into the snow like a light-blind moth. She lowers her hand and leans against a paddock fence post. Behind her the boy lifts the corner of a tarp next to the slurry lagoon's cement ramp. Axel picks the white off the pasture to go again. Knowing that Axel is about to fail makes it both sad and funny. How can it not be? A damp firework.

AXEL

The white sat on the lower perches. He should have seen that. Other falcons fly from one perch to another in the flight pen. The white only hopped down. He took her on the fist and fed her, but as a breeding bird that wasn't for sale, there was no reason to train her alongside the juvies to be sent to Doha and the East. With another bird, he would have noticed. With any other bird. The white struggles to walk in the snow. It beats its wings, but can't clear its legs, and lurches sideways like it's broken. He bends and lifts it.

"I told you." Kendra zips her coat. Cloaked like the Argentinean nuns, head to foot, hair tucked away under her winter cap. The bird he flew at the convent—the reason he still keeps hawks around now—was speckle-breasted, brown, with yellow legs and beak—sun-yellow, the colour of a spring siesta. Above the wings, chestnut shoulders. A fondness for snakes. For landing next to the sisters with the snake. Well, that was him. So easily trained, that bird, all it needed was opportunity and out shone a spirit of alert, high excitement. Keen-pitched enjoyment. The bird shot from his fist and exploded pigeons to feathers. He flings the white up. It falls, wings spread, in the snow.

"Isn't it enough?" Kendra nods toward the kid, who

wipes his nose and tucks the tarp back under the dismantled slurry poles.

Enough? It's too much. All his plans. The books
of charted mating history, documentation of which
falcons from which continent at what time, family
oddities and traits he explored — white deck feathers,
striated quills, ceres and nares without their usual waxy
blue. He scoops the bird from the wet snow. Falcons
have been flown for centuries. His Argentinean hawk
would have been a bird for a poor man, but the lift it
had. The chalky girl now on his fist — perfectly plumed,
sleek and unruffled feathers. Black-eyed. White toes and
pounces. A bird for a king. Has about the same use as a
king. She hangs from her jesses and flashes him seven
thousand white feathers. Bleached bitch. He hurls her
skyward.

MILO

On the road, in the middle of the road, across the highway by the river, over the driveway, in the paddock and
in front of the slurry lagoon, almost everywhere but in
the pasture. Cows. His fault. He left the gate ajar after
moving the tractor to the driveway, and opened the
barn to get to the garage without remembering he'd
left an escape route. He thumps a cow on the side. No

response but the hollow sound of its lungs. Get off the damn highway. He clasps his hands, raises his arms, and chops down behind its shoulder. The cow swivels its ears. He leans on the cow and it leans back with all its brickish bovine heft. "Move!" It takes a step or two sideways when he pulls away, then drops a pile of crap that burns into the salty highway slush.

Cursing. At first he thinks it's his own voice echoing off the wide valley walls, but there's Axel in the dairy field—barely through the pasture and paddock fence—with a big, impressive bird on his fist. Kendra yells, Axel yells. Their boy mills, a bit back from the two of them, beside the slurry lagoon.

Maybe if he corrals the cows closer to the gate, the highway band will follow them in. He walks down the drive, his boots skidding on the sodden layer of melt and mud under last night's now-wet snow. The bird is bigger than Axel's standard breed. Makes sense now why Axel's been so secretive, and why he was so angry at Melanie in the hatchling barn. Milo hasn't seen a bird like it his whole life.

As he passes his house, Melanie runs onto the porch. The door flails on its hinge, slaps the wall and bounces back. She bends over the rail, sees him, straightens, and pushes clumps of snow off the banister. The sleeves of her sweater are visibly darker than the rest of the material—wet or filthy or wet and filthy. She's in her pyjama bottoms and boots. He'd hoped to get the cows in before she woke.

He claps his hands and hollers. "Go cows."

"They been milked?" Melanie asks.

"Not yet," he says.

"You turn on the machine and they'll wander back."

Of course. Of course they will. He looks at his kid. Day two, he imagines telling her. Hasn't had a drink for two days. He kicks snow over the puke and gasoline holes beside the tractor.

"When the power comes back on I'll do it." Melanie opens the door and reaches for her coat. She slips it on and laces the toggles through their loops and walks along the driveway toward the barn. As she goes she shoos a cow, a big tan, swollen at the belly, into the paddock and next to the lagoon. The cow's probably in late gestation, though he's not good at judging birth times.

Oh God, the still. "Wait." He runs after Melanie. She can't learn he made another batch. The heifer shies away, antsy — now they listen to him — and heads through the paddock to where Axel and Kendra argue at the pasture fence. Axel holds the bird on his fist and turns toward Milo and the paddock and driveway. Axel's not in his everyday jumpsuit. Instead he wears grey sweatpants — the outline of his thigh and missing leg visible under the worn fabric — and a faded green canvas coat. He's Austin's age, and still all that muscle in a stump. Milo stops and rests a hand on the tractor seat. "Melanie."

"What?" Melanie turns and faces him. All her hair is sheared now, short and pretty, and darker blonde without the length. Her glasses perch crooked on her nose—have they always been twisted? Did she sleep on them?

"What do you want?" She claps her palms, then raises them above her shoulders like she's giving a blessing or a long-shot prayer. "What is it now?"

"I only," he starts. "I brewed to pay Axel and Kendra."

She bites her upper lip then says, "You don't think they'd take milk?"

The boy, to his right, plays with his bangs, then his kilt, and tucks his fingers into his sleeves and rubs his elbows. The slurry stretches snow-covered and bright behind him. Ahead of Milo, on the other side of the open gate that separates pasture from paddock, Axel lifts the bird. "Go. Get."

Kendra puts her hand to her head, either to help her gaze or out of exasperation. The bird falters, then rises, goes up maybe ten feet—Axel punches his palm—then the white bird snaps down, quickly, like all falcons do. For a moment Milo thinks it's coming for him, but the bird smacks the pelvic bone of the tawny milker in the paddock, halfway between him and the boy at the slurry. That does it. The cow bolts. Away from Milo, from Melanie, away from Axel and Kendra. The boy cringes to almost a kneeling position as the cow stampedes his way then veers right, hoofs it onto the slurry ramp, and stops at the metal gate—the only rail around the lagoon still standing after yesterday's "fixer." The bird, with its body half-sunk in the snow, tries and fails to fold its wings. The boy backs slowly and trips onto the tarp-covered posts.

"Girl," Milo says. "Cow. Come on." Come down now. Please. The cow jumps. Its front legs pop over the short steel gate and land on the snow-covered pit like the animal thinks it can walk on water. Its front half sinks. The cow seems surprised, at least momentarily, then its head and entire front half disappear under the manure—its back legs remain hooked over the gate.

Axel runs first, then Kendra and Melanie. Axel pushes them back from the cow's rear. "She'll kick your legs."

"You're already down one," Kendra says, but shifts her approach from the side. She puts her shoulder under the hip and tries to lift.

Melanie unlatches the gate, and the rail, supported only by the hinge, bends with a groan under the cow's mass and lowers the animal further into the slurry.

Kendra starts swearing like she hasn't cursed for days.

"Hoist her in." Axel strains on the opposite side. "Hoist her in. So she can get her head up."

He should run forward. The legs from the front of the hooves to the hocks scrape pinkly along the cement. The skin over the spine and barrel spasms. Around the abdomen the clean scrub of snow browns. He would run forward, but how can they lift a cow?

V

—

MELANIE

The cow has dipped into the slurry lagoon and died, hips hooked on the bent gate. Melanie rubs her hands. Her skin stuck to the frozen metal when she pulled the pin to let it open, and it stings a little. Is a bit red. Anywhere else along the pit, the cow would have been able to step her rear in the pit, get her head up, and they might have had time to help her out. Melanie squats next to the cow and rocks forward onto her toes. A chocolate line of shit clings to the animal's hair. What a stupid way to die.

"Bird hit a cow." Kendra flexes her jaw and chews on her cheek.

The pretty-boy, on his butt on the tarp, his black kilt flipped and showing off his skinny denim, raises the back of his wrist to his nose and turns away. How dare he.

"Should have stayed in the training yard." Kendra talks without direction to the distance—the pasture, or the mountain trees subdued by snow—so it's hard to tell who she's addressing, or if she's merely stating the obvious. Axel takes his shoulder out of the cow's hip and uses its rump to help himself stand.

Melanie runs her fingertips over the cow's short hide, following the swirling patterns around the hips and belly. Whorls like grass blown prostrate, or, in the late summer, where the cows have lain down in the shorn hayfields. Scratched the wrong way the hair bristles untidily.

"Rope?" Axel unbuttons his coat. Yellow-grey streaks the sternum of his T-shirt.

"Yeah." Milo sounds out of breath.

"Sling," Kendra corrects.

"Yeah." Her father, now that she listens, sounds quiet. Not breathless—reserved. Maybe he's babying a head-splitter. Is he off the hooch? Don't tell her he's attempting abstinence again.

"Rope could rip right through her." Kendra tosses her toque to Cody and pulls her hair into an elastic on the top of her head.

Milo unzips his jacket, stretches his tube scarf, then zips the coat halfway up again. "In the garage."

Axel cups his palm over the cow's pelvic bone where the bird hit, spits, and heads to the barn for Milo.

Melanie shifts from a squat to her knees. How would a rope cut through the cow? Would it be like squeezing dough, with head and butt bulging and the waist becoming thinner and thinner, stretching out to a thread, then to nothing? That's how the end of Axel's leg looks like it was separated—she's seen it. In summer when he relaxes on his veranda he sets his leg beside him under the bug zapper and sips ginger ale. Or would the cut be more like a roast on the chop-board, a clean anatomy lesson of muscle? She balances with a hand on the rail. She should feel sorrier for the cow. But screw that—what good has sorry ever done?

Axel walks back from the barn with both rope and sling. Kendra checks her hair, tugging the bun at the top of her head to make sure it's fixed.

A car horn echoes off the mountain. Melanie stands and plants her hands on her hips, squinting over the lagoon and field into the cloud-dulled sun and the turn behind the trees. The school bus—her old one, complete with coloured toques on heads that gape out the windows—drives by on the highway headed to town. On their way to school.

KENDRA

The cow hangs tan-assed to the sky. Her udder bulges over the paint-stripped rail, the bag so squashed that Kendra — despite the way the teats dangle about like limp dicks — wouldn't be shocked if it blew. One more thing to haul out of a ditch.

"A cow." She unzips her vest and tosses it to Cody, who's crawled off the tarp and stands twisting her toque beside the slurry. "How stupid can you be."

Axel hands the rope to Milo, lifts the bird from the snow and slips a hood over its head. The bird can't be totally blind. Hooded, it has poise — the talons pick over the leather glove, minute adjustments are made by the tapered tail; except for the breeze-ruffled breast feathers, the bird's ceramic. Could it be depth perception that confuses the thing? How it beats one wing and over- or undershoots the lure? And, is there still hope to breed her? The issue could be an injury, environmental. And if not, well, bloodhounds have bloat, German shepherds dysplasia. White gyrfalcons with eye issues? The bird lifts a ropy leg, talons and toes fist under the belly feathers. Two hundred kph into a cow's ass. The bird's porcelain, but so's a toilet. "Well?" she says.

Milo feeds the coiled rope through his hands and stares at her feet. Of course he won't be the one doing the reach-around in the manure. Why'd she think he would? If she leaves the cow for him to deal with, Melanie will be the one to strip down and take the shit.

She pulls off her sweater and shirt, balls them and throws them to Cody, then adjusts the straps of her undershirt and bra. She holds out her hand. Milo passes her the rope. She fastens the end of the rope to the sling and lies on her front beside the cow. Her arm barely stretches under the heifer's barrel. Can't even reach a quarter under the belly without going face-first into cow-pie. She stands up and unbuttons her jeans with her clean hand. Cody hangs them over his shoulder. Kid's pretty much a clothes rack anyway.

She sits on the edge and swings her legs in. She lowers herself to the waist. Crust, liquid, then solid ground. Or semi-solid sludge that sinks with her. She strings the rope under the heifer, bending down to reach, and when she stands again the warm muck hugs up to her pits. "Can you reach it round the other side?" She holds her breath. Barn-loads of mealy cow flops, hay, and runoff. Probably ammonia seeping out.

"Axel, can you reach it?" Her face is against the warm udder, its skin — softly scrolled with raised mammary veins — swells above her head, and beyond that the velveteen arc of hide slices an upright horizon along neutral clouds. The white's bell jingles. "Axel." Under her feet, nothing, but she can't wiggle them sideways.

She plants her palms on the ramp and thrusts at the elbows and shoulders. Too much suction.

"Get me out." She tugs the rope. "Jesus. Axel." Cody runs forward and grabs the sling and starts to reel her in. "Now. Please. Now." Cody offers his hand and she grabs his sleeve and then the rail. She kicks off her boots and gets enough air to alleviate the vacuum and slide onto the ramp.

"What now?" Cody wipes his hands on the snow, then on the gate and on the snow again.

She lies back and bends her knees. What now. Last meet, when she camped in the desert, Sanders opened up about his methods. Half of them were fake, flirtatious—rheum, supposedly, could be cured by feeding a hawk meat soaked in the excrement of an unweaned boy. To stop a falcon's shrieks, stuff a bat with hot pepper and hang it in the mews. She can't recall any cure for poor sight. Blindness—sewing the eyelids, or hooding as the modern equivalent—is the solution for fright, and will keep a bird calm even packed in hay, ten per crate, as smugglers do. Where the hell did all the crazy come from? Off is off. And Axel himself is—well, he's off.

What now? The cow is easier. "There's a pump, no?"

"Yes." Milo's voice.

Clouds knead into each other over the entire sky. They've pulled up from the mountain and set off the

trees with a uniform grey glow. It's not possible to pinpoint the sun beyond. She rolls onto her side. Milo coils
the rope. She should lecture him, say, Get your own
damn cow out.

Axel loops the white's jesses around a fence post.
The falcon spreads its wings and clenches the wood.
Melanie goes into the house and comes back with a
pair of Milo's boots.

"Fine." Kendra stands and takes the boots. "All right.
Go get the pump."

Milo backs the tractor to the garage. Kendra and
Milo latch the trailer and the pump. She and Melanie
unroll the thick canvas hose over the pasture. The few
cows in the field glance at them, then return to brows-
ing the churn of dirt, tufted grass, and snow. Kendra
signals to Axel and a rush of raw waste animates the
hose. Half the morning passes before the shit level drops
low enough that she can reach under the cow without
getting sucked into the lagoon again. Axel shuts down
the pump. Milo unlatches the trailer, loops the rope on
the hitch, and drags the cow onto the ramp with the
tractor. Melanie takes the creased blue tarp from the
fence poles and covers the cow.

CODY

A rumble off the valley walls. The highway's been quiet all day — all day he's crouched next to the hooded bird and Kendra's clothes on the fence, and his digits have iced over — so his first instinct is to think, idly, some sort of howl off the mountainside? His fingers are coated with what looks like coffee grounds, is probably poop, but there's a chance it's dirt because he wiped them down with grubby snow. He's going with dirt. His toes, for sure, are white, the blood pushed out by cold and poor circulation. Can't see them under his sneakers and socks, but can't feel them either. First step is the waxy yellow-white, then blue, then gangrene — Explorer Green, his mom joked the first time he had to soak his feet in the tub. He should tell Kendra about his feet now that the cow's on the ramp.

The sound builds — not a roar, at least not a live roar. A bus rounds the corner — orange, dirt sprayed up the wheel wells, the same bus that drove past earlier — coming into view from the direction of town. A school bus. Maybe his mom took pity and signed him up for school. What would she say to that — So you want school now, smart mouth? The bus turns down the driveway.

"Christ," says Milo. "Christ."

The bus brakes screech and kids spill off. He crosses the paddock and stands next to Kendra at the pump.

"Christ." Milo kicks snow over the half-covered puke holes.

"Ready for that tour?" The teacher, last off the bus, rubs his hands together and stomps.

"The power." Milo turns a half circle and runs his hands through his beard. "The power's not working."

"Can't you milk by hand?" Cody asks Kendra.

She taps the pump with her boot. "If you know how."

The kids sprawl over the drive and cluster into groups. A girl, from a clump of girls in fitted jackets, lifts the corner of the tarp and squeals and drops it.

"What've we got here?" The teacher squats next to the cow. His collar, un-ironed, sticks half under the ribbing of his sweater vest. His jeans rumple cigarette-style over his ankles and steel-toed boots.

"Drown. Hey." Milo points at the bus driver, who's lighting up beside the bus. "Hey, not here."

The teacher twitches back the tarp. "How about an anatomy lesson?"

"No way." Kendra swears audibly under her breath.

"What's wrong?" Cody asks.

"What's wrong," she says. "What's wrong." She starts toward her clothes on the fence and stops. "Bring those with you when you come home." She stomps, covered in manure, wearing her long johns and under-shirt and a pair of Milo's boots, over the field toward Axel's. She jerks her arms as she goes, like she's talking to herself, or berating someone, or conducting.

Axel takes Kendra's clothes and looks at Cody over his shoulder. "Stay if you want," he says. He unwinds his bird's jesses and heads back home.

He should follow, but there's kids laughing and mill-ing around. A few of them point to the bird on Axel's fist and he finds himself explaining. "That's my uncle, sort of. A gyrfalcon. The rarest one." No one listens. The teacher pulls the tarp from the cow and the cow hulks vulnerably on the bare ramp. Melanie stands next to the cow. She stands straight and her mouth is cracked open like she's about to ask a question. He'll ask her about it after he washes his hands.

AXEL

"The rarest one," his brother's grandson brags behind him. A compliment that the boy is proud. Says maybe the boy will shape up. He turns, walking backwards while looking at the dairy. The cow tan beside the blue tarp. The raw waste from the sewage pumped over a good section of the field. All that shit on the snow. The boy in the kilt with his hair in his eyes, chatting to no one. The school kids around the boy ignore him. Pah. His arm sags. The white has never felt heavy before. A bird plays with gravity, mocks it. This lump of chalk—he jerks his arm upwards and the bird, hooded, dips a wing and collects its balance. No doubt now there's a screw loose between mind and eye.

He opens the door to the bird yard and heads for the mewses. Screeches from the other gyrfalcons on their perches. There's her stock—a white male with pale grey peppered over his back, and a female near perfect with only blue tarsus and nare, the ankle and nose. Each worth well over fifty thousand. But it's not the money. All the birds here are related except the hawks. His charts fan from that first gyrfalcon, the bird he scooped from the nest and lost his leg for.

He opens the door to the white's mews and sets her on her perch. Loosens the draw on the hood and slides it forward over her beak. She swivels her head round and plucks at the feathers on her shoulders. Across the drive at the hatchling barn, Kendra sits on the steps in her long johns, waiting for the power to kick on and heat water for a shower. He shuts the door to the mews. He's losing something else, now.

MILO

He didn't drink, but he didn't fix the generator. Didn't secure the gate. Allowed the cows to escape, and didn't help haul the dead milker on the tarp. And now the class visit. He forgot.

The teacher has asked for knives — he carries Austin's butcher set from the barn.

"Be my guest," the teacher says. The man's young, enthusiastic, oblivious to the pasture full of watery shit and Milo's discomfort.

The knife case is a heavy-duty camo roll-up, and inside, the four-piece set: caping knife, curved boning knife, flexible straight boning knife, a skinning knife and sharpening steel. He nearly forgot about these knives and the farm goats Austin used to put down himself.

"Stand close in case she moves," Austin would say, and make him shoot the animal. That's as far as Milo went. It was Austin who'd squat — almost sit — on the back of the goat, tilt the head, and slice the throat to let it bleed. Slit the skin from throat to anus, string the animal from the "gallows tree" — a spruce at the edge of the pasture. It's impressive that his old man managed the farm as long as he did.

Take the cow apart and she'll be easier to dispose of. Milo — if he can't do anything else, at least he'll do this.

VI

—

MELANIE

THE YARD IS full of Kratz twins and jocks and nerds and ditzes and idiots and Mr. Friessen, who holds a pack of dusty latex gloves that pull out of a box like tissues. Kendra strides home, in her underwear, across the paddock. Milo's half-buried puke piles scatter the driveway, and this woman—presumably a chaperone—puts her arm around Melanie's shoulders and says, "Aw, dear, the hair will grow back." The woman's own hair is a wad of coarse brown curls and a good inch of grey roots. Thread-veins redden the bridge of her nose and upper cheeks. Her down vest is stained, but still she's smudged on lipstick—a faddish coral shade she's either way too old for or never grew out of. The woman gives Melanie a shake and a kiss to the temple and tucks a pair of gloves into her hand. The chalky powder makes her skin crawl and her lungs close up. She'd hyperventilate but her throat would rather vomit.

Kids dawdle and fall from a single school crowd into their standard cliques around the yard in the muddy snow. One girl uses the bathroom and comes out pinching an eight-inch chunk of blonde hair, her hair. Of course. She left it all over the floor and vanity. The girl throws it at a jock, who flings his arms up and overplays his jump backwards.

Cody, hands aloft, walks past the twins and Angelique and the other girls who've swapped bracelets and hair clips to some code. These girls, they wouldn't last a lunch hour against her old school and Candice, not with their catalogue parkas and knowledge of hay and horses and potato guns. Angelique—the tall brunette whose winter boots curve along her ankle and leg, and who, despite Melanie's cut-off galoshes and over-sized winter coat, had hung with her—grabs Cody's elbow and flicks his bangs from his eyes. "Can you see in there?"

Cody blushes and squeezes by the group into her house.

"Maybe Melanie could give you a buzz?" Angelique calls after him. Melanie closes her fists. The girls squeal and whisper like they're besties, "I can't believe you did that," and "Oh-my-god he's adorable. Did you see the skirt?" Angelique steps toward Melanie and says, "Did you want to say something?"

Melanie crosses her arm over her chest and holds her shoulder. What can she say? Candice would have liked the kilt too.

Angelique puts on a concerned look. "No? Your mouth was open. But you know your hair looks great. I mean, it's a lot less greasy short." The Kratz twins titter. Angelique turns and huddles with the group.

She should leave. She's in pyjamas—leave already. But she can't make herself walk up the stoop and down the hall where the old man is, where his parts are. Maybe she should go in there—she could give anyone who walked in a real shocker. "Shut up," she whispers. Shut up.

Milo presents Mr. Friessen with her grandfather's knife case.

"Be my guest," Mr. Friessen waves Milo toward the cow.

The class crowds the cow and Milo selects the old man's butcher knife—long, but widely curved at the tip—and slices down the belly. The settled blood is an astonishing watery pink. She expected a creamy beading around the slit, but of course the cow's not full of milk. Milo pries the flesh back and unfolds a calf—a wet slip of hooves and tacky fur. The eyes are blueish and pearled and useless, although the calf, judging by the size, might have lived if they'd cut it out sooner.

Mid-afternoon and already the sun's jerked behind the western valley wall and let the clouds lower and darken.

"Should be one hundred seventy feet of gut." Friessen and Milo scoop the heifer's innards onto the ramp. A jock steps over and helps stretch the intestines across the paddock. A trio of nerds lift out the organs. The ditzes and idiots close in. There's hacking and chasing. The eyes are removed — oblong things, filmy black at the front, gripped by red muscles at the sides. They burst and goop sprays down a Kratz sweater. The power flickers back on but there's no talk of milking. Kids balloon their latex gloves into translucent udders and bop them volleyball style. Nose holding. Whining. Piling it all back on the tarp in the three o'clock dusk. Then her friends are back on the bus. "Sure you don't want to come, honey?" Melanie shakes off the chaperone. Then they're gone.

CODY

On the table: a silver sugar dish and a lighter, plates, a bucket of scummy water and a drowned cloth, cups. The kitchen isn't untidy, it's filthy. And cold. The sink is full of dishes, so he looks for the bathroom, where the vanity is covered with long clumps of hair.

Axel's house, cluttered with dyes and leather, bird skulls on the shelves and feathers in vases, is eccentric. His place with his mom is too clean—so scrubbed it's noticeable (his mom scratches the tub enamel with coarse cleaner)—but this house, it's barely a house.

Someone coughs.

"Hello?" he says. "Are you all right?"

KENDRA

The kids across the field are counted—the teacher taps each teen on the head and calls a name—and they pile on the bus and drive away into the dark. Now that the power is on, she showers, wearing her long johns, in the outside stall of the hatchling barn. Heat steams off and streams upward. In the cold afternoon night, the clouds thin and are inhaled south along with the river, leaving the tops of the mountain bare and stippled wintergreen with hemlock and pine. Her underclothes turn brown and clear and heavy.

Axel locks the white in the flight pen and trudges over. He sits on the steps with his back to her. Her jeans and shirt and camera are draped over his shoulder. She peels her long johns and undershirt and underwear and leaves them in a pile at her feet. She takes the hard, yellowed bar of soap first to her hair and nails and then to her body.

He says, "We can clean you a room."

She rinses her face and spits. Rinses again. The muscles in his shoulders are knotted. He's tense. He wants her to stay? To be what the boy isn't? What is he thinking? How long has she been here now? Has she ever been more clear about what she needs from him? That he'd offer her a permanent room. A room, not a bird. The kid's room, too.

She picks up her underwear and slaps them over the side of the sink next to her. "I have a room now?" she says. But it's not even the room that bothers her. It's not that he's writing off the boy, who needs, well, someone. It's that he's asking for help. Asking her. "You talking about giving me Cody's room? You want me to move in?"

She shuts off the shower. Axel stands and turns to her. The heat from the shower is replaced by late-afternoon chill. Is it that she's naked? Is that what makes him think that giving up his role — she's his apprentice — will fix his plans, his bird, anything? He's holding on to her and he doesn't know what he's holding on to.

She takes her clothes from his shoulder and meets his eyes. Blue, set in tanned, weathered skin — not wrinkled, that would imply he has extra flesh. He's bone and leather. "No, Axel," she says.

He limps to the house.

"Shit." She leans on the shower wall. Her shoulder blades stick to the cold plastic. "Just, shit." Across the highway the bare aspen dapple the riverside. Beyond them the black water pushes pallets of ice against the riverbank. Cows, some still on the highway but most of them back in the pasture, stand and fade—dull patches in the dark. The front of her truck, shiny in the snowy ditch down the driveway. She sets her clothes on the steps and turns the shower back on.

AXEL

He limps the steps to the house and sits. Rolls his sweatpants above his knee and removes his prosthetic. Doesn't bother him anymore, except sometimes he dreams the pain—a contorted limb that won't relax.

His brother visited him in hospital when he was scheduled to lose it, like he told the boy. Travelled from the farm to Quebec, where the medivac had flown Axel after he'd landed his kayak at the camp with that smashed leg. The hospital had called his brother, unable to talk sense into Axel.

"How do you expect to hold a falcon during surgery?" His brother leaned over him on the hospital bed. He held the gyr, downy and peeping, to his chest.

"A bird in the hand," he said.

"Two feet on the ground." His brother leaned so close Axel worried the bird would be crushed, and tucked his fingers under the falcon.

He let go. Damn him, he could have cried. His brother kept a hand on his shoulder while the nurses rolled the stretcher into the hall. Locked eyes when he had to let go. Brown eyes. Like the boy, Cody. When he was wheeled back with a freshly severed stump, his brother put down his newspaper. "Was it worth it?"

In the ICU on hospital sheets, the chirps of machines and monitors, the pulse of the bird cradled again at his own heart, he never doubted. Even now it's not doubt.

"Thirty birds in the hand," he says aloud. At his own table, in his own house. The offspring of that first falcon filling the mewses outside. "A bird on the hand of every falconer in North America."

MILO

The school kids gone, he escapes to the garage. Reflex. The still. His father's pet, ordered from Europe, runs on sawdust bricks. Steel base polished at alternating angles to look checkered, the sleek rose-copper boiler and botanical basket, the thick windows the gin condenses behind—his father didn't skimp. Austin used to steep juniper, peach, sarsaparilla, and a few more flora Milo's forgotten, for twenty-four hours, and spend the next day in the garage monitoring optimum distillation temps. What Milo makes can't be called gin officially, but it has the alcohol content. He unscrews the lid from a jar and sniffs it. Not good, except that it smells like alcohol. In fact, it could be called disgusting. He sets the jar on the cement floor.

The mess they made of the cow — a bloody puzzle on the tarp. The tractor in the driveway still has gas, and a backhoe attachment. The keys are in his pocket. If he couldn't prevent the mess, maybe he can clean it up.

VII

—

MELANIE

THE BUS HUFFED the kids off her property, but not out of her space. The cow is spread on the tarp in a pile next to the empty carcass and calf.

She climbs the porch and opens the door. They were in here. Mugs and crusted bowls cover the table and counter. Instant soup packages are set on a melted bag of frozen veggies on the stove. And although the entire farm smells of shit, the human crap smell of the house is worse. Mud. Footsteps. She pinches the hair above her ears and pulls. They went through the kitchen. She drops her hands and heads for the bathroom, then stops. Cody stands in the old man's doorway, in his kilt, with his cutesy bangs and his thin neck, his knees slightly bent like he's trying to vanish or is ready to bolt.

He wipes his cheek, tries to hide his embarrassment of her, no, worse, for her. His whole future life at Axel's flung her in the face.

He starts to apologize. "Sorry, I—"

Sorry? She slaps his mouth. Punches. He curls. She punches again. Pushes. Kicks, then straddles him and beats: fists, teeth, fingers.

The worst, most awful thing she's done, she thinks, was like what this boy is doing. Like Milo. Like those kids on the bus. In grade seven, she opened the door to use the girls' washroom and found this special needs kid rocking in her own throw-up, saying, "I feel sick." And she did nothing. Nothing at all. She shut the door and pretended not to know, even when Candice helped the girl from the bathroom—her hand on the girl's back—saying, "It's okay. It's okay." She hits Cody till there's sticky blood and probably tears. Why apologize? Why be sorry? Should she be sorry? There's black snot down his chin. He's stopped covering his face. What good is that? She slides down his legs. His kilt is up round his hips. She unzips his pants and pulls out his dick.

"Sorry for what?" she says. His eyes are swollen shut, or he's keeping them shut. His cheeks are red—either he's blushing because she's touching him, or blushing from being caught in her house, or from the kick to the face. She puts her lips on his penis—should she bite?—but the kid gives a twitch and pulls his hands back up over his face. She spits it out on his kilt.

She leaves him on the floor. Outside, there's enough moonlight to see that most of the cows have wandered off the highway and back to the pasture. She shuts the door and walks toward the barn. She should be sorry. Walking isn't fast enough. She runs. She is sorry. Still not fast enough.

CODY

Only because of the bathroom, because of the bathroom sink—all he wanted was to wash the cow-pie off his hands—and then because someone moaned in the back room, needing help. And he waited because he wasn't sure what the next step should be. Otherwise he would have left when Axel did, taking Kendra's clothes from him.

Or maybe he went inside to avoid the kids outside, because the kids outside were so mean to her. Or maybe it was because of the cow. His left eyelid is stuck— there's a red pulse through the eyelid from the hallway light. He zips his jeans, rolls on his front, and cringes upright. He washes his hands and face. He walks home across the snow.

He starts to climb over the paddock fence, but hurts,

so he crawls under. His kilt trips his knees and he has to tug it out of the way twice. The motion sensor flickers in the training yard—Kendra, scrubbed pink, back in her jeans and sweater and jacket, with the bucket of feed. He lets himself in. She looks him over and swings the bucket his way. He takes it. The dead chickens are coated in a greenish slime that could be decomp, but doesn't smell like the crime shows on TV back home claim rot smells.

"Vitamin powder," Kendra says. "Remember?" She feeds a handful into a tray and slides it through a slot in the plywood nesting pen. "For the hatchlings—remember I told you about the hatchling room? You'll see them in spring." She furrows her forehead, scanning his sweater and scratches.

"For the hatchlings," he prompts.

"For them, you start the same. Toss the feeders in the cement mixer and get these guys." She taps the bucket. "Then everything goes through the meat grinder—Axel will show you—and next the blender. It'll all come out grey and tufty, but that's normal."

"How many chicks have you gone through?" he asks. "Over the years."

"Over the years." She laughs once, then looks at him and takes back the bucket. "This bother you?"

"Does what bother me," he says, before she can ask what happened to him, or if he's going to be all right here by himself. "Feeding birds birds? Cannibalism?"

She puts a hand on her hip. "Cannibalism," she says. "Good one."

AXEL

The light in the training yard is on, shining through the curtains, and Cody and Kendra are feeding the birds. Kendra feeds the birds. The boy hugs himself. Beyond them, in the distance, the light of the tractor digging a pit.

Kendra — she has pictures. Undeveloped film he needs for the records: the white, centre of the training yard on a post in the snow. And she'll have snapped one of the bird on his glove, unhooded, as he walked her around getting her used to the fist. Only took him a lifetime to breed out the brain.

He lets the curtains fall. He'll have to bring himself to ask before she goes.

KENDRA

Night's calm. No point in rushing. She hops the falcons to her fist to feed them. Wipes the green fluff of the chicks from their beaks and hands them to Cody, who sets them on a perch-scale and calls the weight to her. Returns the birds to their mewses, crops full, lazy. They tuck a blue or yellow leg into their feathers.

The birds each carry their own beauty; if she could sneak a speckled male, or even Lola. No, she laughs to herself, Axel will be at the window. And she doesn't want a bird that way. Not stolen. Nothing that will give her hesitation every time she lifts it.

She's going to miss this place, she realizes. She's going to miss this kid and his kilt. His fear of snorkelling. She's going to miss Axel.

MILO

He climbs off the tractor at the far side of the pasture, slaps his hands on his thighs, and claps the blood back into his fingers in the dark. The drop in temperature that arrived with evening has solidified the ground. The half-frozen dirt has risen like yeast, is full of air and gritty with ice crystals; he stomps his feet at the edge of the pit he's backhoed. The ground crunches crisply. Five or six feet deep. The first two feet good, fertile, grass field, and under that roots and rock. The tractor cools beside the pit, the exposed hydraulic metal of boom and dipper glint oily blue-black, although the rest of the tractor's and world's colours are lost in the night. The cow can wait until morning. So can Kendra's truck. He should close the garage.

He starts to follow the tractor path back then stops. The barn looms, even at a distance. Melanie will be there, she likes it better than home. He plans to apologize, has an apology idling in his head, has this big sorry ready, but when he talks to her he only gets as far as the shit he's done, and then thinks what's the point? He wants to say, What I'm doing to you is worse than the stories I'm telling. Worse than squeegee-ing out the boxes in the morgue. He wants to tell her he wanted to care for her even before she lived with him, before her mom got involved with that nurse and started another family. Remember, he wants to say, when you were little and I picked you up for breakfast—you were so excited you threw up all over your birthday dress. After you finished crying and got changed we drove out of the city instead. Through the suburbs and the big ranches—there were cows then too. But he can't get that far. Not even in his mind. Only gets as far as, A few nights back I shaved your head, and then he gives up.

Melanie. What was she like back in the city? Can't recall. Instead what comes to mind is the loner whose hand burned when he was a teen. That kid running a stick along the chain-link fence every lunch hour, and one particular time when—a month or maybe a year after the fire thing—the kid broke. The kid had stayed out past the bell, and the teacher had gone to fetch him. Milo'd watched through the window as the kid yelled and ran. Looping around the monkey bars, the swings, then sprinting out into the field. The teacher frozen — surprised, probably, like the rest of them, that that timid kid could tear around so fast. Yelling, hollering like his life depended on it. A real roar. That kid, a boy with parted hair and sweaty pits — possibly born cleft palate, one nostril was larger than the other — that's what Milo remembers: staring through the school window. The whole class fascinated. Filled with a weird mix of fear and curiosity. His daughter is that kid, now, he realizes absently. His fault again.

Earlier the clouds were like a tarp, hung low over the field; now they drag south, blackening the moon above the river and leaving for light only the stars and the open barn door. The glow breaks over the snow and mud and on the tufts of bent grass in the pasture. Melanie, setting up the night's milking. The power's fixed.

And suddenly, standing alone in the black expanse of the field so far from his daughter, he's not alone. The cows. Shocking to notice, to remember those huge beasts, their bulk and breath so close in the dark, having been so close all along. Only now they move, a shift like a tide, passing him by on their way to the barn. The heat of them as they walk by in the dark. They were right there, are right here, then they are gone.

VIII

—

MELANIE

AGAIN, ALL SHE has to do is vacuum the milkers to the teats, then there is the grind of chewed cud and the flick of tails and the soft drop of cow pats. She runs her hand over the hip bones of the animals as she walks by their stalls. So big. They'll keep them inside now, for the winter. The grass is snow-covered, and she learned about laminitis last year. So there's those reasons. But also, inside, the bus can't scrutinize them every morning on its way to school.

She climbs up onto the rail of the last stall, swings a leg over, and straddles it so that one foot hangs in the pen. The cow raises its head. Big brown eyes and light hair. Tan down the muzzle, grey on the nose. She scratches its ear.

"Why so sad?" She swings the other leg over the rail too, so that she sits facing the cow, and runs both her hands down its face. There's blood on her knuckles. The garage door rumbles open beyond the wall. Milo. That girl, the one who puked, afterward Candice had whispered, I know you were in there, I know you left her. All she did was deny it. Kept spouting self-defence — I didn't see her, I didn't.

"I hate myself," she says. She waits for Milo's clunks and scrapes beyond the wall to stop before she hops off the rail and opens the adjoining door. The still sits dormant at the back of the garage. The boiler, with its polished copper and circular window, is thankfully off. When active, it looks like a bathysphere, only the water roils around the window on the wrong side.

She turns to go back into the barn, then glances out the garage door and doesn't. Milo stands beside the slurry, jars and pails of spirits next to him. He pours bucket after bucket over the pit and tosses a match to it. Blue and fierce — alluring like the bug zapper in summer. He means well; he won't be able to help himself.

CODY

The mattress in the spare room is shiny, grey-silver with royal-blue floral stitching, and the woven vines and leaves make the bed look like a Dutch plate. He and Kendra stretch a faded mint sheet over it. The creases stay even when the edges of the sheet are tucked under the foot and sides of the mattress. The bedspread, at least, is happy — lively orange and pink and blue. South American, maybe. Wool. Kendra tosses a pillow on it.

"You going to be okay sleeping here?" she says.

"I'm good." He sits, traces a stripe on the blanket, then touches his swollen eye.

Kendra reaches down and opens a cardboard box from a stack of boxes along the wall. Feathers. Bells. Leather. Envelopes of unlabelled photos.

The skin around his eye is taut, not soft like he'd expected, more like his thumb when he slammed it in a car door. "I'm going to wash."

"Sure. This will take a while anyway." Kendra sits cross-legged on the floor and picks out a skull. Her hair is braided again, and now that they're inside and the cold has gone from her skin her freckles have returned to her face, neck, and hands. They'll be the rest of the way down, too — breasts, butt, thighs, toes. She balances the skull on her fingertips. "Crow. Neat, hey?"

In the hall, he stops at the phone. Her machine answers. "Mom. I know you're there." Maybe Aunt Jen is there too, baking apples, or curry, and they're both around the stove and the fan is drowning out the phone. "Mom." Nothing. "Mom I know you're

listening." If she is, she'll be in the bathtub or curled
next to a heater in the dark. There's no way Aunt Jen
is over. "Pick up, please?" She doesn't. "Well," he says.
After another minute of silence he hangs up.

The bathtub is full of Axel's soaking clothes. But
there was that shower outside.

He strips down, folds his kilt and sets it on the toilet. Can he even ask Axel to take it to the dry cleaners?
Underwear, jeans, shirt, and sweater get added to the
tub. He takes the biggest towel from the bathroom
closet—one that reaches from his armpits to his knees
when tucked around him—and puts boots on. Axel sits
with his back to him, absorbed in hoods.

He walks down the drive to the hatchling barn and
the outside stall. The shower's hot. A damp cloud forms
instantly, thickening the air and hanging. The heat and
steam clear his nose. He washes loose scabs from his
nostrils.

Up the mountain yesterday. He drops the soap. He
was stupid to show her the postcard. What can she
do? He shuts off the shower and immediately shivers.
There's a sense of urgency to the dark as he crosses
back to the house. Like, shifting. Like it has pieces, like
a great glom of ants. Like he might shake apart in the
cold. He climbs the porch steps and stops. He's going
to have to live across from that girl.

MILO

The power's on, but he sits in the rocker with the light off. Him and his old man and a lingering jug. There's fragility to the alcohol in the Mason jar; the way it sloshes makes it seem clearer than water. He sets it on his knee. Out the window the clouds have pulled back entirely, and the light from the moon, circling low above the highway, will soon breach the room. "I'm here." He runs his thumb over the lid and metal band. The old man breathes under the quilt. "You got me." He leans back, rocking the chair, and bumps the bookshelf.

Though, what if the old man never wanted him here? The hospital called him, not his father. What if, instead of being added to the old man's pyramid, he's the looter? Robbing the tomb before the body's cooled.

The old man's throat catches and gargles. Milo tips the chair forward and hugs the Mason jar against his gut. "What are you waiting for?" The skin around the old man's eyes is collapsed and purple. His hair—what's left of it—is overgrown, and it occurs to Milo that his father's on a different plane. For all he knows the old man is in pain, or, what if he's not even lucid? Not even there.

Melanie knocks on the door frame.

"I didn't see you," he says. He sets the jar beside the rocker and stands, careful to move slowly. All the light comes from the porch lamp through the window and casts her shadow out into the hall. Her nose is pink, from crying or cold he can't tell because her glasses obscure her eyes, and he doesn't know her well enough, he realizes—standing there she's a petite, blonde stranger in a shitty coat—to guess how she'd react to this morning.

"I know," she says.

He nods. Well, at least she's talking. At least he's quit. The first time he quit was because of his daughter, too, after—a few years ago—her old school had called about her attitude.

"She's ending everything with 'yawn,'" the teacher back in the city had said. "I'll ask her what's the definition of a city-state, and she'll say, 'A city-state? Yawn.'"

"How can she have an attitude?" he'd asked.

"She's twelve," the teacher explained. "And I think she doesn't know the answers. I haven't seen any homework."

"Homework? Since when does she have homework? Kids don't start homework till grade four."

"She's twelve," the teacher repeated. "That's grade six."

What a loser he's been. But now, with Melanie waiting in the doorway, here's his chance. Apologize. "This isn't the worst thing," he starts.

Melanie folds her arms. "You want to know my worst?"

Her worst? She's never done anything. How can she think that? How can he respond to that? "Maybe we'll find him a home." He gestures to the old man then rubs his hand over his own chin and facial hair. Should shave. Should shave the old man, too. "A care home."

She uncrosses her arms, rests a hand on the door frame, then asks, "Can you help me with the cow?"

They go out. Under the moon the field becomes a stark, open bone. Beneath his feet the ground is swollen and full of air and space, the dirt pulling apart from itself—expanding. The ice around the slurry, where he lit the booze, has melted and exposed a tangle of flat grass.

He hooks the tarp to the tractor and drags the cow to his pit. He pushes, Melanie beside him, and they tip the animal in, sliding it off the tarp.

"So long, Bess," says Melanie.

"This one's Bess?" he says.

"They're all Bess."

She tugs her collar closer around her neck, a small neck, like her mother's—her mother, he has no idea where, with her new daughter and new family. The old man dying. In the bigness of the pasture, he and she are all of it. Solo.

The pit smells of good dirt. The night is wide—over the dairy, over Axel's. Kendra's truck—why wait till tomorrow? He leans back against the tractor. Why not start now.

AXEL

At the table he traces the pattern pieces and cuts the leather. Halfway down the crest, he cuts a hole for the beak, then uses a sponge brush and daubs the pieces with brown dye.

Kendra adds another box, lugged from the spare room, to the pile in the living room. She dusts off her hands on her jeans. "You want this in the attic?"

"Mostly junk." He'll sort it later. He sets the wet leather aside and selects pieces he left to dry this morning—forest-green eye panels paired with crocodile crest. He circles their edges with a line guide and stitch marker. "Can bring me a water cup if you want."

She fills a mug and sits beside him.

"Leather listens better moist."

"I know." She picks up the hole punch and indents the stitches to show through the other side.

He aligns the eye panels with matching marks. Next step is hole punching, then sewing. "Where's the floss?" He lifts the leather and the pattern.

"Think Cody took it to the bathroom."

"Where is he now?"

"Go easy," she says.

"Thought he might want to make hoods."

"I'll get him." Sets a roll of film on the table. "Last couple months."

He nods.

"Milo rescued my truck. I'm going to head out." She stands and leans on the chair back. "I know you won't try," she says. "She might breed fine. If you gave it one year—"

He waves her off. She won't. The bird is present— locked in her pen—but only partly. The white's around in the same way his leg is still around. A ghost of what it used to be. "Go fetch him already," he says.

KENDRA

The moon has come up, faint, and like it's stepped into the world after a rough, rough night, and so badly needs to wash its fucking face. She takes her bag from Cody and throws it into the cab of her truck.

The kid will do well with the hoods. So he's not a hunter. Axel needs a helper. A companion, after these last few days.

She finds her keys in her vest. Across the paddock in the window of the dairy house she can see the outline of a person—Milo or Melanie—against the curtains, the window lit orange around the shadow like the house is being candled. That's one thing she'll be glad to escape—whatever hatches there.

Cody wraps his arms around himself. He's changed

into loose khakis and an orange fleece. Wears Axel's extra set of boots. The porch door opens. Axel pauses on the stairs then walks into the training yard.

"Got my bird?" she calls. "That was a joke," she tells Cody. She reaches in the truck and—thank goodness—everything starts. She leaves it running—let the engine warm—and walks to the back and opens the canopy. A mess. Her equipment tub tipped in the crash and dumped her supplies over the box. She slides the live noose trap to the side and throws the fit-all pigeon trap on top. She crawls in. Calcium supplement has spilled, nothing to do about that, but the pedestal scale and tail guards are good. She repacks the tub. Mite and lice spray, hides she picked up from the locals at the meat draw, trainer kite, sand anchor for the kite, swivels and carabiners, duck-wing lure, rabbit-skin tube lure. Gloves she's made, two: winter-lined and spring design. Both calfskin, brown, full cuff.

She flips the gloves over. The truck creaks and she turns. Cody presses down on the tailgate. Kid's cracked lip is swollen, his nose too, though it doesn't look broken—that's a plus. Bruise over the eyebrow and eye. Scratches—bites? What can be done. She crawls over and sits beside him. Hands him the winter-lined calfskin.

There's a knock on the side of the canopy. Axel. She stands and brushes calcium powder from her knees.

"Here." Axel extends his arm—a bird. The white. The big, blind beauty. So white she looks like someone erased a bit of scenery. Hooded in blue.

"Axel." Kendra holds up her hands.

"Take the asshole." He tosses a bag of frozen chicks in the tub with the traps, then goes round to the passenger side and sets the bird on the headrest. Kendra motions Cody off the truck and slams the tailgate and closes the canopy. She walks to the front and to Axel, runs her fingers over the weather strip and then — what the hell—over the white's back. The bird dips and straightens.

Not Lola, not a hunter, but look at her. Well, look at the gesture. Thirty years, over three thousand falcons, and, best guess, one point eight million feeder chicks. Axel won't breed her, but she can give it a go. The bird can be her start. Does he know that, giving it to her? She smooths the feathers at the bird's crop. Does he need to know that?

The night is clear along the western horizon, and the mountain under it looks like a missing patch of sky, black and rough, as if the bottom has been ripped away. The flecked moon hangs half-finished and trails behind it a crush of lavender over the eastern valley.

Cody steps back from the truck. Behind him, the dairy house, the barn, grey and diminutive in the moonlight. They'll survive—no stopping it. She salutes him, then grips Axel's hand. Her right hand in his, then her left on top of his again. Knuckles, calluses. She breathes—pulsed, focused—a shot of eagerness at what comes next, what she doesn't know, can't see, but what will grow, riled and thirsty, out of the flopped and baleful past, into the now, the What Comes Next.

ACKNOWLEDGEMENTS

This book was made possible in part by financial support from the Canada Council for the Arts and the Writers' Trust of Canada RBC Bronwen Wallace Award for Emerging Writers.

Thank you to the literary journals who've published my stories over the years: *The Malahat Review, PRISM International, Little Fiction, Riddle Fence, Granta,* and *Ambit*.

Thank you to Sarah MacLachlan, Janie Yoon, Melanie Little, Maria Golikova, and everyone at House of Anansi Press, and to my agent Rachel Letofsky and the Cooke Agency.

Thank you to the faculty and mentors who encouraged me during my years at the University of Victoria, to my many writer friends who read and helped these stories, and to my non-writer friends and family who gave me places and time to write. Special thanks to Lorna Jackson, Cody Klippenstein, and Bradford Werner.

ERIN FRANCES FISHER's stories have been published internationally in literary journals such as *Granta*, *Ambit*, PRISM *International*, *The Malahat Review*, and *Little Fiction*. She was the winner of the RBC Writers' Trust of Canada Bronwen Wallace Award for Emerging Writers, *The Malahat Review*'s Open Season Award for Fiction, and PRISM *International*'s Short Fiction Grand Prize. Erin holds an MFA in Writing from the University of Victoria and teaches piano at the Victoria Conservatory of Music.